Anthony Gilbert and The Murder Room

>>> This title is part of The Murder Room, our series dedicated to making available out-of-print or hard-to-find titles by classic crime writers.

Crime fiction has always held up a mirror to society. The Victorians were fascinated by sensational murder and the emerging science of detection; now we are obsessed with the forensic detail of violent death. And no other genre has so captivated and enthralled readers.

Vast troves of classic crime writing have for a long time been unavailable to all but the most dedicated frequenters of second-hand bookshops. The advent of digital publishing means that we are now able to bring you the backlists of a huge range of titles by classic and contemporary crime writers, some of which have been out of print for decades.

From the genteel amateur private eyes of the Golden Age and the femmes fatales of pulp fiction, to the morally ambiguous hard-boiled detectives of mid twentieth-century America and their descendants who walk our twenty-first century streets, The Murder Room has it all. >>>

The Murder Room
Where Criminal Minds Meet

themurderroom.com

Anthony Gilbert (1899–1973)

Anthony Gilbert was the pen name of Lucy Beatrice Malleson. Born in London, she spent all her life there, and her affection for the city is clear from the strong sense of character and place in evidence in her work. She published 69 crime novels, 51 of which featured her best known character, Arthur Crook, a vulgar London lawyer totally (and deliberately) unlike the aristocratic detectives, such as Lord Peter Wimsey, who dominated the mystery field at the time. She also wrote more than 25 radio plays, which were broadcast in Great Britain and overseas. Her thriller *The Woman in Red* (1941) was broadcast in the United States by CBS and made into a film in 1945 under the title *My Name is Julia Ross*. She was an early member of the British Detection Club, which, along with Dorothy L. Sayers, she prevented from disintegrating during World War II. Malleson published her autobiography, *Three-a-Penny*, in 1940, and wrote numerous short stories, which were published in several anthologies and in such periodicals as *Ellery Queen's Mystery Magazine* and *The Saint*. The short story 'You Can't Hang Twice' received a Queens award in 1946. She never married, and evidence of her feminism is elegantly expressed in much of her work.

By Anthony Gilbert

Scott Egerton series

Tragedy at Freyne (1927)

The Murder of Mrs
  Davenport (1928)

Death at Four Corners (1929)

The Mystery of the Open
  Window (1929)

The Night of the Fog (1930)

The Body on the Beam (1932)

The Long Shadow (1932)

The Musical Comedy
  Crime (1933)

An Old Lady Dies (1934)

The Man Who Was Too
  Clever (1935)

**Mr Crook Murder
  Mystery series**

Murder by Experts (1936)

The Man Who Wasn't
  There (1937)

Murder Has No Tongue (1937)

Treason in My Breast (1938)

The Bell of Death (1939)

Dear Dead Woman (1940)
  aka *Death Takes a Redhead*

The Vanishing Corpse (1941)
  aka *She Vanished in the Dawn*

The Woman in Red (1941)
  aka *The Mystery of the
  Woman in Red*

Death in the Blackout (1942)
  aka *The Case of the Tea-
  Cosy's Aunt*

Something Nasty in the
  Woodshed (1942)
  aka *Mystery in the Woodshed*

The Mouse Who Wouldn't
  Play Ball (1943)
  aka *30 Days to Live*

He Came by Night (1944)
  aka *Death at the Door*

The Scarlet Button (1944)
  aka *Murder Is Cheap*

A Spy for Mr Crook (1944)

The Black Stage (1945)
  aka *Murder Cheats the Bride*

Don't Open the Door (1945)
  aka *Death Lifts the Latch*

Lift Up the Lid (1945)
  aka *The Innocent Bottle*

The Spinster's Secret (1946)
  aka *By Hook or by Crook*

Death in the Wrong Room
  (1947)

Die in the Dark (1947)
  aka *The Missing Widow*

Death Knocks Three Times
  (1949)

Murder Comes Home (1950)

A Nice Cup of Tea (1950)
  aka *The Wrong Body*

Lady-Killer (1951)

Miss Pinnegar Disappears (1952)
aka *A Case for Mr Crook*

Footsteps Behind Me (1953)
aka *Black Death*

Snake in the Grass (1954)
aka *Death Won't Wait*

Is She Dead Too? (1955)
aka *A Question of Murder*

And Death Came Too (1956)

Riddle of a Lady (1956)

Give Death a Name (1957)

Death Against the Clock (1958)

Death Takes a Wife (1959)
aka *Death Casts a Long Shadow*

Third Crime Lucky (1959)
aka *Prelude to Murder*

Out for the Kill (1960)

She Shall Die (1961)
aka *After the Verdict*

Uncertain Death (1961)

No Dust in the Attic (1962)

Ring for a Noose (1963)

The Fingerprint (1964)

The Voice (1964)
aka *Knock, Knock! Who's There?*

Passenger to Nowhere (1965)

The Looking Glass Murder (1966)

The Visitor (1967)

Night Encounter (1968)
aka *Murder Anonymous*

Missing from Her Home (1969)

Death Wears a Mask (1970)
aka *Mr Crook Lifts the Mask*

Murder is a Waiting Game (1972)

Tenant for the Tomb (1971)

A Nice Little Killing (1974)

Standalone Novels

The Case Against Andrew Fane (1931)

Death in Fancy Dress (1933)

The Man in the Button Boots (1934)

Courtier to Death (1936)
aka *The Dover Train Mystery*

The Clock in the Hatbox (1939)

Lift Up the Lid

Anthony Gilbert

An Orion book

Copyright © Lucy Beatrice Malleson 1945

The right of Lucy Beatrice Malleson to be identified as the author of this work has been asserted in accordance with the Copyright, Designs and Patents Act 1988.

This edition published by
The Orion Publishing Group Ltd
Orion House
5 Upper St Martin's Lane
London WC2H 9EA

An Hachette UK company
A CIP catalogue record for this book is available from the British Library

ISBN 978 1 4719 0986 3

www.orionbooks.co.uk

To Elizabeth, with love.

CHAPTER ONE

DR. OLIVER STUART looked with interest at the last name on his list of appointments for the day. Mrs. Rose East. He knew nothing about her, less than he did about most of his patients since she had not been introduced by a doctor, but had telephoned out of the blue to his secretary asking for an appointment. Miss Lasker had explained that he only saw people through the medium of their doctors, to which she had replied, " I have no doctor. Please ask him to make an exception in my case. I am desperate—desperate."

" She sounded quite young and absolutely at the end of her tether," added Miss Lasker, reporting the message. " I should think she's quite likely to put her head in a gas oven if someone doesn't help her."

" That kind generally puts its head in a gas oven in any event," was Stuart's grim retort, " and I'd as soon she did it on her own responsibility."

Nevertheless, because he was a man who took his calling with great seriousness, he agreed to waive professional etiquette in this instance and fit Mrs. East in at the end of the day.

Now he was waiting for her to come through that door. He supposed it was another case of a maladjusted marriage ; that was usually why wives wanted to consult him. The unmarried ones were often more difficult because it was harder for him to explain to them the source of their distress.

" Mrs. East," said Miss Lasker's voice, and a girl came into the room.

He rose mechanically, putting out his hand, saying, " How do you do ? " and " Won't you sit down ? " but he scarcely realised what he was doing. His first thought was that she was the loveliest thing he had ever seen. She was quite young, not more than twenty-five, he decided, and obviously money wasn't her trouble, not the lack of it anyway. She was dressed in a tailored black suit, very plain, very perfect, with a blouse of some red silk stuff and a ridiculous red hat that came down over one eye and was trimmed with a long sweeping red feather. Rather big red plastic ear-rings matched her lapel ornament ; she had dark red gloves, red shoes of some

1

material that looked like lizard and a red bag to match. She looked indeed as if she had walked out of the pages of the *Parisian Vogue*. Very few women, he thought, would have had much sympathy with a girl who could afford to dress like that. But a moment later he realised too that he had never seen any one more possessed by fear.

" It's good of you to see me at such short notice," she was saying. " It's very seldom I can get away. My husband . . ."

She paused and he said, " Is your husband the trouble ? "

She smiled faintly. Even her obvious misery couldn't disguise her beautiful mouth. " Is it always husbands ? "

" Quite often. What's particularly wrong with yours ? "

" I'm frightened," she said. " Frightened to death—not my death."

Her words startled him out of his normal composure. " What does that mean ? "

" Do you often have people coming to you because they're afraid they may commit murder ? "

" Only self-murder," he agreed. " Are you sure quite you're saying what you mean ? "

" I don't want you to think I'm out of my mind. I'm not—not yet. But sometimes I wish I were. I don't like what's in my mind, and that's the fact."

" What it boils down to is that you're unhappy in your marriage. How old are you ? "

" Twenty-five."

" And your husband ? "

" Sixty-four."

" I see. What made you marry him ? "

" I was frightened."

" Of what ? "

" Not being safe."

" And you thought he spelt security ? "

" The way he explained it—yes."

" I think you'd better begin at the beginning. Had you known him long ? "

" He was a friend of Uncle Ned. Uncle Ned was my guardian. He was Aunt Selina's husband. It's like the House that Jack built."

" And who was Aunt Selina ? " Give her her head, it was the only chance of getting all the relevant facts.

" She was my mother's sister. But she never approved of mother. Mother married the man she loved, and he hadn't much money or any settled position, and they wandered about a lot and they were very happy, mostly in obscure parts of the world."

" And you ? "

" I spent a good deal of time with Aunt Selina, and was with them whenever they came back. Then when I was nine they were both killed in a railway accident. I remember Aunt Selina telling me about it. I was in the schoolroom, and she said, ' I always knew nothing good would come of their queer life. And now we've got to think what to do with you.' She explained that I had no legal claim on her, nobody could make her give me a home, and if she did it was only on condition that I didn't make a nuisance of myself. Whenever I got into any trouble she would say, ' Remember what I told you. There are orphanages for little girls whose parents get killed in accidents and don't leave any provision for their children. I don't believe you'd like them.' The very name filled me with terror. I didn't like Aunt Selina, but her house represented some sort of background. Whenever I was tiresome or I broke anything valuable or got a bad report from school Aunt Selina would remind me of the orphanage."

" What about school ? Didn't you like that ? "

" I didn't go for a long time. I had lessons with a backward girl in the neighbourhood. Her parents were very well off, and they thought it was a good thing for her to have someone to work with, so my lessons didn't cost very much. But when I was thirteen she died, and then I did go to school, but I didn't like it very much. I never felt quite the same as any one else. I could never make plans like the others, because I wasn't sure what was going on in Aunt Selina's mind. In those days I thought if only I could be safe *with any one*, I'd be happy. I don't believe she ever meant to send me to an orphanage," added Rose East, after a moment. " I think she just held it over my head, because she liked to feel she had power over someone."

" What about her husband ? " asked the doctor.

" He was a disappointment to her. I mean, he didn't get on and make money and give her a car or any of the things that show you're prosperous and successful. And sometimes he drank a little too much. She despised him, and she didn't make any secret of the fact. She despised me, too. I wanted to go on the stage when I was fourteen. I dare say most girls do, but she wouldn't hear of it. She said there had been too many gipsies in the family as it was, and I could do some steady respectable job. It wasn't decided what I should do when she died of pneumonia when I was sixteen, and though I'd never liked her I wished she was alive again, because at least she kept a home together. I asked Uncle Ned after the funeral what was going to happen to me, and he looked at me for a minute and then he said, ' Since you ask me, Posy, we're going to have a bit of fun. Life owes it to us. But not here. Not in this long-faced community. And we aren't going to wear mourning either ! ' I had the best two years of my life after Aunt Selina died."

" Safe ? " asked the doctor.

" Looking back, I suppose they were about as insecure as they could be, those two years. We lived in a hugger-mugger way Aunt Selina would have deplored. Uncle Ned sold all her furniture, he said he'd always hated it anyway, and we lived sometimes in boarding-houses, and sometimes in furnished rooms, and sometimes we went abroad. I thought it was wonderful, it was so free, and we did what made us happy. For instance, Uncle Ned loved music and he showed me how to love it, too. I know people would have thought him a queer sort of guardian for a girl of sixteen, but then I wasn't quite a usual sort of girl, and I didn't want to change. People generally took us for father and daughter, and he used to say I was like a daughter to him."

" He had no children of his own ? " interrupted the doctor.

" Oh, no. I don't think Aunt Selina really liked children. Another of Uncle Ned's weaknesses, if that's what you like to call it, was that he was a gambler. That didn't matter so much when we were in England, because the most he could do was put a little money on a horse, but when we were abroad he went to the casino, and he got into real trouble, and that's how we met my husband."

" At the Casino ? "

" James didn't gamble, but he used to go and look on. Uncle Ned said that was the most cold-blooded sport he'd ever heard of, but I think James got quite a lot of pleasure out of it. Then, one night, Uncle Ned looked more serious than usual. He told me he really was in a jam. He had a system, he said it was infallible, but, of course, like all systems it did break down sometimes. The long and short of it was we owed our hotel bill and we'd got nothing with which to meet it. Then to our amazement, because we hadn't thought he was that sort of man, Mr. East offered to help. Uncle Ned was the kind of person who thought nothing of accepting help, though I don't believe he ever asked for it. When he was in funds, which wasn't often, he would help any one else, and—it's difficult to explain without making him sound quite different from what he really was—he never thought of owing money any more than he thought of people owing things to him. That was something my husband never understood."

"It's something a great many people don't understand," agreed the doctor dryly.

"Then came the war, and we were back in London. Uncle Ned thought that people who went out of London because there might be raids were incomprehensible. He said if you lived in London and had your fun and your friends there you'd no right to get out because it became dangerous. I had taken the usual courses in first aid and gas drill and I went to a Post the day before war was declared. Uncle Ned tried everywhere for work and at last he made them take him on as warden. He wasn't very young, you see—fifty-four—and there were rumours that he wasn't very steady. But the people who thought that didn't know Uncle Ned. He was wonderful, once the raids began. Even when it wasn't his night on duty, he always turned out. We were living in a boarding-house, and every one was doing something, fire-fighting or watching or Red Cross . . . You got used to the odd kind of life. Uncle Ned had been in France in the first war and he'd have liked to go back but of course he was much too old for overseas service. Anyhow, he was extremely useful where he was."

"Did you see anything of your husband during this time ? "

"Oh, yes. He didn't come to London much, he said frankly he didn't like the raids, and he wasn't a young man, but he used to ask us down to the house we've got now at Hinton St. Luke. Though he was such a rich man, much richer than we'd realised at first, he didn't offer the house or any part of it for evacuees."

"I thought people in evacuation areas had no choice." The doctor looked puzzled.

"It wasn't an evacuation area from the Government's point of view. When the raids started the planes went straight over the village, and they even dropped a bomb now and again. He said his doctor had warned him his heart was in a poor condition, and he must be careful. Then there came the scheme to provide rest and recreation for wardens who were worn out by raid experiences, and he took two or three, Uncle Ned among them, but the scheme didn't work very well, he said his cook didn't like it and anyway the wardens didn't feel at home, so after two or three experiments they didn't go again. Then we had the bad raid, the raid when our street was hit, the raid when Uncle Ned was killed."

" Were you there at the time ? "

" I was at the Post. I went on duty at three and left at eleven. Uncle Ned wouldn't let me be on night duty. It had been a bad night and I was late anyway. A bomb had fallen not far from the hospital and they brought in a number of casualties to the Post. Several of them were more shocked than hurt, and one of them was hysterical. She kept on babbling of what she'd seen and it was all horrible. It was about one o'clock when I got back and I found a policeman barring my way. He told me there had been an incident and the road was closed. I tried desperately to get through but it was no good. They couldn't even tell me if Number Fourteen had been hit. I went to a Rest Centre and from there I went to Uncle Ned's post, but no one knew anything. It was forty-eight hours before they dug through to the base-ment of the house and found him and a woman who lived on the top floor. They said both of them must have been killed at once, but I've never been certain."

" And that worries you still ? " he asked keenly.

" No. No, I don't think of that any more. It's all over, and whatever he suffered is over, too. But at the time I was absolutely dazed. I didn't know what to do or where to go. I'd no other relatives and no home, because the house was completely wrecked. I hadn't even any clothes except what I stood up in. I went back to the Post because I didn't know where else to go, and I slept in a shelter that night. Then Mr. East appeared again. He said he'd heard the news and he wanted to help me. He suggested that I should go down and stay at his house while I got over the shock, and they gave me a week's compassionate leave, and said I could apply for a second week if the doctor sent in a certificate. Mr. East was so kind to me it seemed to take away every bit of moral back-bone that was left in me. Although the war was on, he had servants and a car and good food, and he insisted on treating me as though I were an invalid, until I began to think that I was different from other people, more delicate, more highly-strung. We talked about what I should do and he asked me how I was off for money, and I had to say I had only the two pounds a week I earned at the Post. When he inquired into Uncle Ned's affairs, it turned out that, far from leaving any provision for me, he was in debt when he died.

Not that I ever complained about that. He'd given me a wonderful time. No millionaire could have given me more."

" But it did make your situation rather critical ? " suggested Dr. Stuart.

" I couldn't imagine what I should do. I didn't know what happened to girls who weren't trained for anything who suddenly found themselves without a home or a relation and with no money, or anyway not enough to live on."

" Do you know now ? " inquired the doctor.

" I don't know what the right answer is. I know mine was wrong. Mr. East told me that he had sometimes discussed facts with Uncle Ned, and he'd promised that if anything should happen to him, he—Mr. East, I mean—would make himself responsible for me. I asked what Uncle Ned had meant by that, and Mr. East said, ' Oh, he never went into details, that wasn't his way. You should know that.' "

" And then," the doctor judged it time to hurry up the story a little, " he proposed marriage."

" Yes. He said he wanted to look after me as long as he could and leave me provided for afterwards, but it was very difficult to do it unless I was his wife. He said people gossiped cruelly, and they didn't understand the—the chivalry and affection that prompted his offer. He didn't think I ought to go back to London, and he said I should have plenty of opportunity for doing war work at Hinton St. Luke. I suppose now I should have enough sense, enough knowledge of life, to realise that what he suggested was impossible, I mean, that it wouldn't work out like that . . ."

" Are you trying to tell me that he suggested it should be a marriage in name only ? "

" Yes. He said it was only a formality to make things easier later on. He told me I could see for myself he wasn't very young and his health wasn't very good. The doctors had warned him he couldn't expect more than a very few years, but he wanted me to have those few years with him. I didn't understand about law, I was still getting accustomed to Uncle Ned's death, I believed what he told me. You see, I'd never thought of him in any connection but Uncle Ned's friend. The idea of him as a husband wasn't so much repulsive as absurd."

" You didn't think that by marrying him you were putting it out of your power to marry someone else you might come to love ? "

" I didn't think about love. All I knew of marriage was

7

Uncle Ned's and Aunt Selina's, and it had been horrible. I was frightened, that was the plain fact. I felt as I used to at Aunt Selina's after my parents died, that I might be turned out at an hour's notice and have nowhere to go but an orphanage. And then there was so little time. He kept pressing me for an answer. He said if I married him he'd pay off Uncle Ned's debts, and he said he was sure this was what Uncle Ned would have wanted. And between cowardice and a sense of being lost in a wood and only seeing one light in sight, I agreed."

" And—how long did he keep to his side of the bargain ? "

She shivered slightly. " Not very long. He said I must see it wasn't fair to take everything and give nothing, and I should be much happier . . . By the time I'd been married six months I knew that I should never make a greater mistake in my life, and I tried every way I knew to get out of it. But, of course, it was impossible. I was dependent on him for everything, and people aren't anxious to employ a wife whose husband doesn't want to let her go. After a time I realised that he was having me followed wherever I went. He became violently jealous, I couldn't have a friend of either sex. I got so desperate I even went to see a lawyer to ask if there was any chance of getting away, but my husband found out about it. When I got back he asked me where I'd been, and when I tried to deceive him, he—oh, it was terrible."

" He wasn't—violent ? "

" Only with his tongue. If he'd struck me I could have used it as evidence against him. But my home became a prison. Then Mr. Bevin started calling up women from all over the place, and I had to go to the Labour Exchange with the rest. I thought that might be my opportunity to get away. I didn't worry about money any more, I knew I could somehow make a living, looking after children or an invalid or something. But my husband had sent a medical certificate to the effect that he oughtn't to be left, and it was better to release some fully-trained nurse for active service than take me and force him to employ a nurse. So back I went, and presently the two women we had had at the beginning of the war left—one was called up and the other said she wasn't going to stay on alone. The chauffeur had gone and the car was laid up. My husband had never been very friendly with his neighbours, but now he refused altogether to see any of them. Of course, with no servants and with part of the house closed, we had no evacuees. The billeting officer, Mrs. Hilary, did come once or twice, but each time he insisted on seeing her and telling her he was a very sick man and he referred her to Dr. Ventnor."

" Was he really ill ? "

" He had definite heart trouble. He couldn't have been called on to do any war service. I don't know," she caught her breath sharply, " I don't know why I'm talking of him in the past tense, he is still alive, or was when I left him to-day."

" Does he know you've come to London ? "

" He doesn't worry so much what I do now. Dr. Ventnor told him a short time ago that I couldn't carry on, doing the housework and the cooking and the shopping, and looking after him. He had rather a bad attack a short time ago, and he spends a good deal of his day in bed, which means carrying trays and cooking special food."

" Doesn't this Dr. Ventnor suggest a nurse ? "

" He did. He said either James must give me a servant or he must have someone to look after him in the sick-room, and he said he'd sooner have someone in the sick-room. He has a great fancy for medicines of every kind. I sometimes think if he took a dose out of every bottle one would counteract the other, and he'd be back where he started. He looked at Dr. Ventnor and laughed in a queer sort of way and said he understood it was every woman's ambition to be a rich widow, and it would probably be wisest for us all to relieve me of some of my responsibility."

" This Dr. Ventnor," asked Stuart. " Has he ever suggested to you that your husband's mind may be affected ? "

" I did ask him once if he thought James was sane, and he said no doctor would dare certify him. There wasn't any proof to the contrary. It was just on this one subject—myself. He manages the household, arranges about paying the bills, makes me keep accounts for my allowance, and complains of my extravagance."

" And he arranged to have a nurse ? "

" No. After Dr. Ventnor had gone he said to me that it was absurd that I couldn't manage. It wasn't as if he needed any real nursing, and quite soon he would be up and about again."

" And that's where the position remains at present ? "

" Yes. Except . . ."

" Well ? By the way, has your husband been hardly hit by the war—financially, I mean ? "

" I'm sure he hasn't. In fact, I believe he is an extremely rich man, though he never discusses business with me."

" What were you going to tell me before I asked that ? "

" My husband is perpetually saying to me that wives who are in sole charge of their sick husbands have innumerable opportunities for poisoning them or getting rid of them in other ways. It's becoming a sort of obsession with him, but when I once said something about it to Dr. Ventnor he pooh-poohed it, said I shouldn't give it another thought, said it was just his rather grim idea of a joke."

" But—it's stopped being a joke to you ? "

The girl turned to him desperately. Her expression was oddly at variance with the sophistication of her appearance, it was so wild and helpless.

" When I can't sleep at night, and often I can't, I keep remembering what he says. I think how simple it would be, I open the paper and read how some man or woman has done that very thing, tampered with food or contrived some accident. I don't really believe I should do such a thing, but my mind becomes more and more filled with the idea. When I saw him the other day leaning rather far out of a low window to see how the garden was being tended, to see if the vegetables were doing well—you can see it from the landing window—it went through my mind how easy it would be to give him a push and every one would think he had fallen."

" I wouldn't be too sure of that," observed the doctor, dryly. " It's surprising the notions people get into their heads when a rich man dies suddenly and it comes out that the only person in the house at the time of the accident was his wife."

" It's James's fault really," she persisted. " If he wasn't always trying to catch me out—or perhaps he only wants to drive me to the point of desperation—I simply don't understand. He didn't have to marry me . . ."

" One presumes he married you for the usual romantic reason that he had fallen in love," hazarded Dr. Stuart.

" I think he had, but I was honest with him. He knew there was nothing of that sort on my side. How could there be ? A man older than my Uncle Ned. And then, when he saw I— I shrank from him, his feeling for me seemed to turn sour. Dr. Stuart, can't you help me at all ? "

" Is it possible for you to leave him ? " the doctor inquired.

" In times such as these, when he's sick ? Oh, I've thought of it a thousand times. If there was any one else, it would be different, but there's no one . . ."

" Then get someone," Stuart advised her curtly. " What about this nurse Ventnor suggested ? By the way, I'll write to him if you like—I believe I know him as it happens, we're both Harton men—and say you've been to see me and I consider you quite unfit to continue under the present strain. He can quote me to your husband if he likes . . ."

" No, no. James mustn't know I've been to see you."

Dr. Stuart gave her a long, intensive stare. " You're afraid of your husband, aren't you ? "

" Yes. I don't know how his mind works. Sometimes I think it would be better if he were cruel in the ordinary way. Anyway, it would be easier to understand. But his mental processes are never still. I'm sure of that. Even when he's laid up as he is at present his brain's working and working, he's laying plots, setting traps. Sometimes I think I shall end by going mad."

" You can put that notion out of your mind right away. I'll write to Ventnor, tell him not to mention your visit to me to your husband, but insist on his own account on your having some help in the house. If that doesn't ease the situation, then he must prescribe a holiday for you, but the very fact that there's someone else on the premises will probably make more difference than you realise."

After she had gone, he told his secretary he wouldn't want anything more that night, and he sat thinking about the girl and her situation. It was clear that the old ruffian, James East, had made an infamous bargain, taking advantage of the girl when she was utterly distraught, and then breaking his word. Of course, a more experienced girl would never have expected him to keep it. Now it looked as though the tale might have some disastrous ending unless Nature mercifully intervened, but it was Stuart's belief that Nature wasn't interested in benevolence.

He took his pen and wrote a line to Ventnor. As he had told Rose, he remembered him quite well, a handsome, ambitious chap. It was funny to think he had ended in a place like Hinton St. Luke, a little village half the county maps wouldn't think worth mentioning. But it could be that he was nursing James East, had expectations in that quarter. For some reason Stuart was unwontedly interested in the case. That girl now, she had something that held your attention, not simply beauty, that mattered to most men far less than most women appreciated, but personality, some distinction for which there were no words. It would be a pity if she came to grief, as she so easily might.

" I might go down to Hinton St. John this year," he mused. " I believe there is an excellent links there. Then perhaps I could go over to St. Luke and just take a look round. In the meantime, I'll get Ventnor to insist on some sort of nurse-companion, ask for a report. It's not three months to my leave and Heaven knows I could do with it."

He remembered sombrely that few people understood that the man who is wounded in battle, no matter how grievously, is often much less of a responsibility than the man or woman on the home front whose wounds are of the mind.

He wrote to Ventnor, and Ventnor wrote back that he had persuaded James East to engage a nurse of sorts, which should relieve Mrs. East of part of her burden. He added that if Stuart was coming down in the summer he'd be delighted to meet him again. But before the time for Stuart's vacation came round the case had changed. Picking up *The Times* one morning the specialist saw that James East had died of heart failure at Hinton St. Luke, and thought with a sigh of relief that that was a problem solved. Presently he wondered precisely how the heart failure had come about, and what was happening to that unforgettable girl, who was now presumably a rich widow. The odds were that she would marry again presently, someone of her own age this time, he hoped. He saw that the funeral was private and the widow desired no letters.

CHAPTER TWO

ALTHOUGH he had lived quite obscurely for some years James East was sufficiently well remembered in Fleet Street to merit a short paragraph in the obituary notices of the press. It was recalled that he had made a fortune by great audacity many years before the war ; he had bought up a vast number of shares in an apparently derelict mine, and some time later it was made known that gold had been found there. There had been some ugly rumours, though naturally the press was discreetly silent as to these, to the effect that the mine was worthless, and some outspoken critics declared that James East had rigged the whole story. There was, however, no ground for legal action, and he retired with a considerable fortune and prudently made no more speculations. The press merely observed that he had made a fortune speculating in mines many years before the war, had spent a good deal of time abroad prior to 1939 and the last years of his life in poor health in the country. His sole remaining relative was the wife he had married five years previously, and for good measure several papers added that she was forty years her husband's junior.

The majority of English folk are law-abiding people, accepting a monotonous existence and on the whole living virtuous if uninspired lives. They enjoy their excitement by proxy, by reading detective stories and seeing gangster films and following with breathless excitement the more sensational stories in the press. The casual comment—that Mrs. East was forty years her husband's junior—appealed to a great many imaginations, and in bus queues and potato queues and bread queues and cinema queues, and round teashop tables where men and women sipped ersatz coffee, and at bridge parties, a remark would be made about this odd case of a girl marrying a man forty years her senior. Something fishy, they said. Very convenient for her, they said. She can't have married him for anything but his money, they said. And —wonder if there'll be an inquest, they said.

" Very nice," said Arthur Crook, glancing at the paragraph.

" Think there's any my eye about it ? " asked Bill Parsons.

" I'm not being paid to think—yet," said Crook.

" Any one can die of heart failure, particularly a chap of about sixty," Bill offered.

" Every one does," Crook agreed in his amiable way. " I wonder what the girl's worth. The Chancellor ought to be fond of her, she'll bring him quite a slice of revenue in the shape of death duties. Well, it's an ill-wind that blows no one any good."

But if this particular wind had brought any one any good it certainly wasn't Rose East.

The public was permitted to realise this a few days after the original announcement of James East's death. It began with a little paragraph in an evening paper :

RICH MAN'S DEATH MYSTERY
Nurse's Statement

The nurse in question was a Miss Monica Beake, who was the direct result of Dr. Stuart's advice to the widow.

" Insist on having another woman in the house," he had said, and he had written the same to Frank Ventor. It had been difficult to get a fully-trained nurse for such an out of the way village since, though the war was over, shortage of labour was still very great and not many nurses wanted to go down to look after a tiresome but not very sick elderly man at Hinton St. Luke. Miss Beake, however, was beyond the age limit of the Ministry of Labour. She was forty-nine years old and therefore could not be directed. Miss Beake explained that she was like a practised amateur actress ; she couldn't claim professional status but she knew her job a great deal better than an inexperienced pro. She seemed to have spent most of her life moving from the sick-room of one relation to another.

" What happened to your mother and your Aunt Teresa and your Cousin Alice ? " Rose East asked her one day.

" They died," said Miss Beake.

It was from one point of view an encouraging reply. All the same, she had to work a stormy passage at Hinton St. Luke, for James East at first set his face absolutely against her appointment. It was an unnecessary waste of money, and proof positive of his wife's disloyalty and indifference. A good wife would strain every nerve to keep things going without outside assistance, and indeed at the beginning he suspected that the two women were hand in glove.

" Where did you first meet this Beake woman ? " he demanded sullenly of Rose.

" She answered the advertisement. I'd never heard her name before."

" I suppose she thinks there's something in it for her."

" It's a job," Rose pointed out.

" Don't be so simple. She could get plenty of jobs, or so they tell me, but they won't all be jobs with rich men. You can make it clear to her that if she thinks she'll feather her nest at my expense she's making a great mistake."

Monica Beake was certainly a trier. She wasn't young, she had very little money, she had no connections to speak of, but she went to work on James East like Monty going to work in Libya. She took a great deal of pains about her appearance. She could have had no illusions as to her looks ; she had been born with large plain features, but she had taken great care of her figure, and she was very careful about her clothes. She had her hair permanently waved, took a lot of trouble about make-up, never wore stockings with runs in them, and if her clothes were a little startling she did contrive to give the impression that here was someone a little out of the ordinary. She made it quite clear from the start that she had come to nurse, and though she was prepared to look after her patient's room she could not be asked to cook or do any form of housework generally. James began by being unco-operative, not to say rude, but she treated him with cheerful friendliness, and sooner than Rose would have thought possible the two were exchanging life histories. She had a way of telling hard luck stories with a smile and a pat of her careful coiffure that James East found inspiring. She could evoke sympathy without ever appearing sorry for herself, and within a few weeks she was quite securely dug in at the household at Hinton St. Luke.

" That proposal of Stuart's was a definite success," remarked Frank Ventnor to Rose a short time after Miss Beake's arrival. " She's smoothed your husband down no end."

" Yes," said Rose, non-committally. " She knows her job all right."

" You don't like her ? "

" I suppose James would say she was sensible to reap as much as she can while the sun's still shining. After all, she has her own future to consider."

" But doesn't it make things easier for you having her here ? "

" In a way," Rose admitted. " It's easier to get the household expenses, which is a help, of course."

" Then," Frank began, and Rose said unemphatically : " I don't trust her. I don't trust her an inch. She's virtually shut me out of my husband's room. He won't even let me mix his medicine nowadays."

" Seeing that's what she's paid for, why should you mind ? Oh, Rose ! " He stopped. " I could be crossed off the medical register, I suppose, for trying to make love to my patient's wife, but—I can't stand seeing you look so miserable. If ever a woman was made for happiness, it's you."

" But, Dr. Ventnor—Frank—I never guessed . . ."

" Didn't you ? Or don't you ever imagine being in love ? "

" I never look beyond the day," Rose confessed. " I'm afraid to. Still, in a way you're right. It is a good thing having her here. James doesn't taunt me as he used to. Miss Beake's a new interest for him. They spend hours talking together. Did you notice she was wearing a new ring, a pearl and diamond affair ? "

" I hadn't," Ventnor admitted. " Did your husband give it to her ? "

" Yes. She had a birthday a few days ago. She told him

she has no relations and she's stopped keeping birthdays, and he said, ' What nonsense.' She brought me the ring to show me ; she said she could cry at being remembered again by any one. And then she asked me if I minded her having it. She said I had so much, and women who owned jewellery had no idea what it was like to love beautiful things and know you'd never possess them."

" But did you mind ? I thought you didn't really care very much about jewellery ? "

" I don't—not very much. But any wife would mind being made to look a fool to her husband's nurse. Oh, I don't mean he's trying to make love to her or anything of that sort, though I do wonder sometimes, if I died suddenly, would he marry her ? "

" Very morbid of you," said Dr. Ventnor crisply.

" I know he's pretty old and in poor health, but he certainly seems better since she came."

" He is better," the doctor agreed. " She's provided a stimulus."

" Yes." Rose hesitated for moment, then said courageously, " I'm going to ask you a question, and if it's unprofessional you mustn't answer it. But—precisely how bad is James ? "

" Do you mean, how long is he likely to live ? "

" Yes. I suppose that's what I mean."

" It all depends. His heart's not at all sound. If he takes things very quietly he may go on for a considerable time, but any sudden shock or upset might finish him off. That's another reason I was glad when he agreed to Stuart's proposal. It halves your responsibility. Now, if anything happens, no one can point at you—at either of us, come to that—or suggest that we neglected any conceivable precaution."

She looked so white, so miserable, so strained and devoid of youth, standing there facing her own hopeless future, that impulsively he caught her arm and drew her towards him.

" Courage, Rose," he said. " It won't be so very much longer I'm certain of that. Don't let your heart fail at the last lap."

She stood very still, her heart beating thickly, in the circle of his supporting arm, without speech, almost without breath. Then at last she whispered, " I'm so tired, Frank, so desperately tired. I'm not sleeping well . . ."

" I'll give you some stuff. You must sleep. Remember, you're still young, you've still got so much of your life ahead.

Don't mortgage it now, simply because you feel you can't carry on."

There was a shocked sort of giggle from the doorway and the two moved quickly apart. Miss Beake had pushed the door open unnoticed, and now she stood bridling and simpering on the threshold.

" Oh dear, I hope I didn't come in at an inconvenient moment. Mr. East sent me down to look for Mrs. East. He understood you'd gone some time ago, doctor."

" I'm prescribing for Mrs. East," said the doctor, briskly. " She's run down, Miss Beake, I want her to take things easy for a little." He turned back to Rose and held out his hand. " I'll send that stuff up during the day, and mind you take it every night till you've got back into the habit of sleeping."

" Will you be coming in to-morrow, doctor ? " inquired Miss Beake.

" Not unless you send for me, and I hope that won't be necessary."

" I'll tell Mr. East that. He seemed quite anxious—I thought perhaps you found he was worse . . ."

" Not at all. Under your care he's flourishing. I believe you'll keep him alive long enough for him to follow all our funeral coaches to the tomb."

" Well, naturally that's in my interest." She giggled again. " If anything happened to him I should lose a most generous employer. Now, Mrs. East, don't look so worried. I'm here to take the worry off your shoulders. If you go on frowning like that I shall think you're dissatisfied with the way I carry out my work."

" Of course not," said Rose stiffly. But all the same there was now an element in the house at least as unwelcome as her husband's previous suspicion. She was convinced that something was, as Crook would have said, ' cooking ' between her husband and this unscrupulous woman. Ventnor saw and recognised her suspicions.

" You must appreciate her position, Rose," he said. It was only recently that he had begun to address her by her Christian name. " She has a living to get, and she means to consolidate her position here. Well, you can't really complain of that. Anything's better than that you should be left alone with him."

" Do you think he might do me some harm ? " There was surprise in her voice, as though this contingency had never hitherto occurred to her.

17

" Not in the sense you mean, but I'm far happier to know there is a third person on the premises. There's not much sense your being sound in wind and limb if your nerves are shot to pieces."

As the weeks went on Miss Beake's attitude towards her employer's wife begun to undergo a change. She had been at first aloof, if not actually hostile, but now she manifested a breezy friendliness that seemed to say, " We're in this together. We both know he's impossible, but we both of us think it's worth while putting up with present discomfort for the hope of future benefits."

Rose came to loathe her, but under that loathing was a shoot of fear. Something in the woman's manner, in the tone of her voice, the significance of her glance whenever Ventnor's name was mentioned, made her apprehensive. She had no illusions whatsoever about the woman, and if Miss Beake thought it would suit her book to poison her employer's mind, Rose was convinced she would not hesitate to do so. It seemed to her, too, that James East's attitude towards his amateur nurse was undergoing change. He had resented her at first, the expense she involved and what he described as her damnable cheerfulness.

" She's delighted I'm ill," he complained to Rose. " The longer I'm in bed and the iller she can persuade that nincompoop of a doctor I am, the more pleased she'll be. I'm simply a bread ticket to her. I never met such an inhuman creature." That had been at the beginning. But now, a few months after her arrival, the pair had reached a pitch of mutual confidence that might have alarmed any wife. It was some days later that James began to speak of going up to London.

" But, James ! " Rose was appalled. " Are you fit ? You know what Dr. Ventnor said, that you must keep very quiet, avoid all possible shocks."

" I'm no more likely to have shocks on a carefully carried out journey to London than in my own home," returned James. " I should go by car, of course. Thank Heaven, some of these absurd petrol regulations have been removed, though doubtless they will be reimposed before long." (This was the summer of 1947.) " Miss Beake would accompany me . . ."

" Miss Beake ? " The words burst from her in an exclamation of dismay.

" Certainly." He regarded her with cold malice. " She's my nurse, isn't she ? You were very anxious to be relieved of your responsibility, so what have you to complain of now? Naturally, she would explain to the driver that I must make the journey as comfortably as possible, and I could take a good rest for some days, if necessary, after my return."

"But why are you going to London, James?"

Her husband laughed at her dismay. "Business affairs," replied he, airily.

"But couldn't your lawyer come down here?"

He looked at her for a minute without answering, wearing that twisted, mocking smile that she hated and feared.

"Perhaps it would be as well for him to be preserved from your influence, my dear. Now, you mustn't think either I or Monica is a fool. And you're a very pretty young woman and men, particularly middle-aged men, can easily be made to lose their heads where youth and beauty are involved. Well, I should know, shouldn't I? You quite bowled me over. Already you've got that conceited popinjay of a doctor on your side. Oh, yes, I can see what's in the wind as well as the next man."

She said, in an agony of apprehension, "There's nothing in the wind, James. But at least, if you stick to this ridiculous idea of going to London, you'll ask Dr. Ventnor first?"

"After you've primed him? My dear, is it likely? How do you suppose I became a rich man out of nothing? By being a fool? Not at all. By seeing which way straws were blowing and following them."

Rose spoke to the doctor. "Can't you persuade him to have his lawyer down here?"

"Can I change the direction of the wind?" asked Ventnor dryly. "I suppose, if I were unscrupulous enough, I could give him an overdose of Epsom salts, disguised as heart mixture, and tell him it was a stimulant. But if anything unexpected did happen and he were to pass out, I might find myself indicted for murder, or at all events accused of it by our friend, the Beake."

Plans, therefore, for the London visit went on with as much preparation as though an expedition to a foreign country were under consideration. Miss Beake, now promoted to being secretary-companion as well as nurse, came downstairs carrying some letters in her hand. Rose, about to go out, said spontaneously, "Does my husband want those posted? I'll take them."

But Miss Beake shook her head roguishly and said, "A good secretary never gives away Master's secrets."

Ventnor came in the next day and Rose repeated the incident. She sometimes wondered if she confided in him too much, she knew how doctors shrink from the confidences of their women patients, but there was no one else.

" I shouldn't make too much of it," said Ventnor. " Oh, I agree there's no doubt about it, the Beake's feathering her own nest, but fortunately the law doesn't allow a husband to cut his wife off without even the traditional shilling these days."

" It isn't only the money," said Rose, " though I suppose that's part of it. But the very thing for which I married James, the need to feel safe, to have some refuge, that's precisely what I've lost. I never had it very long, but now I feel suspicion and hate on all sides. And it frightens me. Sometimes when I'm in my husband's room I feel him watching every movement, and I know what he's thinking, and I feel he's laying plans, and she's hand in glove with him."

" Don't give your imagination too much rein," said the doctor, curtly. " You know, I think it might be a good plan if you were to take a holiday."

" Where ? " asked Rose, forlornly. " Besides, I doubt if James would agree. He'd say he gives me a perfectly good home, and holidays cost money."

" He's back on that lay, is he ? Does he talk much about money these days ? "

" Doesn't he to you ? "

" Oh, he tells me I come here to make my fortune without any trouble, and warns me that if he thinks my bill's unreasonable he won't pay it. But he's always been something of a monomaniac where money's concerned. I wonder if he says much about it to Miss Beake."

That night when Miss Beake came down to dinner, the dinner Rose had bought, prepared and served, she said in a kind voice, " I do hope you don't think I'm unsympathetic, Mrs. East. Believe me, I do appreciate the difficulties of your position, but after all, I'm here to look after your husband, so that, professionally, I'm bound to side with him. You do see that ? "

" There's no question of taking sides," said Rose, disgustedly.

" I understand that it must be embarrassing for you to feel your husband's confiding in a stranger and, as it were, leaving you out of things, but we nurses take a professional view of that sort of behaviour. As a matter of fact, I did ask him if he wouldn't consider your coming to London, too. It would be a little jaunt for you, and I'm sure it must be bad for you being cooped up here all the time with no one young to play with. I don't count the doctor," she added slyly.

Rose wanted to be sick, but Miss Beake went on unconcernedly, " Couldn't you get away for a little ? You really are looking very peaked, and there must be some reliable woman in the neighbourhood who'd come in and look after the house during your absence. We could shut up the rooms we don't use, and have a grand spring-clean when you came back."

" Did my husband ask you to say that to me ? " Rose inquired. She detested herself for asking the question, but she had to know.

" No, but I'm sure he'd see the point if you made tentative arrangements and, so to speak, sprang it on him. I'd back you up, and I'm sure Dr. Ventnor would, too."

" When I want a holiday I'm quite capable of making my own plans," said Rose, quietly. " But that reminds me, what about you ? Aren't you entitled to a change ? "

" I couldn't leave my patient at the moment, and as a matter of fact I'm feeling quite fresh. I shouldn't know a moment's rest if I walked out on him now. Perhaps later on he'll be able to dispense with the services of a nurse, and then I'll fly to Switzerland or something. I've always wanted to go abroad, but I've never been able to afford it. But Mr. East is so generous . . ."

She was so sure of her own position she didn't even trouble to hide her satisfaction.

The day after that Ventnor's periodical bill came in, and when Rose went up to her husband's room he threw it across to her.

" Tell your friend I've no intention of paying professional fees to increase his opportunities for dalliance," he said coarsely. " I could have a man down from Harley Street twice a week for what he's charging me."

" You'd better tell him that yourself," returned Rose crisply. " I don't know anything about fees, but if you're not satisfied you could call in someone else."

" And have him going round the place telling every one I'm a lunatic and ought to be certified ? Oh, I know the stories you've been feeding him. Luckily for me I have a responsible woman who can refute all your lies. You thought you were very clever marrying an invalid, someone who couldn't keep an eye on you, didn't you ? But for once you've overreached yourself."

He had never shown quite that degree of malice and hostility before. " I dare say," he continued, picking up the doctor's account and flapping it furiously against the eider-down, " if I hadn't had the forethought to provide myself with Miss Beake, I should have been in the churchyard before now."

He got short shrift from Ventnor, however. " If you like to dispute my bill, you can take the case to court, if you're such a fool," the doctor told him. " And in case you'd for-gotten, there's a law of slander in this country. I sympathise with your wife, as I'd sympathise with the wife of any invalid, but your suggestions are preposterous and malicious and if I hear you making them again to any one I shall take action. If you think I've charged you too much, call in another doctor, and I wish him joy of such a cantankerous patient."

James East was astounded, but he said in equally furious tones, " If you think I shan't call your bluff, you're quite wrong. I know you're much more interested in my wife than you are in my health, which, strange as it may seem to you, is the reason for your being under my roof at all."

" I really believe the old boy is going off his rocker," reflected Ventnor. " All the same, he's going to pay my bill, and he isn't going to switch his medical attendant. Heaven knows, there aren't many rich patients in this hole. I ought to have foreseen that at the start."

" I suppose," said he sarcastically to his patient, " your private inquiry agent supplies you with all these details." He crossed the room as he spoke and jerked open the door. Miss Beake stood outside.

" I thought as much. Come in, won't you, Miss Beake ? Much more comfortable than standing in that contracted attitude in the passage."

" I was just coming upstairs and I thought I heard Mr. East call out. I quite thought you'd gone, doctor."

" I shall be gone in a minute. When do you propose to go to London, Mr. East ? "

" The day after to-morrow. Why didn't you ask my wife ? "

" She doesn't happen to be here. In any case so long as you're not officially *non compos mentis* it's more reasonable to ask you yourself."

" He's going to take a very easy day to-morrow," continued Miss Beake, " then he'll feel thoroughly refreshed for the journey. As a matter of fact, we're both looking forward to it very much. We were so much afraid you would forbid it."

" Not likely," said James East in disagreeable tones, but he didn't amplify his remarks.

Rose was just coming in when Ventnor came down the stairs. " I hear everything's set for Wednesday," he said. " Look here, think over my suggestion about getting a holiday. This isn't a healthy house for you just at present. And if you're afraid of leaving a clear field to that Beake female, believe me, she's got less powder and shot to play with in your absence."

But Rose shook her head. " No. I don't like being spied on, but if I must, then let it be in my own house. Even if James didn't post someone to watch me, I could never be sure. No, I'll wait a little, anyway till he gets back from London, and find out just what he has in his mind."

" Well." He shrugged uncertainly. " Watch out for yourself. I don't like the look of the man. I don't suggest for an instant that he's certifiable, but he's in an ugly frame of mind and, quite unprofessionally, I tell you that woman he's got is egging him on."

" I know. She keeps coming down and trying to persuade me to confide in her. I don't trust her an inch. It seems queer that I married to be safe, and now I feel less safe than I've ever done in my life."

" You don't look up to much either," he acknowledged. " If you take my tip you'll lie down and take some aspirin. Got any ? "

" James will have a chest full. He takes three tablets after every meal ; he even carries three tablets in his wallet in case he's ever caught without them. It's no wonder he and Miss Beake get on so well. Between them, they must have practically everything that ever came out of a chemist's shop."

He smiled faintly. " I didn't realise they were such fanatics. What's her particular solace ? "

" Oh, some sort of indigestion mixture, not because she has indigestion any more than James has headaches, but as a sort of preventive. The instant they've swallowed their last morsels they both dash to their bottles like—like dope fiends.

" I don't suppose there's anything very dangerous in any

of their mixtures." He laughed more frankly now. " You poor dear ! Are you tormented with visions of corpses clutching bottles in their stiffening hands ? "

She turned, her eyes frantic. " Don't joke about it. It's not a bit funny. Oh, forgive me. I seem overwrought to-day. I'll take your advice and see what some of James's aspirins will do for me."

She heard the front door close behind him and began wearily to ascend the stairs. At the turn of the staircase a door flashed open and there was Miss Beake peering down at her.

" Is that the doctor going ? You know, I think he ought to prescribe for you. I shall tell your husband, you're the real invalid in this house."

" Please don't," said Rose, colourlessly. " It's simply that I have rather a headache and Dr. Ventnor has suggested I should take some aspirins. I expect my husband has plenty . . ."

" Oh, well," Miss Beake looked arch, " I'm his nurse. I know how he counts on them and I see he always has a bottle in reserve. I dare say he'll spare you a few." She went back into her patient's room and said girlishly, " You'll have to yield pride of place to your wife, Mr. East. She's looking like a ghost, and she wants to know if you'll spare her a few aspirins."

" Don't run me short," exclaimed James East on the instant. " You know how dependent I am on them. I expect Headley's still open," he added disagreeably.

" Why, you've only just opened a new bottle, you greedy old man," Miss Beake reproached him. She snatched up the little bottle from beside the bed. James East always had his aspirins supplied in bottles of twenty-five, because he said then they were small enough to be carried in the pocket. Miss Beake passed the bottle to Rose, saying kindly, " Don't bother to bring it back just yet. We shan't be wanting it again till after dinner."

She followed the girl out on to the landing to say earnestly, " Mrs. East, don't think I'm trying to interfere, but honestly, why don't you give up smoking so many cigarettes for a little while ? It really can't be good for you. I haven't liked to say anything, but, of course, I couldn't help noticing . . ."

Rose threw back her head. The woman was right, of course. She was smoking too many cigarettes. But she resented what she considered her insolence.

" Really, Miss Beake, there is no need," she began, but the woman did not allow her to finish her sentence.

"You mustn't think I don't understand. I do. I've had some bad times myself. Well, who hasn't? And I used to smoke far too much, until I was afraid of becoming a slave to the habit, so I resolved to cut it right out—like that." She made a gesture with her hand as of someone slicing—no, slashing—a loaf of bread. "Of course, it was hard to start with, but I persevered. No half measures for you, my girl, I told myself. And now," she wound up triumphantly, "I haven't touched a cigarette for over a year. Just as well," she added more dryly, "seeing the price they are now. I certainly couldn't afford them on what I'm able to earn." Then, seeing that Rose had gone chalk-white, and apparently fearing some outburst that would upset the entire household, she added hastily, "You will try and get some sleep, won't you? I'll come and call you when it's time to start thinking about dinner." Because, however sympathetic she might sound, it was quite clear that Miss Beake had no intention of taking over the cooking even for one evening.

"It won't be necessary," said Rose. "I don't expect I shall sleep."

"You should try and relax, Mrs. East, for your husband's sake as well as your own. You want to feel your very best to-morrow. As you know, I'm having Tuesday afternoon this week instead of Wednesday, as I have to accompany your husband to London on that day, so you'll be absolutely in charge, and I don't deny that the old gentleman can be a strain."

Rose turned and hurried to the room she had occupied since Miss Beake's arrival. This was at the farther end of the house, right away from James's apartments. She used to sleep in the dressing-room after James took to his bed, but the newcomer had turned her out of that, saying she needed the room for herself, and anyway if she was the nurse it would be better for the wife to be a little farther off. Rose hadn't minded —much—not then, but now she thought it was the thin end of the wedge. She had no doubt at all that Miss Beake intended to do her harm if she could, was steadily elbowing her out of the position she should rightfully occupy.

"I dare say I'm being unfair to her," she acknowledged, lying on her bed, her arm across her eyes. "Even before she came I wasn't the meek adoring wife. She's simply making capital out of the situation, which I suppose is what one should expect. She knows I've no friends, no one to turn to. If I'm to be rescued from my slough of despair it must be by my own efforts."

She lay wondering about the London visit. Presumably James intended to alter his will, to disinherit his wife so far as the law allowed. Possibly Miss Beake's name would be found in the new version. She didn't know. The probability was Miss Beake didn't know, either. James was so twisted he could have made a corkscrew look like a straight line. For a while she felt too tired even to unscrew the cap of the aspirin bottle and take the dose Ventnor had recommended. The struggle had gone on so long, the odds were so uneven. Few people, she knew, have much sympathy with the wife of a rich man. Suppose he is a bit difficult, a bit cantankerous. Nobody gets everything, and a bit of bad temper isn't a great deal to pay for a comfortable home and a secure future.

" But that's just what I'm not sure about," she acknowledged to herself, turning over and fumbling in the dark for the aspirin. " He's perfectly capable of any meanness out of revenge and, short of pushing him out of a window, there's nothing I can do about it."

She shook three small white tablets out of the opened bottle into her palm, then realised that there was no water in the room with which to swallow them. Reluctantly she got off the bed and went into the adjoining bathroom, still carrying the little bottle. Perhaps it was some sixth sense that made her glance at the label in the very act of conveying the tablets to her mouth and see, with a stab of apprehension, that in the dark she had picked up the bottle of sleeping tablets Ventnor had given her some months before. The bottles were almost identical, and by some mischance the tablets had been left on the bedside table instead of being locked up in the drawer, as was customary. Slowly she lowered her hand and stood looking at the little white lozenges, so small, so innocent-looking, yet containing in their tiny content the seeds of certain death. " One only " the bottle said, and Ventnor had explained that more than one would be dangerous, if not actually fatal. Three would have written Finis to the story, and for an instant she could regret the instinct that made her consult the label. When she had considered various ways of getting out of her prison, strangely enough this one had never come into her mind. And yet—how simple it would be. One small gesture, and she would be past everything, past humiliation, anxiety, the constant nagging wear and tear, the appalling sense that life had come to a permanent standstill, that she was like someone paralysed. And because personal grief always seems separate and particular, she never saw herself as one of a great army of disappointed wives, all of whom were enduring their circumstances with as much grace as they could muster, a contemplation that might have reduced her unhappiness to something so commonplace it wasn't worth making a fuss about.

"All the same," she told herself, returning to the three sleeping tablets to their bottle and taking up the aspirin instead, " I shan't take that way out, not yet. It wouldn't be fair to James, giving the impression that he and Miss Beake between them had driven me over the edge." Besides, even when things are at their worst, the average person is secretly persuaded that something better must be on the way. It's only in later middle-age that hope fails, in spite of what Mr. G. K. Chesterton has said to the contrary.

She was so much taken aback by the narrowness of her escape that it was some time before she could bring herself to put the harmless aspirins into her mouth, and even then she could not sleep. She took up one of the slender books of poetry that she kept beside the bed and opened it at random.

> The chaffinch speaks and then the dove.
> Then the blackbird. This is spring.
> There they wake and talk of love—
> Here I lie, remembering.

She closed the book and slipped it under her pillow. That was another thing Miss Beake used to smile about.

"All this poitry," she'd say. " I can't think what you see in it, Mrs. East. I never could understand what it was about myself."

When Miss Beake read, which was not often, she chose books with titles like " Not Wooed but Won," or " Twice Betrayed." Rose turned over, stretched, looking through the half-drawn curtains at the fading light. It was so quiet at this end of the house you might imagine you lived in a separate dwelling. She wondered what Miss Beake and James were discussing at this moment. Herself perhaps. Or the real intention behind James East's surprise visit to London. It was so much more sensible, so much more characteristic of James, for Merridew to come down to Hinton St. Luke. And surely, surely, even when you had allowed for all conceivable expenses a lawyer could incur on such a journey, it would work out more cheaply for James.

"There's something here I don't understand," she assured

herself. She wondered if Miss Beake understood. How much did James confide in her? Or was he, as they say, leading her also up the garden path, making vague promises he never intended to keep?

"Not that I need worry about Miss Beake's future," she told herself grimly. "She's perfectly capable of looking after herself."

As for her own future, that hardly bore thinking of. Unless —suddenly she was quite wide awake—unless she refused to be dominated by her circumstances, pulled herself together before it was too late and struck out for herself. She had always said, "I married James because I was afraid and because I wanted what he could give me. So, of course, I couldn't leave him now?"

But was that the truth any longer? Did he give her anything she wanted? And wasn't it, perhaps, rather feeble for a young woman in excellent health, to sit back and let life, in the person of James East, ride roughshod over her? That was the mistake so many women made, accepting their situation as inevitable, whereas really what they lacked was not opportunity but courage and energy. Opportunity? She turned the word over on her tongue. She had supposed she had none left. But if she pulled herself together, wasn't there an opportunity now, almost at this instant, gaping at her feet? Her metaphors became mixed, while her interest quickened.

"I may not get another chance," she thought. "James won't go to London again. And Miss Beake will be out of the way. She said so."

The more she thought of this idea the more it appealed to her. Of course, it meant taking risks, but life was a risky affair, real life anyway. She began to plan. It would be simpler than she had at first supposed. For a considerable time she lay tense on the bed, making and discarding plans until at last sleep overwhelmed her.

It was late when she woke and Miss Beake was standing by her bedside.

"Well, that's a good girl," she said in her odiously familiar way. "Why, you look a different person. I was beginning to wonder if you were ever going to wake up, and then what would your poor hubby do for his dinner? He wants keeping up just now, with that long journey ahead of him."

And with a beaming smile and a reminder from the doorway not to go to sleep again, the triumphant Miss Beake returned to her happy, self-imposed task of home-breaking.

CHAPTER THREE

THE NEXT MORNING Monica Beake was up even earlier than usual, and she was at all times an early riser.

"It's got to be a very wide-awake lark that beats me to the breakfast-table," was her coy way of putting it. This was going to be a busy day for her; when she had 'straightened up her patient' as she expressed it, and had a final word with the doctor, who was coming in that morning to make sure that James East really could face to-morrow's journey, she intended to catch the 12.30 bus into Hinton St. John, where she would lunch, keep an appointment with her hairdresser, have her nails manicured and perhaps buy a hat for to-morrow's jaunt. She left everything ready for James, and was assiduous in reminding him that he must husband his strength for the next day.

"If things don't go quite as smoothly as usual, don't worry," she warned him. "Remember it's to-morrow that matters. We can't have you collapsing on the journey up."

She even debated whether she would give up her afternoon off, but decided against this. In his present mood, it would probably be a good thing to leave East with his wife for a few hours. He'd be all the more ready to carry out his plans next morning.

Ventnor came in and had a brief interview with his patient. He told Miss Beake she needn't stop if she was busy, and she hurried off to find Rose and give a few final instructions.

"You won't let him get argumentative while I'm away, will you, now?" she said importantly. "I know it's very difficult for you, because he has these perverse fits when he seems to want to make trouble, but you know what the doctors say, and of course I can support it from my own experience. When people are ill, especially if it's an illness connected with the heart, they always seem to turn first against those they care for most. I suppose that isn't very much consolation to you at the moment, but what I always say is, we don't see the whole picture, and any change, in a way, would be a change for the better."

"I don't know what you mean by that," said Rose freezingly, but Miss Beake had her ear cocked for the sound of the doctor's departure. Ventnor was caught in the hall.

" I think he's doing a fool thing going to town," he said brusquely. " If he does collapse, don't blame me, but at his age and in his condition, all this excitement—you'd think he was going courting—is the worst possible thing for him."

" You'd be surprised," said Miss Beake in a vulgar, oracular way. After Ventnor had gone she ran up for a final word with the old man. " Now, be good," she said to him, " and leave all the worrying about everything to me. That's what you have a nurse for. Ta-ta for now, and I'll be seeing you again soon after six."

But when she returned at six-thirty James East was dead.

As she let herself in with her latch-key the door of the morning-room opened and to her amazement Mrs. Hillary, the Vicar's wife, marched into the hall.

" Oh, there you are," said Mrs. Hilary. " I began to think you must have missed the bus."

" What's happened ? " demanded Miss Beake, sharply. " Where's Mrs. East ? "

" Just at the moment she's at the Vicarage with my husband. She's had a bad shock."

Miss Beake stood perfectly still. " Mr. East ? "

" Yes. He died very suddenly of heart failure this afternoon."

She spoke in a perfectly cool way, but she kept her eyes on the other woman's face. For a moment Miss Beake said nothing, then suddenly she flung down her bag and gloves and broke out furiously, " I suppose I might have guessed it. The one afternoon I was out. Her own husband, and she couldn't . . . What happened ? "

" You'd better ask Dr. Ventnor. I wasn't here."

" Was he ? "

" No. That was what was so dreadful. Apparently he was rather restless, but she put that down to his proposed journey to London and she gave him his aspirins as usual. After that she left him to sleep for a time and she went back to her work about the house. She looked in once but he was sleeping peacefully, so she didn't disturb him. But when tea-time came and he still hadn't rung for her she felt a little anxious and went up to make sure that all was well. She said at first she thought he was all right, but when she went nearer the bed she realised he had had some crisis."

" You mean," interrupted Miss Beake in a tone charged with feeling, " she decided he was dead ? "

"She feared so. I tell her we should really be grateful that he did pass in his sleep, without pain or—or apprehension. We all knew his life was limited in any case . . ."

"All our lives are limited," snapped Miss Beake.

"But his rather more definitely than most of ours ; that is, so far as our knowledge goes. And it should be a consolation to her that it was quite painless. I have experience of heart disease—perhaps you have, also—and sometimes the sufferings of the patient are quite heartrending."

"A consolation ! Grateful ! " Miss Beake's fury was like a river whose pent-up force suddenly bursts its dam and comes down like a cataract, destroying everything in its path. "Oh, I don't doubt she's grateful. What could be more convenient ? But she needn't think she's heard the last of this. Heart failure, indeed ! "

"Miss Beake ! " Mrs. Hilary's nice voice was suddenly as hard and cold as an icicle. "I'm afraid the shock has been too much for you. You can hardly realise what you are saying. All of us who know Mrs. East have nothing but sympathy and admiration for her and the way she has endured her very difficult life with her husband. A sick man takes fancies, and, of course, Mr. East had been ill for a considerable time before you came. I don't think you have any conception of the steadfastness that has been needed to keep up appearances. Mr. East was, to be candid, an impossible patient . . ."

"I have never found him so," flashed Miss Beake.

"Because his wife bore the brunt of his moods and fancies. It was most distressing for her that he should die when she was alone in the house, and I am afraid we may presently get a condition of delayed shock."

Miss Beake appeared to consider. Then she asked, "Who says he died of heart failure ? "

"His regular medical attendant." Mrs. Hilary's voice was aloof, dangerously so, as though she might any minute forget her Christian vocation and remember that in nearly every woman there is a streak of the feline.

"Dr. Ventnor ? I thought as much. Where is she now—Mrs. East, I mean ? "

"At the Vicarage with myself and my husband. Dr. Ventnor agrees that she should not remain in a house that must have many painful memories for her, at all events until after the funeral. I don't know what your own feelings are, of course, about staying in the house with a dead man, but if you prefer to move out I believe The Pheasant makes visitors

31

very comfortable. In fact, I once stayed there myself; in the circumstances I am sorry Mr. Hilary and I cannot offer you accommodation."

" I haven't any intention of going to The Pheasant," said Miss Beake, rudely. " Someone shall stay on the premises and see to it that justice is done."

She looked down at her nicely-manicured nails, touched her carefully-waved hair and flung down on the table the ridiculous but somehow very engaging little hat she had bought that afternoon, saying she wanted something fashionable to wear to London. Mrs. Hilary, looking at the name on the box, said dryly, " I should have thought, if you were going to London to-morrow, you would have done your shopping there. By the way, Dr. Ventnor seemed rather surprised you were not on the premises this afternoon."

Miss Beake flung up her head. " So it's going to be like that, is it ? It's my fault Mr. East died. The wily old fox ! " She meant Ventnor by that, of course, as Mrs. Hilary recognised. " What does he think I am ? A slave, never to have any time to myself ? I had my own reasons for wanting to go out this afternoon. Anyhow, I didn't want to arrive in town looking like last year's model."

Mrs. Hilary, dismissing the subject of Miss Beake's appearance as one of supreme unimportance, continued evenly, " If you meant what you said about remaining on the premises, naturally you will do as you think best. Personally, I should advise The Pheasant—in the absence of Mrs. East, I mean." Her voice said, " You're not one of the family. Why should you stay here ? "

Miss Beake's resolution hardened. " I shall certainly stay here. I have my own reasons. I suppose Mrs. East won't be seeing any one to-night . . ."

" Mrs. East will see no one unless it is absolutely essential for the next few days. My husband and I intend to do everything we can to help her. Dr. Ventnor . . ."

" Dr. Ventnor ! " Miss Beake practically spat out the words. " What about this lawyer in London ? Does he know what's happened ? "

A stranger might have supposed that Mrs. Hilary could not register a lower temperature, but he would have been wrong. Even the enraged amateur nurse was a little abashed by her manner.

" I am sure you are actuated by a desire to be of all possible assistance," commented the Vicar's wife in a tone that said of course she didn't really believe anything of the kind, " but Mrs. East and her friends will attend to all matters concerning Mr. East. My husband will look after the funeral, and a message has already been sent to London to warn Mr. Merridew not to expect his client to-morrow."

" And he has been told why ? Well, you may be pretty sure he'll smell a rat."

Mrs. Hilary had the reputation of being the worst-dressed woman in the county ; she slouched in tweeds that, though old, were seldom well-cut, her hats were ruins from the word Go, and she knew less than nothing about make-up or modish hair-do's. But when she chose to assume it, she had an air of such withering authority that even Monica Beake was impressed.

" Are you aware that these expressions of opinion could be translated by an expert, by Mr. Merridew, for example, into actual slanders ? "

" I have to do my duty," insisted Miss Beake. " There are steps to be taken . . ."

" I have already assured you that all necessary steps will be or have been taken by the appropriate people. I quite appreciate your concern for your employer's affairs, but the lamentable fact must be faced that he is no longer your employer, and you are therefore under no further obligation to him. Obviously, Mrs. East or her representative will see that your enthusiasm is adequately rewarded, and you must regard yourself as free to make any other arrangement that suits you whenever you please. I think I said there would be no inquest—naturally. Dr. Ventnor has been attending Mr. East regularly, and I understand that he is not at all surprised at the development. These things are always something of a shock at the moment, but . . ."

Once again Miss Beake cut across Mrs. Hilary's steady voice. " You don't understand, nobody understands but me. Why do you imagine Mr. East was going to London instead of his lawyer coming down to him ? "

" I have no idea," returned Mrs. Hilary composedly. " It's no concern of mine. If he wished to change his will, as Mrs. East seems to think . . ."

" His will. Yes. But that wasn't the half of it. He was going to instruct the firm to make inquiries with a view to divorcing his wife."

Having cast this tremendous bombshell Miss Beake waited, panting like a slavering dog, to see its effect, and was furious

33

and disgusted to watch it fizzle out under her eyes. Mrs. Hilary didn't turn a hair.

"Oh, come, Miss Beake," she railled her, "that's quite absurd. I don't accuse you of inventing it, but if Mr. East really proposed such a thing, and he wasn't joking in rather doubtful taste, or you didn't understand quite what he said, it would simply be additional proof of the deterioration of his mental faculties."

Miss Beake was so angry she let her mantle of polite gentility slip for a moment, and stood naked and not very attractive before her companion.

"So that's the game, is it? I might have guessed it. James East was mad. Therefore nothing he said or planned is to be taken seriously. I suppose that hussy put you up to that."

"If by hussy, Miss Beake, you are referring to Mrs. East, and it is difficult for me to see who else you can mean, I can only assume that you don't know what you are saying."

"I know all right," shouted Miss Beake. She would have added details, but Mrs. Hilary closed the conversation by saying firmly, "Then I can only suppose you are intoxicated. I must go now, but I have told you your alternatives for the night. And I should perhaps warn you that the law of slander is a very serious one. If you take my advice, which is worthy of consideration, as you will agree when you have cooled down a little, you will lie down for a time, and when you have thought things over I am sure you will wish to apologise for what you have said and withdraw it unreservedly."

With no appearance of hurry and wearing an awful dignity that silenced the fuming Miss Beake, she strolled out.

"I quite understand how it is people commit murder," she told her husband later. "I could have put my two hands round that woman's throat with the greatest of pleasure, and watched her die by inches."

"Quite, my dear," agreed Lionel Hilary with an equanimity few people had seen disturbed. "But it is one of our privileges as Christians to deny ourselves unlawful pleasures for righteousness' sake."

Mrs. Hilary refused to be soothed. "I wish I were a witch," she said. "Isn't there a spell that covers the enemy with vermin that never goes away? I think that would be very suitable."

"It would be most unsuitable," returned her husband in firm tones. "And the R.D.C. wouldn't be at all pleased. They know, if you don't, that you can't play fast and loose with insured persons with our present Minister of Health in charge of the department."

" Of course," continued Mrs. Hilary, " I told that creature there was nothing in it, that it was simply an invention of her own poisonous mind, but where do you suppose James East got the idea ? "

" Where human nature gets all its foul ideas, from the devil," said the simple-minded Vicar. " By the way, I telephoned the lawyer, as that poor child is in a state of collapse, and the fellow's coming down as soon as he can get away. It's just as well we aren't having an inquest—a jealous woman can do as much harm in a small community like ours as an atom bomb."

" Ought I to warn Frank Ventnor ? " Mrs. Hilary wondered.

But the Vicar said firmly that it wasn't her job.

" You mean, you think Providence will ? " Mrs. Hilary's long mouth twisted.

" If by Providence you mean Miss Beake, I have no doubt you are right."

Dr. Ventnor had no surgery on Tuesdays. He said that a man who worked seven days a week in an age when men of other professions were clamouring for a week of not more than forty hours, and in some cases no more than thirty-five, was entitled to a little time off, though he was wont to add that he got precious little co-operation from his patients. But Tuesday evening he kept firmly to himself. Now and again people got some alarming symptom and telephoned to him, and then most reluctantly he would turn out, but on that evening his surgery was firmly closed and nothing would induce him to open it. On the night of James East's death he had made no engagement for outside, but promised himself a quiet evening on accounts. He had, he decided, reached the cross-roads in his career. Stuart remembered him as a man of infinite ambition, and there were times when he was surprised at himself that he should still be in what he called this tinpot community. He had meant to go in for research, but lack of means had hampered him, and through the good offices of a friend of his father's he had started in practice in Hinton St. Luke, intending it to be merely a step along the road. Then the man who had taken him into partnership was killed in a mountaineering accident, and Ventnor was by this time so popular locally that the dead man's patients all

transferred themselves to him. This presented him with a
smug little practice and he resolved to stay and work it up a
bit before he moved out into some more enterprising sphere.
But one thing had followed another, and although he was
doing quite well he had little opportunity of saving money.
Lately, however, the limitations had irked him almost beyond
endurance, and he was going into the figures and considering
the future when his housekeeper came in to say there was a
lady asking for him.

" A patient ? " he asked sharply, looking up from his papers.
" I don't see people on Tuesdays, Mrs. Pye. All the locals
know that."

" This isn't surgery," said Mrs. Pye, woodenly, " it's the
lady from East House."

" Good Heavens ! " He pushed his papers to one side.
" Ask her to come in."

" I'm glad you've got that much sense," observed a sharp
voice and in marched, not Rose East as he had anticipated,
but the redoubtable and (to him) odious Miss Beake.

" Miss Beake." He stepped back. " I don't understand
why you are here . . ."

" You will," said Miss Beake, taking a chair, uninvited.
" It's about James East's death."

" I've nothing to say to you on that subject. I shall be
giving the death certificate to the undertakers to-morrow, and
they will make all the necessary arrangements with Mr.
East's legal representatives. So far as I'm concerned, that's
the end of the matter."

" Of course, it isn't," retorted Miss Beake, settling herself
scornfully. " If you think I'm going to let that young woman
get away with it so easily, you were never more wrong in
your life."

" I don't know whether you appreciate what you're
implying," began the doctor, and she said calmly, " Certainly
I do. I mean I'm not satisfied about Mr. East's death."

" Too bad," said Ventnor smoothly. " Still, I happen to be
the doctor . . ."

" I'm a citizen with a citizen's privileges."

" Meaning, Miss Beake ? "

" That, if I'm not satisfied and if you can't dispel my
doubts, it's my right and my duty to go to the authorities,
in this case to the coroner, and ask for further inquiry."

" I see." His hand clenched over the papers on his table.
" And that's what you propose to do ? "

" Tell me one thing, Dr. Ventnor. What actually did Mr. East die of ? "

" Heart failure. We always knew he would sooner or later."

" And it happened to suit someone's book that it should be sooner. You must admit that it's extremely convenient for Mrs. East that her husband should pass out just before he alters his will."

" We've no evidence that he intended to alter his will, unless of course he had written to that effect to the lawyer."

" He had told him he wished to see his will and reconsider his dispositions."

" You won't get very far with that in a court of law," said Ventnor, contemptuously. " How do you know he didn't mean to leave his wife more than he originally intended ? "

" I don't, of course, but it's obvious that he wasn't satisfied. In fact, he was going to institute proceedings for divorce."

Dr. Ventnor let out a great hoot of laughter. " What, here, in Hinton St. Luke, where you can't post a letter without half the village seeing you walk down to the Post Office ? You'll have to think of something better than that, Miss Beake."

" You forget," said this forbidding woman. " I've been in the house and on Mr. East's instructions, I've been watching Mrs. East's movements. I don't think he would have had much difficulty in raising doubts at all events."

" Who was he going to cite ? The Vicar ? Or the gardener ? "

Miss Beake said in a level, poisonous tone, " You're rather fond of Mrs. East yourself, aren't you ? "

The doctor got to his feet. " I should warn you, Miss Beake, that if I hear of your repeating that statement to any one whatsoever, whether an official or merely an acquaintance, presuming you have any acquaintances locally, I shall immediately take action. You know perfectly well that a statement like that constitutes criminal slander. Or had the idea of blackmail entered your mind ? "

" Of course not. But Mr. East certainly thought . . ."

" What Mr. East thought is no longer of any importance. What you say may land you in jug. Just remember that, and don't imagine for one instant you can intimidate me or injure Mrs. East by your foul assertions."

All the same, he was worried. He could put up as bold a front as he liked, but no one knew better than he how quickly that kind of gossip goes around.

Besides, there was something about Rose East that he liked very much indeed.

Miss Beake was a formidable opponent. She refused to be quelled by the doctor's anger.

" Maybe it won't do you any good to go to court," she told him spitefully, " and if questions are asked, it's going to look rather odd that on the one day I wasn't there Mr. East should have a heart attack and not be given any of his heart medicine. He wasn't. I examined the bottle before I left. There were three doses left in it, and there were three when I came back."

" Mrs. East doesn't claim that she gave her husband a dose, and in any case, as I keep on telling you, the old man didn't have a heart attack. He died in his sleep of heart failure. And if it comes to things looking queer," he added, sharply, " a coroner might think it a little odd that, on the eve of what I consider a foolhardy experiment, you weren't at your post."

" I suppose you'd expect us nurses to work seven days without a break," flashed Miss Beake, who had stood on her own feet for so long she was like a female Little Tich. " I was giving up my usual day, Wednesday, to take Mr. East to town, so it was perfectly reasonable that I should have another day instead. Anyhow, why should you object ? Are you suggesting that it was risky leaving Mr. East in his wife's charge ? "

" Oh, don't talk nonsense," exclaimed Ventnor impatiently. " He was always in her charge when you were off duty, and for a great many months before you came to the house he was entirely dependent on her."

" And I suppose now you're going to point out that he didn't die till I came to the house," sneered Miss Beake. Oh, a stranger could have seen there was no love lost between these two.

" I hadn't thought of it," returned Ventnor caustically, " but now you come to mention it, it is a point."

" And will you kindly tell me what advantage *I* could conceivably derive from his death ? "

" I don't know. But then I'm not much in your confidence, am I ? And if you were a real nurse you'd be glad things have turned out the way they have. Tyros have some idea there's something rather touching and tender about heart trouble. They'd change their minds if they'd attended it in its final stages as often as I have. If you ask me, James East has been damned lucky. He was doomed and he knew it, and he's slipped out by the easy way."

" Mrs. East's been damned lucky too."

" You might have some difficulty in persuading most people about that," returned the doctor. " It can't ever have been much fun being James East's wife, and during the past year or so it must have been intolerable."

" She seems to have found it so, and have found a very convenient way out."

" You'll find it difficult to keep jobs if you don't curb that dangerous tongue of yours," Ventnor warned her. " If you were a qualified nurse you'd know it's not your place to question the doctor's verdict."

" Very convenient for the doctor," said the obstinate Miss Beake.

" Look here," said Ventnor quietly, " if you're making a charge why not do it openly, instead of all this foul innuendo ? Do you really suggest that in some way Mrs. East is responsible for her husband's death ? "

" All I've said is that people don't die of taking three aspirin tablets."

" No one is suggesting that they do. On the other hand, if a man has a seizure three aspirin tablets aren't going to save him. You don't blame a mouse because it can't pull a horse-carriage. Aspirin will neither save life nor take it—except, of course, in enormous quantities."

" I can see you mean to back her through thick and thin. But don't think you've heard the last of this. Just because Mr. East was retiring and had no friends, that doesn't mean he can disappear, as it were, without any comments being made or questions being asked." And she slammed out furiously.

After she had gone Ventnor frowned and muttered to himself. That infernal jade, he said, she's out to make trouble for Rose, and though that girl's as innocent as—as spring, Miss Beake can ruin her if she carries on this campaign. And there are always people who like to believe the worst. He didn't suppose she could do Rose lasting damage, but there would be whispers and nudging elbows and significant glances if the story broke in the form in which Miss Beake appeared to be dying to tell it. It would sound bad, he had to admit. If it could be established that James East had died on the eve of disinheriting his wife and even starting proceedings for divorce, Rose's position would be even less enviable than it had been for the past few years. Of course, under existing law, a husband cannot entirely disinherit his wife and on even a third of James East's fortune the widow must be a comparatively rich woman. Still, most people wouldn't think of that. He wondered if the story about divorce was true. He would dismiss it at once as too fantastic for consideration if he hadn't known James East so well. To that twisted mind such a course might have seemed possible, and in any case it would have ruined the girl and her suspected lover. Ventnor shivered. It was horrible to think of hate like that let loose, and now it seemed likely that Miss Beake was going to carry on where her employer had perforce had to give up.

"All the same, there's no sense looking on the black side of things," Ventnor told himself, walking up and down the room like the chief character of a Victorian novel. "Miss Beake can't really do much, and all this will blow over quite soon. It won't seem at all strange if Rose moves out of the neighbourhood—she's nothing to leave behind but unhappy memories—and later on, when people have forgotten the gossip and Miss Beake's making mischief in some other job, perhaps . . ." He stood by the window smiling and laying plans. It all mattered so much to him, and though of course he couldn't speak of the future to Rose for a little while, he thought there was a good chance that it would all come right on the night, as they said. Forgetting the dead man, he stood there oblivious to the present, wrapped in a rosy dream.

CHAPTER FOUR

MAJOR CONKLING, the coroner, was a retired Army doctor who had established himself in the neighbourhood on his retirement from the Army, and announced that he didn't want to work any more but intended to enjoy himself for the time that remained to him. In the course of years he had acquired a select list of patients, just enough to prevent his being bored with his wife's endless bridge parties and the place he early acquired on the Committee of the Conservative Association, but he had always set his face against evening and night work, so when Miss Beake arrived panting at his door immediately after dinner, which he had at the unfashionable hour of seven-fifteen, he was prepared to say that in no circumstances could he see any one.

" The lady said it was in connection with a sudden death," the general servant told him, returning from delivering his original message.

" A sudden death ? Whose ? No, never mind. I'll come out."

So out he came, and there was Miss Beake in the hall, her hat a little crooked, her face flushed, her voice hard and resolved.

" I have something to tell you about the death of Mr. James East, who died this afternoon," she told him. " The doctor's prepared to give a death certificate, but I am—was—his private nurse, and I'm quite convinced there has been foul play."

" You'd better come in," said Conkling irritably. He didn't experience the smallest thrill of excitement at the thought that the village might become a focus for national curiosity. To begin with, he knew Ventnor and knew he wasn't the sort of fellow to give a certificate unless he was pretty sure of his verdict, and for another he knew, or believed he knew, women, and in Miss Beake he saw another jealous female out to make trouble for someone younger and prettier than herself. Because even he realised that when she said foul play she was thinking of the young widow.

" Now," he said in the same ungracious tone when they were seated in his uncomfortable regulation hide armchairs, " what grounds have you for your suspicions ? "

Miss Beake poured them out in a steady stream. She had rehearsed her speech so often that she didn't get confused or repeat or contradict herself, and Conkling had to confess, though not aloud, that she had put up quite a good story. Nobody supposed young Mrs. East had married her husband for love, and most people thought him a cantankerous old curmudgeon and wondered how on earth such an attractive girl put up with him. It wasn't even as though he were generous ; village people are like weasels, nothing can ultimately be kept from them. And, if Miss Beake's story could be proved, about the visit to the solicitor and East's intentions in that connection, it certainly looked a bit fishy that he should die when he was alone in the house with his wife just in time to prevent action being taken. However, there was no proof of any sort of foul play and he pointed this out to Miss Beake, brushing aside her repeated statement that a woman with her husband's interests at heart would have mixed a dose and left it by him for emergencies.

" I understand you were the nurse in the case," snapped Conkling, who had taken an immediate dislike to this pushing, dogmatic woman. " That being so, wouldn't it have been a good idea for you to mix him a dose before you left the house ? I really cannot see how you can hold Mrs. East responsible, and certainly no jury would hesitate in their verdict."

" Then you refuse to make any move ? It looks as though I should have to approach the police."

" I can't think why you didn't do that in the first place."

" I would, if we'd been in London or one of the big towns. But this man, Turnbull, is such an idiot it would take all night to try and get the idea that there was some funny business going on into his thick skull."

" You must think mine is equally thick," returned Conkling with an evil courtesy. " I'm afraid I don't believe your cock-and-bull story any more than the constable would, and I might warn you that you're laying yourself open to considerable misconstruction, if nothing worse, by spreading this unfounded suspicion."

" You wait," said Miss Beake, undaunted, and marched back to East House. She had already told Mrs. Hilary that she had no qualms about sharing the place with a dead man, though Rose might choose to cower in the vicarage. Somehow or other, she resolved, as she settled herself with a book and a tea-tray in the drawing-room, she would compel the authorities to take her seriously. She hated Rose East as she had never hated any one in all her life.

She had not been back long when the telephone rang, and Mrs. Hilary's voice said, " Thank Heaven, you're in at last. I'm coming over for Mrs. East's sleeping-tablets. The poor girl is in a wretched state, and the doctor says she must get her sleep."

" I'll get them for you," offered Miss Beake. " I'll bring them up, too, and have a word with her."

But Mrs. Hilary vetoed that at once. Dear Rose was completely exhausted ; it would be quite impossible for her to see any one else to-night.

" They're certainly keeping her locked up like a pearl in an oyster," Miss Beake told herself grimly. " What are they afraid of ? That she'll break down if she's tackled ? "

She went upstairs to the room Rose had occupied since her husband's illness and began to look for the bottle. It should, presumably, be in the drawer of the Queen Anne commode table by the bedside, but this was empty. As Miss Beake knew, it was usually kept locked, and the fact that it was locked no longer and that the tablets had disappeared began to put a notion into her head.

She went back to the telephone and told Mrs. Hilary she couldn't find the tablets. They weren't in their usual place, and was she, Mrs. Hilary, sure that Mrs. East hadn't taken them with her ? Mrs. Hilary asked her to hold on and went to talk to Rose. A minute later she came back to say that the bottle was in the pocket of the overall Rose had been wearing during the afternoon.

" That's a queer place to put them," commented the outspoken Miss Beake. " She must be dotty."

" If it wouldn't be too much trouble to fetch them," insinuated Mrs. Hilary, and she added, " No doubt Mrs. East has her own reasons for keeping them there."

" They're not there as a rule," retorted Miss Beake.

But she couldn't draw Mrs. Hilary, who merely waited to hear that this odious woman had located the bottle and was going to bring it up. In no circumstances, reflected the Vicar's wife, would she be allowed over the threshold.

" Bitch ! " said Miss Beake, after she had hung up the receiver. " I believe she'd back that girl through thick and thin. There's no religion about it. No wonder so many people are leaving the Church."

She stood staring at the bottle in her hand.

" Now why should it be in her overall pocket ? " she demanded of herself. " You don't carry sleeping tablets about as though they were aspirin." And as she spoke she felt her heart give a tremendous leap. It was as if she had been looking for something and suddenly she had found it where she had never thought of searching.

" You fool ! " she said under her breath, and this time it was obvious she was not addressing herself. " You're delivered into my hands. Now at last I can pay you back in your own coin."

She stood perfectly still, oblivious to the fact that up at the Vicarage Mrs. Hilary and Rose were waiting for the tablets. She was working out a plan of campaign, and she had to be very careful. It would never do to make a mistake now, for there would be no opportunity to amend it, and once she set this ball rolling (as usual her metaphors were hopelessly mixed) it would gather impetus and go bounding down to the foot of the hill far faster than she could rush after it to stop it. Carefully she counted the tablets. Fourteen. She poured a few into the palm of her hand, then poured them all back save one.

" Does Mrs. East know how many there should be ? " she wondered. Whatever happened, she repeated to herself, she mustn't make a mistake. Her face was so hard that if someone had bashed it with a hatchet, the hatchet would have come to grief. Smiling in a way that would have made Ventnor's blood run cold, she put on her hat and walked up to the Vicarage.

Mrs. Hilary opened the door. " Here they are," said Miss Beake brightly. " Fourteen. Two weeks' supply ; and I don't suppose Mrs. East will be with you all that time. Do," she added, as Mrs. Hilary with a curt word of acknowledgment, began to close the door, " remember me to her. And tell her to get a good rest. I'm afraid she may have rather a difficult ordeal in front of her."

Her voice and her smile when she said this would have made a black mamba shrink.

Mr. Headley, the chemist of Hinton St. Luke, had been closed for a considerable time and, as befitted a man who had had a busy and honourable day, had settled himself in a state of unbuttoned relaxation with a cross-word puzzle. When he heard the side-door bell ring he said aloud, " Shan't answer that." There were many advantages in being a widower, but it did mean you had to answer your own doors if you only employed a working housekeeper who slept out, as most of them did these days. Not that Mr. Headley would have had any trouble in getting a housekeeper to sleep in, and he had the accommodation, but she would probably want to sleep in permanently, and not in the alternative accommodation, either.

" Let her ring," said Mr. Headley. It was usually a woman who had run out of some absurd commodity that could perfectly well wait till the morning. Anyhow, it was eight o'clock, or precious near it. However, the mysterious ringer had no intention of being so easily choked off. Ring. Ring. Ring. Mr. Headley couldn't stand it. He got up and threw the cross-word across the room, he stooped and pulled on his shoes and laced them up, he buttoned all the buttons he had previously undone, and in a furious temper he went down to the door. Whoever was there seemed to have glued a finger on the bell. It rang and it rang and it rang.

" This isn't the fire station," shouted Mr. Headley angrily as he unslipped the catch. " Who on earth . . . ? Oh, it's you, Miss Beake." Not the most optimistic person could have construed welcome into his tone. It was a sad thing for the poor lady ; wherever she went she was unwanted and plainly shown it. " Whatever's the matter ? " continued the chemist. " Ringing away like that. Any one would think it was murder."

" Any one might be right," retorted Miss Beake sharply. " And if we're not quick they'll get the body shovelled underground without a post-mortem, thanks to that idiotic doctor— or criminal, I'm sure I don't know which—and every one knows how hard it is to get an exhumation order, particularly out of this government."

Mr. Headley would have been more than human if he had not felt a stab of the most intense curiosity at these words. A socialist himself, he wanted to explain that the type of government had nothing to do with exhumation orders, but Miss Beake was in no mood to listen and he tactfully let the point go.

" Whatever are you talking about, Miss Beake ? " he inquired. " Who's dead now ? "

" The same one who was dead a few hours ago," retorted Miss Beake in her uncouth way. " Don't you ever hear the news ? "

" You can't mean Mr. East."

"Why not? Unless there's been another sudden death in the past two hours."

Mr. Headley pulled the door a little wider open. "Won't you just come into the passage, Miss Beake? I mean, if you think there's anything I can do to assist."

Miss Beake came marching in like the army of the Reich, as the chemist told one of his friends later, and pulled a little bottle out of her pocket. It contained three small white tablets.

"See these?"

"Yes. Of course."

"What should you say they were?"

"Why, they're aspirin. I mean, it's on the bottle."

"It's a good thing you haven't got a wife who wants to get rid of you," commented the unscrupulous Miss Beake. "There's such a thing as being too innocent. You know what they say, all is not gold that glitters, and all isn't aspirin that you find in an aspirin bottle, whatever the label may say."

Mr. Headley looked completely at sea. "What is it you're trying to tell me, Miss Beake? You've brought me three aspirins ."

"That's what you're meant to think," agreed Miss Beake. "That's what Mr. East thought."

Mr. Headley looked so startled he nearly lost his balance. "Are you suggesting . . . ?"

"If somebody handed you that bottle and you were in the habit of taking three aspirins after every meal you'd empty the bottle without thinking, wouldn't you?"

Mr. Headley cautiously admitted that he would.

"And that, if you ask me, is what Mr. East did."

"Dear me!" Mr. Headley had a long white face with a reddish moustache and looked something like a horse, though less noble.

"Are you suggesting that in some way something that is not aspirin found its way into the aspirin bottle? But that's absurd surely. And in any case . . ." he hesitated delicately.

"Yes?" snapped Miss Beake.

"Well, Miss Beake, you are—were—the nurse in charge of the case. Surely you would accept responsibility . . ."

"I can't accept responsibility for what happens when I'm off duty," retorted Miss Beake crisply. "The bottle of aspirins was all right when I left the house."

"Then—whom do you suggest . . . ?" Since it was obvious whom Miss Beake had in mind he hurriedly changed the shape of his question. " What do you suggest happened ? In some way some noxious body was introduced into the bottle of aspirin ? "

" Don't talk as if you were already in court," said Miss Beake in her hectoring way. " It's perfectly obvious to my mind what happened. Did you ever supply Mrs. East with her sleeping-mixture ? "

" Once." Mr. Headley was so surprised by now that he was jolted into a monosyllabic reply. " Do you say that these tablets came out of that lady's bottle ? "

" One of them did." Miss Beake looked as sympathetic as a tigress on the prowl. " The other two are genuine aspirin. You're a chemist, a man of experience. You sell aspirin over your counter most days of the week. You also made up Mrs. East's tablets. But when I show you a mixture of the two you don't detect any difference."

" Really, Miss Beake," protested Mr. Headley, " you are putting me in a very difficult position. If you were to give any man—yes, even Dr. Ventnor himself—that bottle with its present contents and ask him off-hand to say what they were he would almost certainly give you the same reply as myself."

" I'm quite sure of it," agreed Miss Beake heartily. " And of course, Mr. East made the same mistake, the chief difference being that in his case it was fatal."

" But," objected Mr. Headley, whose mind appeared to work slowly, " how did the tablets get confused with the aspirin ? "

" They weren't—at least, I don't think they were. Mr. East never took his own tablets. I used to abstract three from the bottle and give them to him and he would put them in his mouth and swallow them down with a glass of water. Now, I'll tell you a very strange thing, Mr. Headley. If you were Mrs. East or any one else for that matter, where would you keep a bottle of sleeping-tablets like these ? "

Mr. Headley, convinced that this appalling woman was laying a trap and the he was probably going to walk straight into it, hesitated before he answered. Finally, he said, " The safest course would be to keep them under lock and key, but in the circumstances Mrs. East may not have thought this necessary. I mean, there was no one else in the house but her husband and yourself, so . . ."

" Well, tell me this," broke in Miss Beake who would never have had an instant's patience with the Circumlocution

Office, " you wouldn't carry them about with you in your
overall pocket, would you ? Or, in your case, your waistcoat
pocket."

" I certainly should not."

" Nevertheless, that's where I found Mrs. East's bottle, in
the pocket of her apron. How do you explain that ? "

Mr. Headley's face, which had been grave enough before,
now assumed an expression of tragic intensity. " I see," he
breathed. " That is, I believe so. Mrs. East mistakenly took
this bottle from her room believing it to be a bottle of aspirins
—you have yourself pointed out how easy it would be to
make such an error—and when the time came to give her
husband his customary dose . . ."

" Oh, you're hopeless. If you're not careful, Mr. Headley,
you'll live to hear yourself described as an obstructive witness.
Mrs. East didn't have aspirins. The only time I ever remember
her taking them she had to come and ask me to give her some
of her husband's. If Mrs. East gave her husband any tablets
out of the bottle in her overall pocket, she did it knowing
exactly what she was doing."

Mr. Headley's indignation momentarily overcame the
extreme apprehension his visitor aroused in him.

" Consider what you are saying ! " he cried. " That is
tantamount to an accusation of murder."

" That is precisely what it is. Nor shall I be satisfied till the
whole matter has been investigated by the authorities. You
don't really believe, do you, that people die so conveniently
for their heirs as Mr. East has done ? I tell you, someone didn't
mean him to make that trip to London, and took the opportunity to put it out of his power once and for all."

Mr. Headley was looking thoughtful. At all costs, he was
deciding, this malicious woman must be prevented from
spreading her story. Once the rumour had gone the rounds
of the village Rose East might just as well have poisoned her
husband and announced the fact from the housetops. People,
thought Mr. Headley, are not actually bad, but life is monotonous and never more so than at present, and a possible
murderer in one's midst does make a change. Mr. Headley
didn't like murder himself, but he prided himself on being
broad-minded, and he did in such instances as these, see the
point of the man in the street.

After a moment, during which Miss Beake eyed him like a
rat looking at cheese, he said quietly, " I take it, madam,
you have no witness of what you allege."

" People don't generally commit murder in the presence of witnesses."

" I was not referring to that. I meant these tablets. You say you abstracted one of these out of Mrs. East's bottle."

" So I did."

" No one saw you do it."

" They didn't, but if you can tell me where else I could have got such a tablet . . ." She didn't finish her sentence. There was no need. It was clear that Mr. Headley took her point.

" In any case, until they have been diagnosed we can proceed no further," continued the pedantic little man.

" I'll watch you diagnose them," was Miss Beake's instant rejoinder. " Or if you're going to say it's after hours, I'll take them round to the police and explain the circumstances."

This was precisely what Mr. Headley wished to avoid, so, very reluctantly, he agreed to his visitor's suggestion. The result of the diagnosis came as a surprise to both.

All three tablets proved to be aspirin.

Mr. Headley drew a deep breath of relief. " If this is your idea of a joke, Miss Beake," he said severely, " I must say I consider it in very poor taste."

Miss Beake, however, was thinking too deeply to take offence. " Don't talk to me," she said. " There's something behind this and I mean to find out what it is. Because, whether you believe me or not, one of those tablets did come out of Mrs. East's bottle. Now why, why should she have aspirin tablets mixed with the others ? She didn't take aspirin, so there's no sense . . . Of course. I see it all. The fox. The sly, cunning vixen." Miss Beake was of those who think nothing of repeating themselves. " Surely you can see it too ? " she demanded, turning imperiously on her nervous companion. " It's all perfectly clear now. Nobody but Mrs. East had access to that bottle of tablets, so that nobody but her could have substituted the aspirins for the real thing. Since she never took aspirins in the ordinary way it's obvious that the substitution was deliberate. And the only reason I can see, and I should imagine that the police will be on my side in this, however prejudiced other people may be in Mrs. East's interest, is that she knew there might be some question about the number of tablets in the bottle. Actually, there were fourteen."

" Since you claim to have abstracted one there will now be thirteen," interpolated Mr. Headley coldly.

" Nothing of the kind. I, not knowing, followed her example

and when I took a tablet out I put an aspirin in, so that it still looked as though she had fourteen tablets left. You admit yourself they are so much alike that no one who wasn't looking for some difference between them would realise what had happened. Now, it's of the utmost importance that we should get hold of that bottle this evening." She pasued, quite carried away by the position she envisaged. " Mrs. Hilary said she was going to take a tablet immediately and go to bed. Most likely she'll shake the bottle up so as to get the aspirins to the bottom, so they should be there still to provide evidence."

" If you would be good enough to explain what you are driving at," said Mr. Headley in crushing tones, and left it at that.

" I should have thought it would be obvious to any one. I told you, Mr. East never took his own aspirins. He waited to have them given to him. Mrs. East had simply to hand him three of her tablets, which would be a fatal dose for any one, and put three aspirin tablets into her bottle, just in case anything should go wrong and questions be asked."

" You are making some very dangerous assumptions," said Mr. Headley, his heart sinking to his boots, because really it did all sound so plausible.

" You wait," threatened Miss Beake. " A lot of people are going to have a shock over this."

" I understood that Dr. Ventnor had given a death certificate of death from heart failure," protested Mr. Headley.

" That can easily be overset. Every one knows what Dr. Ventnor's feeling for Mrs. East is, and that in itself is enough to get him crossed off the register. Oh, I don't doubt for a minute he'd connive at a crime if Mrs. East was implicated."

Mr. Headley was a little man, but when he heard those words such a gust of indignation and loathing filled him that he seemed to swell into quite a considerable fellow. " Miss Beake, I must warn you again that you are making quite ungrounded assertions which may well land you in a police court. You are virtually accusing Mrs. East of murder and Dr. Ventnor of being her accomplice."

" I don't say he knew anything about it in advance," conceded Miss Beake. " I dare say he didn't. He wouldn't want to risk his precious career. He sees himself as the doyen of Harley Street, you know."

Mr. Headley was not sure what doyen meant so he kept his mouth shut, and Miss Beake went on, " What I do say is that if he knows his job at all he must know that Mr. East didn't die of heart failure, and it's his duty to say so. The fact that he hasn't is proof enough for me, and I should think will presently be proof enough for the police, that he knew there'd been some hanky-panky but he wants to keep Mrs. East's name out of it for reasons of his own. Oh, he's been sweet on her for a long time, and rich widowed Mrs. East is much more useful to him than downtrodden Mrs. East, the wife of James East, who could, I dare say, be a very ugly customer on occasions. Anyhow, it'll be simple enough to find out if I'm right by raising the issue and having a post-mortem, before that creature can get the coffin screwed down."

"You are setting in motion activities you may most bitterly regret within a very few hours," began Mr. Headley. Miss Beake terrified him, but he was a staunch chapel man and he backed his conscience against Miss Beake any day.

"Not in the least. If I'm not satisfied with the situation and have any grounds for suspecting foul play, it's my duty as a citizen to inform the authorities. Then a full inquiry can be made, and if I've made a mistake, no one's any worse off. And if I haven't, and in this case I'm pretty sure I haven't, then we can see justice is done."

She marched over to the door, having snatched the tablets back from the chemist, but on the threshold she turned to fling a last bitter word over her shoulder.

"You better be ready for the inquest, Mr. Headley," she assured him. "You're certainly going to be called."

After she had gone the unhappy man felt very perturbed, very perturbed indeed. He didn't like this sort of thing ; indeed, nobody but the amateur does enjoy being mixed up in a murder charge, and he was pretty sure Dr Ventnor wouldn't like it either, particularly if it could be shown that there was any substance in the charge.

"Even suppose there is it wouldn't be difficult to make the mistake, seeing how like the pellets are," he tried to reassure himself. But there was no consolation to be found that way, because it simply didn't explain how the sleeping-tablets, which were normally kept locked in Mrs. East's room, had ever found their way into her husband's. Everybody knows everything in a village, and Mr. Headley, like every one else, knew that the Easts had been separated ever since Miss Beake's arrival, and bottles can't walk from one end of a house to the other all by themselves.

"We must only hope it doesn't get as far as the courts."

Mr. Headley told himself, picking up the cross-word again. As the author of the Dolly Dialogues observed, hope is not yet taxed.

But it was no good. He couldn't let matters rest there. He hadn't much time or much courage or much influence, but his conscience, like a nagging wife, drove him on. So with infinite reluctance he became involved in a case that was shortly to be a topic of burning interest over ten thousand breakfast tables.

CHAPTER FIVE

MR. HEADLEY was not the only person in Hinton St. Luke who was having a bad time that evening. Dr. Ventnor also was feeling more troubled than he cared to admit by Miss Beake's slashing attack. When, late that evening, he heard his telephone ring, he took off the receiver and barked, " Who's that ? " He felt a bit sorry for any one who wanted his professional services to-night.

" It's Headley, Dr. Ventnor," said a hurried and apprehensive voice. " Headley. Yes. I've had a visit from Miss Beake . . ."

" Damn the woman ! " exploded the doctor. " Is she going the rounds of the village ? "

" I feel I should warn you what her lay is," continued the chemist, more disheartened than ever by the doctor's violent reception of his news. " She is trying to put it about that Mr. East was poisoned by sleeping-draught tablets given in place of aspirin."

" It would take Miss Beake to think up a thing like that," commented the doctor bitterly. " Hasn't that unfortunate girl had trouble enough as it is ? "

" I rather gather from what she says that she is—hostile— to Mrs. East."

" British gift of under-statement," said Ventnor in the same tone. " Did you gather whom she proposes to accuse ? Mrs. East, I take it ? Or does she suggest that the widow and I were in collusion ? No, Headley, I'm not joking. I wouldn't put anything beyond that harridan. She's a public danger, and how a shrewd fellow like James East let himself be bamboozled by her, I shall never understand."

"I thought," stammered Headley miserably, "I ought to let you know."

"Thank you very much," said the doctor. "As a matter of fact, she's already been round here trying to rake up trouble. Did you gather where she proposed to make her next call?"

"I think—she did say something about the police. She seems insistent on a post-mortem. She says that as a citizen . . ."

Dr. Ventor called her something much less polite and rang off. He lay for a long time considering.

"If that hell-cat has her own way," he said aloud at last, "it's all UP with Rose. And it wouldn't look too good for me either, not knowing the difference between death from heart failure and death from an overdose."

Because he hadn't been deceived from the first. But if it hadn't been for Miss Beake and her beastly jealous temperament nobody would have asked any questions. As it was, the position was just about as bad as it could be.

He had reached this stage in his reflections when his front-door bell rang and Mrs. Pye came in, looking part excited, part alarmed, to say, "It's Inspector Finch from Hinton St. John, doctor. He'd like a word with you."

"Bring him in," said Ventnor, struggling out of his chair. "Miss Beake hasn't wasted any time," he added grimly to himself, coming forward to greet his visitor.

"What brings you over to us?" he asked pleasantly. "Don't say the news of our current mystery has reached you already?"

"Which one's that, doctor? Matter of fact, there's a rumour that that fellow, Baddeley, who escaped from Morton Jail, has been seen heading in this direction. One of the warders winged him in the arm, and it's thought he may be trying to get some doctor to bandage him up—Baddeley, I mean. You've not had a stranger in to-night?"

"I don't have a surgery on Tuesdays. Anyway, he'd probably go a bit further afield into some big town where there's a hospital with an Outdoor Patients' Department. So much less noticeable."

"Except for the identity card," demurred the Inspector. "A doctor like yourself wouldn't be likely to ask for it."

"That's true. Well, he's not been here yet."

"What was this private mystery you spoke about?"

"Oh, a woman scorned, or rather, a woman disappointed, trying to make trouble for a younger, better-looking one. I've reason to suppose she's at the police station now, or has just left it."

There is an injunction in the New Testament to the effect that whatsoever thy hand findeth to do, that do with all thy might, and that injunction the tireless Miss Beake had taken well to heart. During the twenty-four hours following James East's death she scurried round Hinton St. Luke voicing her suspicions to every one, whether she knew them or not. It was expecting too much of human nature not to anticipate that where she sowed the seed there the tares would spring. And it was generally admitted, even by Rose East's well-wishers, that the finding of the bottle of tablets in the pocket of the widow's overall was a very peculiar circumstance, very peculiar indeed. Old Lady Boothroyd said vaguely, " Well, I dare say she was afraid of her husband getting hold of them," but since every one knew that East now never left his room, that didn't cut much ice. At the end of twenty-four hours everybody knew that the coroner had ordered a post-mortem, and people metaphorically held their breaths waiting to know the result. Miss Beake was grimly triumphant. She at all events knew what the result was going to be. So, actually, did Ventnor, and he wondered how on earth Rose East's counsel was going to steer her through this shoal. He refused to discuss the case, was aware of queer, sidelong looks shot at him as he went on his rounds ; Rose, to the acute disappointment of the sensation-mongers, kept to the house, and Mrs. Hilary firmly told all callers that she was unable to receive visitors. Major Conkling cut Miss Beake dead when he met her in the street, but no amount of unpopularity could affect the issue. Dr. Burton, the police surgeon, made the post-mortem in due course and announced to all concerned that James East had died of an overdose of sleeping-tablets corresponding to those supplied by Dr. Ventnor to the widow. Excitement now reached fever-pitch. Tongues wagged in a way to make every wandering cur envious. People reminded one another of the many curious circumstances of the case, and, say what you like, it was odd that death should occur the very day before the momentous visit to London. The police, they knew, had been in touch with the lawyer, who had not so far put in an appearance. And still Rose remained invisible, and there was more speculation as to whether she would follow the corpse to the cemetery as chief mourner. Normally nobody would have turned out for the funeral, since nobody had liked the old man, but if there was a chance of seeing the widow the whole village was prepared to line the streets.

And they wondered over and over again just what the Inspector, who was in charge of the case, had asked Rose East, and just what her replies had been.

When Mrs. Hilary heard the verdict of the post-mortem she was horrified. Immediately she sought the advice of her unworldly husband.

" This is a terrible thing for Rose," she said in great agitation.

" Only if she is in any way responsible," argued Mr. Hilary.

" What does that matter ? If people think she is responsible, it will be almost as bad as though it were true."

" That is nonsense, Clara. Of course, it will mean an inquest, which in a way will be an excellent thing, since all the relevant facts will be brought to light, and it will be impossible for ill-natured people to go round spreading rumours that are without foundation."

" How dense you are ! " cried his desperate wife. " Can't you see that the bare suggestion that she may be responsible will be enough to drive that unfortunate girl out of her mind ?"

" The police," began Mr. Hilary, and his wife, holding him by the arm so fiercely that next morning he was black and blue, almost shrieked at him : " That's just it. They're here already, talking to her. I'm sure she oughtn't to see them without talking to a lawyer or someone, but when I said something about it to her she looked at me like a blind person and said, " Oh, but why ? He wouldn't know the facts and I do."

Inspector Finch, going along rather reluctantly to interview the widow, found a grey-faced girl, giving no sign either of relief at the sudden ending of her wretched married life or any fear of his examination. Mrs. Hilary need not have feared that he would take unfair advantage of her ignorance. At the very beginning of the conversation Finch said, " There is no need for you to answer any of my questions without advice, if you would rather not. That is to say, you can see your lawyer first."

Rose said again, as she had said to Mrs. Hilary, " There's no sense my seeing my lawyer. He couldn't tell me what to say, seeing he wasn't there ; and I have nothing to hide. And anyhow," she added as an afterthought, " I haven't a lawyer. Mr. Merridew belongs to my husband."

Finch felt anything but reassured. During the short time he had been investigating this affair he had heard a good deal of freely expressed opinion, and no one had had a good word to say for the dead man. Several people had observed frankly they didn't know how the girl had endured the situation so long, particularly since the advent of Miss Beake. So all he said was, " Quite so, Mrs. East. Naturally I appreciate that. On the other hand, we like people to know their rights. Still, if you're satisfied and have no objection, there are some points I should like to raise."

" I've thought and thought," said the girl, " and I can't come to any satisfactory conclusion. It seems to me it must have been an accident. There simply isn't any other explanation. James would never have done such a thing on purpose ; anyway, not just then."

" You mean, the tablets were given by mistake, Mrs. East ? " Finch looked puzzled. He couldn't quite see how she was going to brazen that out.

She nodded. " Yes. That seems the only answer. And it would be easy to make a mistake if you were thinking of something else, as I dare say he was. I nearly did it myself the other day."

" Nearly did what ? "

" Took the sleeping-tablets instead of the aspirin. The bottles are about the same size, and though of course they're labelled, one doesn't often look at the label on a bottle, does one ? There's one thing that troubles me, and that is, if perhaps I'm to blame. I keep asking myself if I should have stayed instead of just putting the bottle by the bed. But it's what he asked, and when my husband asked for things, he meant that was what he wanted, and it was a waste of time to argue." She stopped, her brow wrinkled painfully.

" Perhaps it would help if you went quite simply through the events of that afternoon," Finch suggested. " I don't quite understand about the sleeping-tablets. I didn't know that he had any of his own."

" Oh, he hadn't, he hadn't. But I had some that Dr. Ventnor prescribed for me some time ago. I had never mentioned them to my husband before, but Miss Beake knew I had them. I had given my husband his lunch at his usual time and I was just carrying off the tray when he asked for his aspirins. It was stupid of me to forget he took them and he wasn't very pleased about it. He thought—he thought I had done it deliberately in the hope that he wouldn't be well enough to go to town the next day."

" And had you any reason for wishing to prevent Mr. East going to London ? "

" No. But, of course, Miss Beake—people think that if he was going to alter his will I should want to stop him."

" Was he going to alter his will, Mrs East ? "

" I don't know. He didn't tell me anything about it, but Miss Beake says he meant to change it, so I suppose that meant I should be the loser. At least," she hesitated in some confusion, then went on, " when I married James he told me he meant to leave me everything, so I suppose if he meant to change his will it meant he was going to leave some of it at all events to someone else."

" Did you ever see that will, Mrs. East ? "

" No, never. My husband didn't talk business to me. He said women didn't understand it."

" He didn't tell you why he was going to London ? "

" He just said he had to see Mr. Merridew. Shall I go on ? I took the tray down and then I went back and gave him the bottle of aspirin and said I hoped he would sleep. He said of course he wouldn't, aspirins weren't a sleeping-draught, certainly not when you were innured to them as he was. Then I told him I had some sleeping-tablets that Dr. Ventnor had given me, but I didn't know if he ought to have one—more than one would be dangerous for anybody—without consulting the doctor. You see, if his heart was bad—my husband's, I mean—even one might be unwise. He said, ' You never told me before. Isn't it extraordinary that people who can't sleep for a night fly instantly to drugs ? What was it ? Indigestion or a guilty conscience ? ' He—he made that sort of joke quite often. I don't think it meant anything."

" I see," said Finch, woodenly.

" It's just a thing people say," the girl amplified. " He asked me to bring him the tablets, so I did, and he said something about—about it being like a living arsenal, something might go off at any minute, and he asked me how often I took them. I said whenever I couldn't sleep, which was most nights just now, and he asked how many would be a lethal dose. I said it wouldn't be safe to take more than one, so he said, ' I suppose three would be quite fatal.' And I said.

' I wouldn't dream of taking more than one,' and I asked him to give me the bottle back. But he wouldn't."

" Did he give any reason ? "

" He said he didn't think it wise for people who were—who were emotional—to be in possession of such dangerous drugs, and if he had known I had the tablets he would have told Dr. Ventnor I wasn't to have a second supply, and he wanted to know how long I had been taking them. I said that was the third bottle, and I didn't always take them every night, but the last two or three weeks I had been sleeping so badly I had been pretty regular with them. I told him he needn't worry, I wouldn't dream of taking more than one."

" Mrs. East, had you any special reason for not wishing your husband to know you had them ? "

" Yes," said Rose, rather defiantly. " He—you could never be absolutely sure how he would take things, and he might tell the doctor I wasn't to have any more, and even get Miss Beake to take the ones I had got."

" Where did you keep them ? "

" Locked in a drawer in my room. And I never meant to get dependent on them, but things had been a little difficult just lately, and I simply couldn't face lying awake hearing the clock chime quarter by quarter."

" I see," said Finch, suppressing a feeling that he ought to have insisted on this guileless creature having legal advice before she plunged into this morass of explanation, and then recalling cases where women who looked as innocent as cherubs have proved to have the hearts of fiends. " And did your husband take one ? "

" Not while I was there. But he kept the bottle. And— don't you see ?—he didn't take the aspirin either, not while I was there. I didn't want to leave the tablets with him. I said I had better put them back, but he grinned in a way he had and said he thought they'd be safer with him. I begged him, but it wasn't any good. And presently I went away."

" And after you'd gone you think he took the tablets ? "

" In mistake for aspirin," insisted Rose East. She looked at him wildly. " That's the only possible answer. I'll never believe he did it on purpose. Why should he ? He wasn't in great pain and he hadn't had any news to make him— desperate. Besides, he had all his plans set for the next day, and he never changed his plans if it rested with him."

" So you think he inadvertently took the sleeping-tablets believing them to be aspirin ? Did you *never* hear him speak of suicide ? " He must give her every possible chance, he thought, but everything pointed in the one direction.

" Never, in a personal connection." Rose's answer was instantaneous. " And on the two or three occasions that the subject ever was discussed he said it was only a way out for cowards and fools, people who throw in their hands and admit defeat. Inspector, I couldn't bear them to bring in a verdict of suicide. It's so unfair to him, now he can't defend himself. It must have been an accident. You do believe that, don't you ? "

Finch hesitated. The girl sounded so sincere, so eager that her husband (whom she didn't pretend to have loved) shouldn't be buried with the slur of suicide on his name. She wasn't trying to shape the story so that it exonerated her, she just seemed to be telling him what happened. Of course, if she was being subtle, she was doing it extraordinarily well, and she could hardly have hit on a better story. It covered everything. And how could any one swear that, beyond all reasonable doubt, she had herself administered the tablets, when there was a thousand-to-one chance East had, as she declared, taken them himself in error ? He continued his leisurely examination. The story rambled all over the place, like a country road, he reflected, but sometimes that was the only way of getting your evidence, let your witness go his own pace. Pulling them up too often was apt to make them cautious or put them on the defensive, and then more than half your chance of learning the truth was gone. He moved to another point.

" I don't remember your saying anything about the sleeping-tablets until after the post-mortem, Mrs. East," he observed, and she replied at once, " I didn't see any necessity for mentioning them. Dr. Ventnor said my husband had died of heart failure in his sleep."

" Then you had removed the tablets before the doctor arrived ? "

She seemed surprised, even a little perturbed. " Oh, yes. I forgot that. When I went up about half-past two to make sure my husband was all right—that's when I took them."

" What made you go up at half-past two ? Did he ring ? I thought he didn't like being disturbed unless he rang."

" He always said that, but suppose he had a heart attack and couldn't ring ? Miss Beake—every one—would blame me for the rest of my days."

" Did you think he might have a heart attack ? "

" It's always possible with any one in his condition. And

then, too, I did want my tablets back, and I felt sure he meant to keep them. They were on the table by the bed when I went in, so I just picked them up and put them in my overall pocket. I was so afraid he would tell the doctor he wasn't to give me any more ; he was even capable of ringing up the chemist and telling him he wasn't to make up the prescription."

" You got them from the chemist, Mrs. East ? "

" Once. Doctor Ventnor brought them as a rule, but of course Mr. Headley could make them up from his prescription. And I had to have them by me, even if I didn't take them every night. It gave me a sense of security to know they were there. Like putting the chain on the door at night. You don't really believe the burglars will come to *your* house, but you feel safer with the chain up."

" So, when you took back the bottle, you didn't notice if any tablets had been taken out of it ? "

She turned a rosy red. " I never thought—I didn't count——"

" How many should there have been ? Can you remember when you began the bottle ? "

" I think it was the previous Wednesday. Yes, I remember Dr. Ventnor bringing them in the afternoon."

" You're sure it was Wednesday ? "

" I remember Miss Beake was out of the house, and she was never out except on her afternoon."

" I see. That seems to fix it. Do you remember how many tablets there were in the bottle on the Tuesday night ? "

" Mrs. Hilary said Miss Beake told her fourteen. Would that be right ? "

He looked at her sharply. There was such a thing as overdoing this dewy innocence.

" Quite right. And you took one on Tuesday night ? "

" Yes."

" And last night ? "

" Yes."

" So there should be twelve left. Have you the bottle with you ? "

" It's in my room."

" I should like to see it, please."

" I'll get it." Finch rose with her, and she stopped abruptly on her way to the door and said, " Perhaps you'd rather Mrs. Hilary fetched it. I'm sure she would."

Mrs. Hilary gave Finch a glare that should have turned him to stone and went upstairs. Rose went on patiently, " He still hadn't rung by five o'clock, so I went up again. I remembered Miss Beake saying that people with heart trouble often go out like a puff between one minute and the next. I thought it such a silly thing to say, because, of course, everybody dies between one minute and the next, but I knew what she meant. James was very still, in a sort of stupor, I thought, and then I did wonder if he had taken a sleeping-tablet, because he always says he's such a light sleeper. I stood by the bed and said ' James ! ' twice, because I was beginning to feel apprehensive. And then I saw it wasn't just sleep. I'd never seen any one dead—my uncle wouldn't let me see Aunt Selina—and I'd only seen the injured at the First Aid Post. The others went to the mortuary—but I was quite sure. I wished I wasn't alone in the house. I didn't know when people die they have such an empty look, as if they'd never lived at all. I went downstairs and rang up Dr. Ventnor, and by good fortune he was in and he came round at once. He wouldn't let me stay in the room, he told me to ring up Mrs. Hilary, and she said I must go round to them. I never thought again about the sleeping-tablets in my overall pocket."

There was a haughty tap at the door and Mrs. Hilary came in, carrying the little bottle. She offered it to Rose, but the girl shook her head.

" The Inspector wants it," she said. Finch took the bottle and waited till Mrs. Hilary had left the room.

" I'm still rather in the dark, Mrs. East, as to why you didn't mention the sleeping-tablets even to the doctor."

" I had forgotten all about them in the shock of finding James dead, and when Dr. Ventnor said it was heart disease and nobody was to blame and really it was a fortunate way out, I still didn't think about them. Afterwards it didn't seem to me important. If he had died of heart-disease he couldn't have taken the tablets, and then . . ." she paused, colouring again.

" Yes ? " prompted Finch.

Her words came with a rush. " I thought if everybody knew about them Miss Beake might think I'd tried to persuade him to take one in the hope that he wouldn't be fit to go to London the next day. I know that must sound far-fetched to you, but you don't know what life was like at the house. As it was, things were bad enough—and there was never any suggestion at first it was anything but a natural death."

" Quite," Finch agreed. And if it hadn't been for that

woman, so full of malice and resentment, James East would
have been buried quietly, and even if there had been a moment
of local gossip at the aptness of his death at that particular
moment it would soon have died down. No, Rose East had
Miss Beake to thank for all this trouble, and no one could say
yet where it would all end.

"Are the tablets right—the number, I mean?" Rose
wanted to know, and he counted them. Twelve. That was
all right, then.

"I want to take these away with me for a little," he told
her, and she said at once, "Oh, but why, now you know the
number's right? I need them. I can't do without them."

"I hope to let you have them back quite soon," he said.
"In any case, we could probably arrange for you to have a
tablet to-night, if that's what's troubling you."

The light died out of her eyes. "It doesn't really matter,"
she said. "I've reached the stage where even they aren't
much good. I lay awake half last night, envying James
because he was out of everything, though, of course, I know
I shan't feel like that for ever. It's just everything coming at
once."

"Quite," said Finch again. "I take it you'll be staying
here for the next few days."

"I couldn't go back to the house till after the funeral," she
told him sharply. "I wish I need never go inside it again."

"Then we shall know where to find you if we should need
any more help. You won't try to go to London or anything,
will you? We really need all our witnesses on the spot for the
moment."

"I hadn't thought of going to London. Besides, how could
I? Every one says there's going to be an inquest and I shall
have to give evidence."

When he left the Vicarage, Finch went along to see Ventnor.
The doctor was out, but he came in soon afterwards and his
face clouded when he saw who his visitor was. But he only
said in his normal pleasant way, "What can I do for you
now, Inspector? You haven't got another corpse, I suppose?"

"No, sir." The Inspector looked very grave. "I'm still
on the East inquiry. Now, I understand you ascribed the
gentleman's death to heart failure."

"Seeing that's what I expected him to die of at any
minute, yes, I did. As I've already told Miss Beake and
Major Conkling, I wasn't particularly surprised. He'd

worked himself up over this London visit till he was asking for trouble."

" Still, you'd expect symptoms pointing to death by an overdose, if that's what killed him ? " Finch insisted.

" The post-mortem would reveal those," was the doctor's somewhat evasive reply.

" But in the meantime you never suspected . . . ? "

" What are you driving at ? " asked Ventor sharply. " Do you suggest that I realised he'd died of an overdose and was trying to hush it up ? Heaven knows, a murder case is never jam for a doctor, but it's a picnic compared with the suspicion that he was accessory either before or after the crime. I tell you, if I'd had any reason at that time to think that East's death wasn't a purely natural one I should have called for a post-mortem. Well, you've had one and you've proved me wrong. I have to admit that, and that fact alone won't do me any good. As a matter of fact, I never prescribed sleeping-tablets for Mr. East. Sleeplessness wasn't one of his troubles, and in any case you have to be careful in prescribing for a man with a dicky heart. You should know that the first whisper in a place like this against a medical man's integrity spells ruin for the doctor concerned. I had taken what appeared to me all the necessary precautions, I had no reason to suppose that he would die that particular afternoon, but on the other hand I wasn't surprised when I got the message. I've said that from the beginning, and that's the only information I can give at the inquest."

" But you did know there were sleeping-tablets in the house ? " insisted Finch.

" That I had prescribed for Mrs. East ? " Ventnor sounded impatient. " Certainly. But I had no fear of her taking an overdose, either through carelessness or deliberation. Doctors learn early to make diagnoses of the patients they can trust with dangerous drugs, and I was absolutely sure where Mrs. East was concerned. Personally, in the light of what has transpired, I can only assume that, during Mrs. East's absence, he got hold of her tablets, and unaware of their strength, took an overdose. I don't suspect him of suicide—he was the last man in the world to take his own life—but that he did, in fact, take it I can now have no doubt."

" It's to be hoped, for the family's sake, the jury will take a similar view," was Finch's grim retort.

Ventnor's head came up with a jerk. " The jury ? What are you talking about ? "

63

"The coroner is certain to sit with a jury. As a matter of fact, I've seen Mrs. East and she admits that she gave her husband the bottle of tablets, at his request."

A shocked and fearful look instantly replaced the one betokening nothing more dangerous than impatience that had hitherto shaped the doctor's expression. "She couldn't have done that," he said sharply. "She knew how dangerous they were."

"Apparently Mr. East asked to see them and she brought him the bottle."

"But she didn't give him any? She didn't tell you that. Even one would have been unwise . . ."

"She says that she left him with both aspirins and the sleeping-tablets and she suggests that he took the latter by mistake."

"Yes," agreed the doctor slowly. "That's the only conceivable explanation."

For, he was thinking, if the jury doesn't accept that, it's the end of everything. And he wondered how she could have been so foolish as to mention the sleeping-tablets. Now, of course, people would be inclined to think . . . He bit off the thought sharply, but when he looked up he caught Finch off his guard and saw the end of his unfinished sentence written clearly on the Inspector's face.

When Miss Beake heard the gist of the interview between Mrs. East and the Inspector, she was simply furious.

"Do you mean to say the man's such a fool, he lets her pull wool over his eyes like that?" she demanded in the sort of voice that attracted universal attention. "No wonder so many criminals get away. I was told there are as many as ten thousand undetected crimes every year, and I'm not surprised. Of course, he didn't take the sleeping-tablets; she gave them to him. The thing's as clear as daylight. I've already told that boor of an inspector that Mr. East always waited for the tablets to be put into his hand, he never helped himself, and I shall see to it that the coroner's jury knows that."

When she waylaid Conkling in the street on the night before the inquest, which had been adjourned a further twenty-four hours because of another on the victims of a factory fire which occupied almost a whole day, she attacked him hip and thigh.

"I understand this inquest on Mr. East really is to take

place to-morrow. I'm sure it's hung fire long enough. And I want you to realise that I wish to give evidence."

" If you have any information that's to the point no doubt the police have it already," said Conkling, in tones of absolute loathing.

" I don't believe for an instant that Mr. East asked for those tablets. In all the time I was with him he never once complained of sleeplessness or asked for anything stronger than aspirin. This story the widow is putting about to explain why the post-mortem should have revealed the presence of poison is all poppycock. It's perfectly obvious to me what happened."

" And quite inconsequent to any one else," snapped Conkling. " The only opinion that matters now is the opinion of the jury."

" And they can only make up their minds on the facts. If they're handed a parcel of lies . . . Surely you aren't hoodwinked, too ? Of course, Mrs. East fetched the sleeping tablets—that's why they were in the pocket of her overall— gave her husband three and filled up the bottle from the supply of aspirins. Isn't it a fact that the bottle did contain some aspirins ? "

" I don't know where you get your information," snapped Conkling with truth. Because he knew, though it wasn't common knowledge yet, that when the bottle of sleeping tablets was examined by the police, three aspirin tablets had been found among the rest, and it looked as though it was going to be pretty difficult for Rose East to explain those away.

" She expected to find him dead when she went up at five o'clock," continued his odious companion. " Why, she hadn't even put the kettle on for tea. That shows you."

Conkling had lived in a village long enough to realise that a trivial detail of this nature would carry more weight with the locals than any amount of medical jargon. Everybody had tea, and it stood to reason you put on the kettle before you went up to see if your husband was ready for it. If you didn't put it on, well, it meant you knew it wouldn't be wanted. It was as simple as that. Nevertheless, he put up a bonny fight.

" If you imagine that constitutes proof, Miss Beake, I can only assure you that your knowledge of the law is quite inadequate. And unless you have some more weighty evidence to give I will warn you, though there is no necessity for me to do so, that you are laying yourself open to a charge of malicious slander. In this country, Madam, people are considered innocent until they have been found guilty."

Miss Beake looked as though she were going to have an apoplectic fit. " It looks to me as though there's a plot afoot to defeat justice," she shouted. " Just because she's pretty and people are sorry for her . . ."

" I have always noticed that women have very little respect for the law," began Conkling, fighting hard to hold his own, but she bore him down relentlessly.

" They've too much sense. As for your talk about slander, let Mrs. East bring a case against me and see what happens. But, of course, she won't. She wouldn't dare. Oh, I don't say she won't get away with it, but you and that swollen-headed inspector are the only two people in Hinton St. Luke—except the Vicar, who wouldn't notice it if he was being murdered himself—who don't know she's responsible for her husband's death."

When Ventnor heard about the aspirin in the bottle of sleeping-tablets he looked more worried than ever.

" Nothing to show Miss Beake didn't put 'em all in," he protested. But that didn't meet the case and he knew it. As it happened, the inquest was a very short affair, just evidence of identification and a medical report, and then it was adjourned. Permission for burial was given, and Mr. Merridew, who turned up rather late on the scene, made the necessary arrangements for the funeral. But when it came to ordering a coach for the chief mourner, this proved to be unneccessary. Because James East had no living relatives but his wife, so far as any one could ascertain, and before the cortege set out for the windy little cemetery outside the town, Rose East had been arrested for murder.

CHAPTER SIX

UP IN LONDON Dr. Oliver Stuart read the result of the post-mortem and its consequences in the *Record*, which gave a good juicy report of the whole affair. Like most of his profession he took *The Times*, partly to read the obituary columns and see how many patients he had scored, and partly because the people who consulted him expected to find *The Times* in his waiting-room, but for information and entertainment he subscribed to the *Record*.

What he read shocked him. He had never been able to put the memory of that lovely, despairing creature, Rose East, out of his head, and now when he learned she was to stand her trial for murder he made one of his lightning decisions. A woman would have called it intuition, but Stuart was more modest. He did not suppose there was anything he could do —no doubt she had all the necessary legal aid, and no doubt it would be efficient—but nevertheless he resolved to change his normal choice of a holiday resort and go down to Hinton St. John, where there was a golf course of a sort. His friends would wonder what kind of bee was buzzing in his bonnet now, but it was improbable that any of them would be able to identify it. He was due to go on holiday next week in any case, thanks to a recent change of plans, and he told his secretary he only wanted letters forwarded if they weren't from patients. He told her the address, adding that he was going a little further afield this year, and she said gently, " I see. By the way, you remember that Mrs. East who came to see you some time ago ? " And he said, " Yes, I remember her."

" I dare say you've seen what's happened," said Miss Lasker. " I wonder if she did do it."

Stuart signed his last letter and handed it to Miss Lasker to be placed in the envelope.

" That, happily, is something we shan't have to settle."

But he found the thought that they might find her guilty suddenly intolerable.

He was a good man at his job, so he didn't pretend that he never made mistakes. Also he was ready to admit that there are great tracts of knowledge about the human mind of which at present little is known. His instincts protested against the conception of that beautiful trembling girl as a murderess, but his experience and his knowledge of human nature told him it was not impossible. Given provocation, opportunity and sufficient nervous strain it would be difficult to swear that any one was incapable of murder. It was simply that training and circumstance were normally against it, but every now and again society was shocked by some story, often concerning an apparently devoted couple, in which murder played the chief part. He wondered whether this was one of the cases in which his judgment had been at fault. His advice to Rose East had been to get another woman in the house, advice that had been taken, and for all he knew this had simply precipitated the situation. And yet it had been the obvious solution. Presently he was so troubled by the situation and his own share in it that he decided to consult one of the wisest men he knew, in his estimation, an unconventional, rough-and-ready, persuasive fellow called Arthur Crook. Crook called himself a lawyer ; other lawyers called him a number of unflattering things, but he had a bulldog grip and was tireless in his pursuit of anything that could help a client, and the fact remained that his motto—Crook always gets his man—was generally accepted, even by the police. His respectable brethren said they wouldn't have his reputation for a fortune, but when he heard that, Crook used to grin and say, " Ah, but they haven't got my fortune either, and they wouldn't sniff at that. No one," he would add impressively, " pays such poor wages as virtue. The chap who knows he didn't do it is insulted at the idea that he should have to fork out hard cash to prove his innocence, but the fellow with a spotted reputation realises you have to buy your freedom at the same high price as he's bought everything else. These chaps," meaning his legal brethren, " say they wouldn't touch my clients with a poker. My clients wouldn't be represented by them for all the tea in China."

Stuart looked at his watch. Half-past six. Crook might still be in his office. He had been known to be there at midnight. Some of his clients preferred night appointments ; not so many chaps to see 'em come and go, Crook would explain. To-night, however, he wasn't there, and Stuart made a patient tour of the local pubs, eventually running his crony to earth in the Bag o' Nails. When Crook saw him he showed no surprise at all.

" Looking for me ? " he asked. " What's yours ? "

He brought two pints of beer over to a small table and said cheerfully, " Shoot," and Stuart said, with equal brevity, " Interested in the East case ? "

" When I stop bein' interested in crime you can sign me up for the mortician," was Crook's ready retort. " Accused a friend of yours ? "

" She was my patient on one occasion."

" Still interested ? "

" I believe she was afraid of this. I didn't know which way it would break, but I find it hard to believe the police are right this time."

" You could be right at that," was Crook's equable reply. " Takin' any steps ? "

Stuart abandoned all diplomacy. " I thought of going down to-night."

" Wanting a companion ? "

" If you'd feel like coming."

" Count me in," said Crook. " Matter of fact, this is just the sort of case I like. A nice cosy domestic murder. On the surface, everything looks so quiet and respectable, like that box belonging to who was it ?—dame called . . ."

" Pandora," suggested Stuart.

" That's her. Well, you remember when someone lifted the lid out came all kinds of malice, hatred and all uncharitableness, everythin' in short, except hope. And that," added he, modestly, " is me."

" You feel as strongly as that about it ? But . . ."

" I know, I know. You're going to suggest the lady's already got a chap mugging up her case. But what good's he if he couldn't stop the slops putting her under arrest ? "

" I suppose," murmured Stuart, who liked to be fair, " Mrs. East is the obvious person to take."

" And trust the police not to avoid doin' the obvious thing," was Crook's withering rejoinder. For roses would bloom in December to be fretted by the frosts of June before Mr. Crook would have a good word to say for the authorities.

Stuart said, " I thought we might take the 7.40 . . ." but he got no further for Crook said, " You can forget that. No trains for us while the Scourge is still running." Stuart, with an involuntary start, asked what about petrol, and Crook said, well, what about it ? And what about dining at the Embassy at Chawley, where they still brewed beer that wasn't a perjury? Stuart abandoned the argument ; he knew Crook would win, anyhow. And though he shuddered at his recollection of the Scourge, that infamous little red car in which Crook shot all over the country, he reminded himself manfully that somebody had had to be the first person to fly the Channel and cross the

Atlantic, and they'd survived, and going down to Hinton St. John in the Scourge was child's play by comparison.

"One thing," he consoled himself, "at this hour we're not likely to meet any one I know. And even if we do, they'll never believe it's me in that preposterous red beetle."

On the way down they discussed the case. "The trouble is, nobody likes these cases where young wives discover their husbands dead in bed and it turns out that they, the wives, are sole legatees. Apart from the locals, who don't seem to have liked Mr. East, public sympathy is going to be with the deceased. As for this Beake woman, she seems to have got her knife into Mrs. East all right. But for her the affair would never have got to this stage."

"You do see her point," Crook offered mildly. "She ain't so young as she was, and she was never Helen of Troy if she's anything like her pictures, and I dare say she's got about as much faith in what the Government's going to do for the deserving poor when they're past scrubbing as the rest of us, and she thought she'd fixed herself up nicely till Kingdom Come."

"But is there any evidence that East intended to leave her provided for?"

"I'm giving you her story," explained Crook patiently. "You do have to hand it to her, she don't let the grass grow under her feet. Y'know, Stuart, that woman's wasted as a nurse. As a publicity hound or a barker at a circus, or even a Cabinet Minister, she'd be in her element. She may not have created the situation, though I wouldn't put that past her, but Churchill himself couldn't have exploited it better."

"This is a nasty situation for Ventnor," continued Stuart, who inevitably took the professional's view. "People are going to wonder how it was he didn't notice the old man had died of an overdose."

"P'raps he did," said Crook, laconically, "and didn't want to get mixed up in a murder. Come to think of it, the old boy was no loss . . ."

"Only Heaven knows how you've managed to stay on the register all this time," was Stuart's frank comment. "Still, you're very likely right. No doubt he thought the girl had had enough to put up with, and there was no reason to suppose any one was going to question his verdict. It wouldn't be the first time that had happened in my experience. Still, it hasn't broken the right way for him. All the self-righteous are going to say either he's so infernally careless he can't be relied on for a correct diagnosis, or else that he's so sceptical about morality that he was prepared to be an accessory after the crime to protect Mrs. East."

" Hasn't the Beake spread the glad news that he'd hoped to see the widow as the doctor's bride ? "

" I don't think even the police will take all Miss Beake's evidence at surface value," observed Stuart dryly. " I suppose the defence will be that the old man took the tablets by accident . . ."

" If I was the old boy on the box (which was Mr. Crook's irreverent way of referring to the judge), I'd count that out of court pretty early in the proceedings. Chap who's going to town next day and has everything set, down to a hired car and a date with his lawyer, takes a lot of care to see he gets the right dope. Or rather, that he don't get the wrong one. Besides, how about the tablets in the bottle ? How d'you explain those ? "

" I suppose someone else could have substituted them," said Stuart, dubiously.

" Sure," agreed Crook. " P'raps the old man put them there himself. Or the doctor. Or Miss Beake. But till we've got a case against one of 'em, the person with the most motive and opportunity is the widow. That's the way the police would argue."

" And you'd disagree ? "

" So far as we know, it does look most likely to be her, but then, how much do we know ? Just what the police and press like to tell us. The odds are there are a whole lot of things and people connected with the case we don't know yet. (It's funny how attractive a rich old gent is. Magnets have got nothing on him.) And you and me are down here to dig them out of their holes."

" Of course," continued Stuart, after twenty minutes of Crook's intensive driving, at the end of which time he was pleased but surprised to find himself still alive, " there's the chance the defence may plead insanity. From what I saw of Mrs. East, she was almost at breaking point then."

But Crook would have none of it. " It won't wash, my boy. Take the word of the man who knows. To begin with, it don't strike me as particularly insane to do all you can to stop your husband disinheriting you, draggin' your name through the muck and leaving as much of his ungodly wealth as the law allows to a vulgar upstart who's been in for it what it's worth from the beginning. And for another thing, people don't go mad at 12.30 and be as sane as you or me by half-past two—not in law, anyhow."

When Stuart and his remarkable companion arrived at Hinton St. John, where he proposed they should stay, the former booked accommodation for himself at the Park House Hotel, but Crook, who said he wasn't fussy about his creature comforts, while a pub, always gave you the best beer, put up at the Barley-Mow. The next morning he got permission to see Rose East, on the ground that he was an old friend of the family, and learned, as he had hoped and rather anticipated, that she had as yet no one to act for her.

"They told me I could have a lawyer and if I didn't know one they would make arrangements," she told him. "I suppose they couldn't find any one who wanted to take the case on. Unless you . . ."

"Not likely. I'm Dr. Stuart's nominee. Don't tell me you've forgotten Dr. Stuart. And my motto is Crook always gets his man, and I only act for the innocent, so your troubles are mostly over. You do see that, don't you?"

She said in a low, toneless voice, "I didn't kill him, though when I saw he was dead and heard Dr. Ventnor say he'd died painlessly in his sleep, I couldn't feel anything but a sense of relief, of such relief as I can't hope to explain to any one else. It was a feeling of being free. I'd almost forgotten what freedom could be like."

"Do me a favour," begged Crook. "Don't say that sort of thing in the witness-box. You haven't any experience of jurymen, of course, but you can take it from me they're the most wooden-headed people in the world. It takes a fellow a couple of days to get an idea through their bony skulls, and once it's there it's like a penny in an empty money-box, rattles round and round, and nothing on earth will ever get it out again."

Then he got down to brass tacks and got her to tell him the whole story, not at all troubled at its length, letting her take her own path, putting a question now and again, till all the facts she had given to the Inspector were in his possession. When she had finished he said cheerfully, "That's dandy. Now, you regard this place as a rest-cure. No, don't think I've gone dotty. There are a lot of places where you might be less safe than in quod."

"I don't understand." She stared at him as if she thought him guilty of bad taste.

" Well, even if you didn't polish off your husband, and we're agreed that you didn't, and he didn't do the job himself, and the police have decided about that, somebody's responsible, and you're going to be the least popular person in the country, barring me, of course, with that somebody in the days ahead. So if he could manage to put out your light in such a way that it looked like you'd done it yourself, he'd have a good chance of getting clear away. And, of course, so long as you're in durance vile he can't get at you. Count your blessings, sugar, count your blessings."

It was certainly a new idea to Rose East. " You mean someone might try to murder me, too ? "

" Why not ? " asked the imperturbable Mr. Crook. " You can't hang twice."

Crook's next visit was to East House, where he found Mr. Merridew patiently wading through his deceased client's documents, of which there was an immense quantity. Mr. Merridew was not at all pleased to see his visitor. Life had been one frustrating event after another ever since his arrival. First had come the police, who had no respect for legal reticence, and when he had coped with them he had been faced by the pugnacious Miss Beake, who made it clear at once that she had added the lawyer to her Black List. A loyal attorney, she intimated, would have dropped everything and flown, literally, if necessary, to his deceased client's house, whereas Mr. Merridew had remained in London for nearly forty-eight hours after the news was given him. He for his part found it quite impossible to make that unreasonable woman realise that there are occasions when a live mouse may be more profitable than a dead lion, since the latter in the very nature of things is bound to remain stationary, while the former, if it considers it is receiving inadequate attention, may scamper off to a more hospitable hole. He completed his ruin so far as she was concerned by refusing outright her offer to act as his secretary during his stay there. She was an efficient typist and there was a machine in the house that she had often used for her late employer's correspondence. Merridew, however, did not give two thoughts to the proposal. He said at once, and with more brusqueness than was perhaps quite necessary, that he could not consider such a thing. He was dealing with confidential matters. At this stage, if the atom bomb could have taken human shape, it might have looked pretty like Miss Beake.

Merridew experienced none of the exhilaration that always filled Mr. Crook at the prospect of a murder case. It was Crook's boast that his clients never got as far as the courts, he'd always franked them first. Merridew's firm didn't deal with violent crime, and they even disliked divorce, unless they were inveigled into such action by a particularly valuable client. What they enjoyed was contesting wills and fighting remote property claims, and they did a nice sideline in elderly lunatic ladies with persecution manias, always provided the ladies in question had ample means to pay for their fun. He was terse with the police, short as crust with Miss Beake and frankly hostile towards Crook, who proceeded to draw him out as a pin extracts a winkle from its shell.

It was one of Crook's habits to take a bull by the horns. Why else, he asked simply, had the creatures been furnished with such appendages ? Having seen Rose East he went prancing round to East House like Autolycus, to collect any trifles the police might have overlooked. Merridew had heard of Crook, and his manner, when the two met, suggested that he didn't care much for what he had heard.

" Representin' Mrs. East," explained Crook cheerfully, putting out a hand that looked like a pre-war leg of mutton. (They don't come so big since the war.)

Merridew stared at his visitor as though he were a stranger from some mysterious and probably uncouth planet, Mars, for instance. When Crook added, " Hope I ain't poachin' on your preserves," he drew himself up to his rotund five foot three and said, " Naturally I represent the deceased."

Crook thought irreverently he looked like a gnome sitting on a toadstool, perched up on that uncomfortable leather-seated chair, with his hairless face and his bald head and his flashing gold-rimmed pince nez.

" Give me anything you've got," Crook offered. " I've seen Mrs. East and got her story . . ."

" Presumably the same story she has already told to the police," snapped Merridew.

Crook grinned. " Ah, but you'll be surprised how different it'll sound when I start tellin' it. Mind you, I know how unpopular I'm goin' to be. If I can show, as I mean to, that the little lady didn't put her old man under the daisies, she's going to ruin the season for a lot of sightseers, and if I can persuade the authorities she didn't, believe me, I'm goin' to tuck up my tail and get back to London double-quick before they start singing, ' Now the labourer's task is o'er ' over me."

Mr. Merridew put his finger-tips together in the immemorial novelist's fashion and said with studious forbearance, " I should perhaps inform you that I am not personally acquainted with Mrs. East. Mr. East did not bring her to see me when he made the necessary emendations to his will, nor did he subsequently visit town."

" Y'know," remarked Mr. Crook meditatively, " if your client had been an S.S. man or a prison guard or anything in that line, and she'd clumped him over the head so that the angels in Heaven are singing to-day, ' Here's Jimmy, here's Jimmy, here's Jimmy,' the odds are she'd get a medal. But he was just as much of a tyrant—don't it ever seem to you a good thing so few people, apart from ourselves, understand the law ? If they did, they'd be sure to change it."

Mr. Merridew looked like someone who has unexpectedly got out of his depth and doesn't like the temperature of the water. You could almost see him feeling with his toe for the bottom, and being panic-stricken when he couldn't find it.

" What was the position ? " Crook urged. " We know Mr. East was coming to town, no doubt for some good reason, though why he didn't ask you to come down here is nobody's business. As for that human scourge who was all set to accompany him—any idea if she did stand to gain anything and if so, whether she knew it ? "

" If she was and if she was aware of the fact, it would be the strongest possible argument in favour of keeping my client alive," said Mr. Merridew in a tone that would have frozen the Fuel Minister himself.

" Until the will was signed," agreed the dauntless Mr. Crook. " She talks a lot, but what the soldier said ain't evidence, and it's my belief she knew no more about Mr. East's intentions than the Man in the Moon."

" I am afraid I am unable to be of any considerable assistance. My client went into no details. He simply said that he wished to add certain codicils to his will, and he enquired whether the law insisted on his providing for an unfaithful wife, if no action for divorce had been filed."

Crook whistled softly. " I suppose your client was all there ? I mean, he did understand you can't bring that sort of action without proof? "

" If he did not, I should certainly have enlightened him."

" H'm," reflected Crook. " Wonder what yarn this Beake female had been feeding him. Oh, she hated Mrs. East the way the good Christian hates the devil—that sticks out a

mile. If not, why has she run round stirring up all this mud?
Don't tell me because she's a good citizen and wants to see
justice prevail. Citizens don't come as good as that. I should
know."

" If you are trying to involve Miss Beake," Merridew
reproved him weightily, " I must point out that she had no
possible motive for wishing Mr. East out of the way."

Crook jerked up his head. " That so? Meaning she didn't
stand to gain anything if he died? Well, I dare say at this
stage she didn't. Still, you know what the police keep telling
you. Motive ain't essential for murder. Besides, where a
dame's concerned, what do you know? Maybe the old man
insulted her in some way—no, don't ask me what way.
Remember Kipling? There are six-and-forty ways of writing
tribal lays and every single one of them is right—and if my
quotation ain't, skip it. Well, there's more ways of insulting
a lady. P'raps she hoped he'd turn on the tender tap and he
didn't. P'raps he just told her he thought he'd like a change—
nothing to show, is there?"

But Mr. Merridew simply said that romantic suppositions
were not evidence, and in any case Miss Beake had not been
on the premises at the time of the crime. Crook said that made
it all the more suspicious—alibis were three-a-penny these
days, and the police had opened Hendon College to prove
that if you had an alibi you were for it. " If it couldn't be so,
it must have been, that's their motto," he added blithely.

Mr. Merridew looked keenly at his companion, wondering
if he could conceivably be under the influence, but Crook went
on unconcernedly. " Any notion if the old gentleman did
mean to smooth out Miss Beake's latter years?"

" If you mean did he intend to leave her a legacy, the
answer is in the negative. I understand that he held the view,
a somewhat cynical view, but my client had unfortunately
cynical tendencies, that once a man made—er—made . . ."

" Made it worth any one's while to bump him off, then he
might expect a bump at any minute. That's common sense.
Y'know, he may have been a queer old codger, but he had all
his wits about him."

" No one has ever suggested anything to the contrary,"
Merridew assured him, freezingly.

" That's what you say," retorted Crook. " You should get
around the village a bit. You'd be surprised."

" That being the case," continued Merridew pedantically,
" Miss Beake would clearly take every precaution to see that

her patient met with no ill-effects through the agency of a third person."

"Were you," asked Mr. Crook leaning forward and speaking with an air of great interest, " ever on the B.B.C. ? "

Mr. Merridew looked offended. " Certainly not. I trust I do not require that particular form of publicity."

"My error," said Crook. " Only, you know, if you ever had been thinking of it, you'd be a wow."

Mr. Merridew unbent a little. Like most people who have had no contact with the Corporation, he had an idea that it would enhance his reputation in some mysterious way to be sought out by governors. " When we were young men," he said, generously including Mr. Crook in his remarks and making their mutual youth sound as remote as the dodo, " our profession was not regarded as something approximating to the music hall stage."

Crook couldn't help thinking that the producers, announcers and other superior B.B.C. young men would hardly have felt flattered by the comparison. The interlude, however, had been worth while, for there was now a distinct softening in Mr. Merridew's manner. Crook settled down to be cosy.

"Now, tell me a few things," he suggested. " You haven't spilt many beans to date. This visit to London, for instance. Did it surprise you when you heard about it ? "

"To tell you the truth, it did. I knew Mr. East had been ill, and if he merely wished to change his will it would have been simple to send his directions by post. If he had more intimate matters to discuss with me, I should have expected him to ask me to call on him."

"Maybe he was thinking of your petrol coupons."

"It would not have occurred to my client that I had petrol coupons for any purpose but to serve him. No, no, there was an ulterior motive behind the suggestion, though I am not in a position to divulge precisely what it was."

"Meanin' you don't know ? Then either he was afraid somebody at this end might overhear what he was going to say, or else he had a secondary interest in coming to London. Meaning, of course, that he was planning to pay another visit while he was in town. I understand Miss Beake was coming with him ? "

"Merely as a sop to the doctor and because it was her own wish, but she was not accompanying him to my office, though she was to pick him up there in the afternoon. As a matter of fact, I question whether Miss Beake was quite so much in my client's confidence as she had supposed. There is a reference to her in his letter to me to the effect that women appear to know as little about men in an age of sex equality as they did when they went (quite rightly in Mr. East's opinion) in blinkers. Nurses, in particular, he observed—I believe I have the letter by me; yes, here it is. 'Nurses in particular seem to labour under the delusion that, because a man is sick bodily and is no longer young, he has forfeited his brain and his senses. Personally, I am always in favour of giving a man all the rope he requires. The unjust thing is when he contrives to hang himself and then blames you.'"

" Is he talking about his wife there, or is he still on Miss Beake ? " Crook speculated.

" I fancy the latter, for there is a footnote. ' In any case,' he says, ' I consider that Miss Beake has done very well out of me, and though gratitude was never a feminine virtue, I think I may take it that she will remain with me for so long as I want her.' "

" Hold on ! " said Crook showing his first sign of excitement. " You may have something there. Quite sure he didn't mean to leave her a bit ? "

" I am afraid my reading of the passage was that he had been, shall we say ?—er—leading the lady up the garden."

" Lettin' her think she was coming in for a bit and really she wouldn't even be mentioned ? Well, that gives us, as you say, a motive for her wanting to see Mrs. East hanged. But—what does he mean by saying that she'd done well out of him ? What did he pay her ? "

" As little as possible," said Merridew dryly. " There is one occasion when he appears to have given her a lump sum, but that, I understand, was for his personal expenses. Although . . . " He hesitated.

" Come clean," Crook invited him. " You're not tryin' to tell me that even a forsaken female like the Beake loved little Jimmy for himself alone."

Mr. Merridew decided to be indiscreet. Crook was a queer sort of lawyer, but there was no doubt about it, he knew his onions. Also he had a motto, " I only defend the innocent," and Mr. Merridew personally had no feelings at all where the culprit was concerned. If a jury brought in Rose East guilty, he wouldn't lose an hour's sleep at the thought of her being hanged on the gallows-tree, but on the other hand he had no personal animosity against her. So far as he was concerned, any one else would fit the bill quite as well.

"I will take you into my confidence," he announced to his companion. "There is admittedly one rather strange feature of the case which has not been cleared up, and on which Miss Beake can give me no assistance. I find that on two occasions in the past eight months my client has drawn cheques for a considerable sum of cash, which he has apparently fetched himself from the bank, in each case asking for single notes. That, of course, was before he took to his bed."

Crook whistled. "Now we are going places," he approved. "No notion who was going to benefit?"

"On the counterfoils of the cheque-book I find a note in each case—E.C."

"But no information as to who E.C. was?"

"None whatsoever."

"And Miss Beake can't assist?"

"The cheques were drawn before she came to Hinton St. Luke, the second just over three months ago."

"Not likely they were meant for her then. And the widow?" —"Mrs. East's initials are not E.C."

"You know all the answers. How much were they for?"

"The first for one hundred and fifty pounds, the second for two hundred and fifty."

"No receipts, of course?"

"None."

"No further demands?"

"If so, they have been destroyed. Always assuming they ever existed."

"Well, you're not askin' me to believe that an old codger like James East drew a whack of pound notes to send anonymously to the Crippled Kids' Home. No, if I win my bet, here is X, the mystery no one has yet fathomed, the voice from the past. Y'know, it's ominous, as the whodunits always say, that the next instalment was just about due. And at that time he makes a lightnin' decision to come to London, sayin' he's got to see his lawyer, though every one knows it 'ud be a damn sight more sensible for his lawyer to visit him. I begin to see light in the tunnel, Merridew, on my sam, I do."

Merridew looked pained. "May I remind you that my client was a man of over sixty, in delicate health? It is improbable . . ."

"He hadn't always been over sixty or in delicate health. And you know what they say about old sins havin' long shadows."

" In this case, extremely long. Mr. East had been married over five years."

" That still gives him half a century to get into trouble. Now don't spoil my fun, Merridew. By the way, how did the old man make his pile ? "

" I understand he was self-made."

Crook nodded. " Another amateur job. I never did have much use for them. Where did he make it ? "

" I understand in South Africa."

" You understand a devil of a lot," Crook congratulated him. " I wish I was as clear about the whole thing. Still, that does explain the delay. South Africa's quite a way off, and X. may only just have tracked the old boy down. By the way, what time was your appointment with him on the Wednesday ? "

" Two-thirty. His own suggestion."

" Hardly give you time for more than a cupper and a biscuit, would it ? " said Crook sympathetically. " What time was the car coming ? "

" I under—I think at ten."

" So he'd be in town at twelve-thirty at latest. Now you'd expect an old miser like that to let his lawyer give him lunch, wouldn't you ? "

" Not if he suspected he would ultimately pay for it himself," was Merridew's dry reply.

" Oh, well, you could charge it to his account in any case, couldn't you ? No, Merridew, I swear we're on to something at last. He came to London because he was goin' to see somebody besides you. Question is, who ? I say possibly E.C."

" And how do you discover the identity of E.C. ? "

" Just you wait," Crook promised him. " Now, didn't he keep a diary or anything ? "

" There is a diary among his papers but it reveals nothing that would throw any light on this situation."

" No note of a lunch date on the Wednesday ? "

Reluctantly Mr. Merridew found the diary among the papers on the table in front of him. Eagerly Mr. Crook snatched it out of his hands.

" Oh, boy," he said. " What did I tell you ? Here's an entry. L.R. Hotel, 12.45. How does that sound to you ? Liverpool Road Hotel. That's a nice big anonymous place. Wonder if he booked a table ? " He picked up the telephone receiver as he spoke.

80

" The number," began Mr. Merridew, but Crook waved him away. " Bless you, I know the numbers of all these station hotels. Most of 'em have got a history that 'ud surprise you. Not their fault, mark you, but if one bad hat wants to meet another what's a better place than a pub at a station ? Such opportunities for a getaway in half-a-dozen directions."

At this stage the lady at the other end of the wire asked for the number, and in a miraculously short time he was put through No table in the name of East had been booked for that day, he was informed, and the management seemed reluctant to tell him even this until he represented himself as the police, after which they couldn't do enough for him. They even discovered that a lady had inquired for a Mr. East on that particular day. The waiter she had interrogated remembered it when the story of the old man's death broke in the press.

" Attaboy," said Mr. Crook, ringing off again, having been assured that no table had been booked in the name of West either. " Well, where does that get us ? East makes the date but don't make the assignation. And for why ? Because by that time he'd handed in his dinner-pail for keeps. You heard me ask the chap if he'd have been lucky if he didn't book a table, and the fellow said there were always some for casual travellers. So I bet you East was counting on that."

" And how do you propose to follow up that information ? " Merridew demanded, in a fever of curiosity.

" For the next instalment of this thrilling murder mystery, see our next issue," pattered Crook rapidly. " Now, let's do a bit more excavatin'. Old Man East says Miss Beake has done pretty well out of him. We know—or do we ? I mean about the first cheque for £150 ? Could she be posing as E.C. ? No. That's out. But suppose she's rumbled the old boy ? Didn't you say there was a sizable cheque made out to her on one occasion ? How sizable ? "

" Ninety pounds," replied Mr. Merridew.

Crook looked puzzled. " That's a damn odd sum. Why ninety ? A hundred's so much more sensible. Or did she see an advertisement in an Oxford Street store for a fur coat price ninety pounds and say artlessly how nice it would be to have one ? Even so, there's coupons. No, I think there's a bit more behind this. Does the lady volunteer any information, by the way ? "

" She says Mr. East often gave her cheques of varying

amounts for his own purposes. I gather she had more or less taken the financial reins out of Mrs. East's hands."

" But ninety pounds," repeated Crook. " No, Merridew, I don't get it. When was this drawn ? "

" About a month ago."

" Got the cheque there ? "

" It's quite in order," said Merridew sharply. " I have the counterfoil, with Miss Beake's name clearly noted in my client's writing, which would be extremely difficult to copy."

" Let's have a looksee," pleaded Crook, and Merridew found the cheque book and passed it over.

" There was doubtless some excellent reason," the lawyer began, watching Crook examine the counterfoil as though he'd lick the figures off the paper. Crook suddenly whooped with excitement.

" I'll say there was. Take a look at this, Merridew my buck. Note specially the nought. Anything occur to you ? "

Mr. Merridew inspected it with care and offered the comment that it was slightly smudged.

" Good man !" Crook knew nothing of good form and dispassionate bearing, none of the legal niceties at all, in fact, " That was the right answer. Now, do you notice something else ? The figure ' 9 ' and the lady's name ain't smudged, whereas the nought is reproduced a trifle hazily, I admit, on the back of the previous counterfoil. What does that suggest?"

Mr. Merridew, with the air of giving a lunatic his head, said it looked as though the book had been closed in a hurry.

" Right again. But in that case, why ain't the rest of the writing smudged ? "

" Because in blotting the entry . . ."

" Wrong," interrupted Crook. " *It hasn't been blotted.* See, it's dried black, whereas the nought is a palish blue. Now, why should everything except the nought be the same colour ? Come on, the kindergarten could answer that one."

Mr. Merridew, not to be outdone by the kindergarten, said slowly, " Are you suggesting that the nought was added later, as an afterthought ? "

" Not as an afterthought," said Crook, " but later—yes. And I wouldn't be surprised if an expert said it was written with a different sort of ink. What kind of pen did the old bird use ? "

" He had one of these modern pens . . ."

" I know. Dry as you write, with no more nib than a modern tea-pot has spout. Just what I suspected. Now you see what happened. Old Man East drew a cheque for nine pounds—what size were most of the cheques he gave Miss Beake ? "

" They ranged from five to eight pounds. Nine is the highest on record."

" Better and better," said Crook. " That Miss Beake's got her head screwed on all right. Five pounds don't give any one any scope. Six is better and seven better still, but she's a believer in the saying that all things come to him who waits, and one day she's rewarded. Her niggardly employer gives her a cheque for nine pounds. She knows she'll never do better and this is her opportunity. So she changes the nine to ninety—yes, I know about his spectacular handwriting, but two letters ain't too much of a risk, and anyway she's going to chance it. I thought first, you know," he added in parenthesis, " she might have found out about E.C. and be asking for payment, but in that case she'd have taken a round sum, and no one can call ninety round. And having put that transaction through she has the wit to see it 'ud be as well if the counterfoil tallied with the cheque. " A bit risky, wasn't it," objected Merridew. " Mr. East was a keen man of business. He might easily have noticed the alteration, and however convalescent he was he would know he hadn't given Miss Beake a cheque for ninety pounds."

" You've got something there," Crook agreed. " But—see here—there's nothing to show *when* she altered the counterfoil. Once the old boy was in the priority queue for the mortuary she'd realise you were coming down hot on the trail, and while everything was in a state of confusion at the house she could get hold of the cheque-book and change the total, so that everything tallied. It could be even she had some conscience or somebody came in when she wasn't expecting it and she shut the book in a hurry, which would explain the smudging. After all, it was one chance in a thousand any one noticing a little detail like that."

" Would the bank cash a cheque drawn to Miss Beake for so large an amount ? " demurred Mr. Merridew. " Of course, she may have paid it into an account—we might inquire as to that . "

" Maybe you've hit it, Merridew. Maybe they did confirm it to Mr. East. Anyhow, we know he was wise as to what was going on."

Mr. Merridew looked hopelessly puzzled. " I don't quite get you."

" Why, he told you so himself in that letter. In fact, he told you twice. Once when he said nurses seemed to think a sick man was blind or an idiot, or words to that effect, and again when he said he thought Miss Beake had done pretty well out of him as it was."

Mr. Merridew shook his head. " Very ingenious, but I doubt if that is the truth. You did not know my client. He was a man who found it positively painful to part with money. He would never have allowed Miss Beake to get away with it, as they say."

" Sure, he was mean," agreed Crook. " But he also knew he wasn't going to live for ever, and it could be he'd discovered there are some things more valuable than money, things it's worth paying quite a price for. And having Miss Beake on the premises for as long as suited his book may have been one of them. Y'see, she fitted into his plan, she was on his side. If she went, Mrs. East might refuse to have another nurse. Or it mightn't be possible to get one. Or if he did she might go all soppy over Mrs. East. Then *he* might have found himself without allies, and that didn't suit his book at all. Ninety pounds would be cheap at the price, and she wouldn't dare leave because she wouldn't get a reference, at least not one she could use."

" And may I ask," inquired Merridew politely, " where all this is leading ? "

Crook seemed surprised. " I've got to find someone to put in Mrs. East's place, haven't I ? " he said. " So far the police can't find any one with a motive for wanting the old boy out of the way but the widow. But suppose East is holding Miss Beake here against her will ? Or here's a better idea. She knows he's going to town, and she knows as well as we do that in the ordinary way he'd get you to come down to see him. So she argues, same like us, he must be meaning to see someone else, and that someone else may be connected with Miss Beake. And he isn't to be allowed to talk."

" You still take no account of the fact that Miss Beake was not in the house when her employer died."

" That's the beauty of poison. You don't have to be. Of course, the danger is that the stuff may be traced to you. Here she had it under her hand. She knew about the sleeping tablets. She only had to watch her chance to get hold of some and put 'em in the aspirin bottle instead of the real thing. You know how it is with these bottles. They always have a wad of cotton wool in the neck, so you shake out the top three.

You remember G.K.C. saying you don't look for a hamadryad in a sideboard, and naturally you don't look for poison in the aspirin bottle."

" But it was Miss Beake who drew attention to the fact that the old man may not have died naturally."

" They often do that. It's called a red herring. Mind you, I don't say I'm right. There's still E.C. to be considered, but I never mind having half-a-dozen strings to my bow."

Mr. Merridew said weakly it all seemed rather far-fetched to him, but Crook, who was by now in a buoyant mood, replied that in his experience nothing about murder was too far-fetched, and if the jury didn't like his theories he could tell them in words of one syllable what to do with them. He then proceeded to instance a number of notorious cases which, had they been presented as fiction, would have been howled out of court by the critics as too improbable for consideration.

" And there's always the chance that the old boy took them himself," he ran on. " No, I know there's no proof, but that'll come. Well, obviously, or we shan't win our case. Y'see it's like a cake."

" A cake ? " repeated poor Mr. Merridew, by this time hopelessly at sea.

" Yes. Look how unromantic it is at the start, just so many heaps of flour and sugar and whatnots, whatever you put into cakes. But when it's been properly mixed and cooked, and the cooking's the important thing, especially about our cake, what a metamorphosis, as some chap has said. Light, tasty, highly flavoured, nicely-coloured, appetising, tempting, irresistible. Yum-yum," he mouthed. " Doesn't that start the digestive juices flowing, Merridew ? "

" I quite appreciate that you see yourself in the role of the cook, but, if I may ask, is there any motive you can offer a court to show why my client should have taken his own life ? "

" Have to contact E.C. before I answer that one. But it could be, Merridew, it could be. Say E.C. has something on him ? "

" The sensible thing would have been to consult his lawyer."

" And make you accessory after the fact ? My dear chap, be your age. Suppose East had come to you and said, ' Look here, thirty years ago I slit my pardner's throat and now the widow's out for my blood.' What advice would you have given him ? "

" Really, Crook," protested his companion. " Your imagination . . ."

" I don't stand out for murder, of course. Maybe he only
swindled him out of every penny and let him cut his own
throat. Or p'raps—didn't you say he came from South
Africa ?—he was mixed up in the I.D.B. ramp and got out just
in time, leaving his partner to take the rap. Whatever it is,
I bet you E.C. is concerned with it. Well, look at it for
yourself. Would a chap with a reputation like your client
part with four hundred pounds unless he found himself in a
pretty sticky spot ? And then p'raps E.C. makes another
demand, wants everything he's got or will go to the police.
The old boy knows he hasn't long to go, his steps are tottering
at a pretty good rate towards that bourne whence no traveller
returns, so he doesn't see why he shouldn't do his blackmailing
correspondent in the eye, and, if possible, put his wife, for
whom he don't seem to have cherished the feelings proper to a
loving husband, on the spot all at one fell swoop. Boy, if you
ask me, this case is a daisy, and I'm going to pick it."

" And if E.C. refuses to co-operate ? "

" We'll pull her in. Oh, I know it's reasonable to suppose
that if she was blackmailing the old man she'll lie doggo, but
dames always do the opposite of what you expect. Besides,
hardly any amateur, male or female, has the wit to copy
Brer Rabbit's example—you remember, he lay low and said
nuffin But if she should be the exception to prove the rule,
then we must pull her out by the ears. And now I'll leave
you to digest all my valuable suggestions and have a word
with Suspect Number 2."

CHAPTER SEVEN

HE WENT bolting down the stairs like a ton of bricks and
found his quarry waiting for him in the hall. There was no
dissimulation about Miss Beake.

" What do *you* want here ? " she demanded fiercely.
" Haven't you got a room at your hotel ? "

" Yes," said Mr. Crook at once, " and it's a single one. And
that's final." He grinned and patted her on the shoulder.
" Now, cheer up, sister," he admonished her. " You don't
have to boil over just because things ain't working out the
way you planned. Remember, that's not my fault."

She seethed furiously. " What do you mean by my plans ? "

" Oh, come," suggested Crook, " you ain't asking me to
believe this is the way you wanted things to break."

" The present situation is none of my making," she assured him.

" And, of course, you didn't want the old man to die."

" Why should I ? It didn't do me any good."

" To date," admitted Crook ruefully, " it don't seem to have done any one any good. Look where it's landed Mrs. East. And it's done you out of a nice trip to London."

" A trip to London's no special treat to me," flared his companion.

" Why, hadn't you been saving up your coupons for a shop-hound prowl ? Don't disappoint me in your sex, Miss Beake. If the ladies don't like the shops there's no sense in keeping 'em open, for the men are dead scared of 'em."

" There's not much sense buying a lot of clothes in a job like this," Miss Beake assured him.

Crook nodded. " You may have something there. Still, what about all the friends you'd dated for the Wednesday ? "

" It may surprise you to know," returned Miss Beake in tones of sheer fury, " that women in my position with a living to earn don't have these hosts of friends."

" No fellow-sufferers ? " asked Crook hopefully. " Besides, if you were thinking of makin' a change, this was your chance to go round the labour exchanges."

" Who said I was thinking of making a change ? "

" Nobody. But if you were planning to stay here for the rest of your natural, it's true what they tell you, women have got more courage than men. A lot more. Makes my blood freeze to contemplate it."

Miss Beake softened suddenly. " That's the first sensible word I've heard from any one since Mr. East died. Every one commiserates with me. Such bad luck, losing a bread ticket. Was it ? I could have got a better job than this a long time ago."

" And you stayed—because you were sorry for Mrs. East shut up in Castle Despair with the ogre ? "

" I was sorry for Mr. East. Poor old man, his money didn't do him much good."

" Better to be miserable with it than without it," returned the optimistic Mr. Crook. " Don't you think so ? "

" I've never had any," retorted his uncompromising companion. " And if you think I was hanging on here in the hope of getting my name in the will, you can put that idea right out of your head. The arrangement for that Wednesday was that I should meet Mr. East at his lawyers' office and witness the new will he was going to make. That'll show you I couldn't be a legatee, because . . ."

" Skip it," begged Crook. " So he was makin' a new will, was he ? "

" Adding a codicil to the old one."

" And going all the way to London for something he could have done just as easily through the post ? "

" There was this question of a divorce."

" Say, you were in his confidence, weren't you ? " said Crook, admiringly.

" Not far enough to give you all the information you want."

" Any idea who he was lunching with that day ? "

" No. Except that it couldn't have been Mr. Merridew, because he told me he was going to his office at two-thirty."

" And reachin' London two hours earlier ? Funny, ain't it ? "

" A man as rich as that has business acquaintances, I suppose."

" Still, if you were acting as his amanuensis . . . You were, weren't you ? "

" I used to type out some of his letters, but not all of them."

" And post 'em ? "

" I didn't post all of them. Sometimes Mrs. East posted them."

" Maybe she could help."

" I don't know what on earth you think you're drivin' at," snapped Miss Beake. " Since Mr. East never got to London, what does it matter who he meant to lunch with ? "

" It could be the brandy in the pudding," said Mr. Crook. " You know, that last little ingredient that gives the whole thing the right flavour. Now, tell me one more thing. Was it ever in your mind to leave East House ? "

" I had thought of it," confessed Miss Beake.

" Mentioned it to the old gentleman ? "

" Yes."

" He didn't take kindly to the idea ? "

" He was very upset. He said at his age and in his condition changes were bad for him."

" Is that," inquired Crook, shooting his arrow at a venture, like the bowman who struck Ahab under the armpit and decided the outcome of the battle, " when he gave you that nice little present ? "

" Present ? " All her suspicions flared up again.

" Well, don't you call ninety pounds a nice little present for a working-girl ? "

" So you noticed that ? As a matter of fact, it was. You see, he felt he could rely on me, and he was so helpless, in a way. Dr. Ventnor was on Mrs. East's side—any one could see that . . ."

" You're so sporty," groaned Crook. " I didn't know there was any question of sides. Like French and English, you know. Well, he asked you if you'd stay for a consideration. What made him choose ninety pounds, by the way ? Like Rosa Dartle," he added quickly, forestalling her indignant inquiry as to what business it was of his, " I only ask for information."

Miss Beake suddenly forsook her aggressive pose. " Naturally, I should have preferred a round sum like a hundred pounds," she acknowledged coolly. " Ten pounds is still quite a considerable sum to me. But—since you've examined his cheque-book I'm sure it hasn't escaped your attention that periodically he gave me small cheques to cash. He didn't need a great deal of ready money, but naturally there were some expenses, and he had come to rely more and more on me. I used to buy his mixtures at the chemist, he always paid for those in cash, and he smoked, though the doctor didn't think it was a very good thing with his heart. On that day, the day I told him I thought I'd like a change, it was so very solitary here, he had just made out a cheque for nine pounds. He listened to me very politely, then asked me if I wouldn't reconsider my decision. He said I was the only person he could count on. He had been quite apprehensive before I came, and he added that he didn't trust Dr. Ventnor. In fact, he intended to make a change there."

" A clean sweep, in short, Doctor, wife, every one except Nursie. Well, go on about the cheque."

" He listened to what I had to say, then he took up his pen and added a ' ty ' to the nine and a nought to the figure beneath it, and said, ' Would that help you to change your mind for a little while ? People like you and me, Miss Beake, who have to earn our livings, can't afford to disregard the problem of old age. You won't always be as spry as you are now . . .' "

You had to hand it to her, reflected Crook admiringly, she did know her onions. She had recognised the trend of his remarks and had spiked his guns before he could get them properly trained on her. If she chose to tell this story, there was no one to disprove it, and she might even say that he had asked her to make the addition to the counterfoil. She had her wits about her all right and he thought more of her for it.

"Very nice, too," he agreed, smoothly. "So you thought it over, and . . ."

"It wasn't the only money," declared Miss Beake. "I did have a sense of responsibility. There was no one but me . . ."

"There was Mrs. East," suggested Crook, mildly. "She'd looked after him quite well before you came."

"And the moment my back's turned, see what happens. I blame myself . . ."

"Always a mistake to do that," Crook warned her. "The other fellow's only too ready to think of that one."

"No one can hold me responsible," she declared, warming up again.

"When you've been on the job as long as I have," Crook assured her, "you'll be surprised what private enterprise can do if it's given its head. Matter of fact, what you ought to have done was get the old man to draw you a cheque for ten pounds and then get him to change it into ten thousand."

Miss Beake laughed harshly. "He'd doubtless have considered it cheaper to waste the twopenny stamp and draw a new cheque."

"He could be right at that," Crook acknowledged. "Well, be seeing you." And off he went, whistling 'Me and the Dark and You.' Miss Beake glared after him balefully. Up to no good, she was convinced. People like that simply existed to make trouble for other people.

Crook's next visit was to the prison, a pleasant run during which he had time to sort out his impressions. Rose East still looked pale and forlorn, and he rallied her reproachfully.

"You're not eating enough, sugar," he accused her. "What's your trouble? Haven't I told you Uncle Arthur's looking after this little bit of bother for you, and you've nothing to worry about?"

"Has anything fresh turned up?" she asked quickly, and he said : "Maybe this is where you can lend a hand. Now, you sometimes posted letters for your husband, didn't you?"

"Not very often. Mostly it was Miss Beake."

"Since there were so few of them it makes it easier for you to remember them. Now, cast your mind back to the last couple of weeks, say, of your husband's life. Did you post a letter to a mysterious lady during that time ? "

" Do you mean Mrs. Carter ? " Rose's response was spontaneous. " Does she come into this ? "

" It could be, honey, it could be." Crook momentarily restrained his jubilation. " Who was—is—this Mrs. Carter ? "

" I don't know. I don't know anything about her, except that she lived—lives—in London. I lon't know," she added hurriedly, " why I'm using the past tense. It's as though, since James is dead, all his contemporary world is dead, too."

" You're letting this get on top of you," said Crook encouragingly. " Just you remember a new world's going to open for you. And I'm not talking like a parson either," he added. " Now, are you dead sure you never heard your husband speak of Mrs. Carter ? "

" Never."

" And you've no notion who she could be ? "

" I did think . . ." began Rose, and hesitated.

" Let's have it."

" I wondered if perhaps James was proposing to dismiss Miss Beake and if Mrs. Carter was intended as her successor. I thought that would explain why he wouldn't let her post the letter, in case she smelt a rat and left before he was ready. James didn't like his plans being upset."

" Who did he think he was ? First Lord of the Treasury ? H'm. More than one letter to Mrs. Carter ? "

" I only posted one."

" Remember just when it was ? "

" Oh, a week or two before James died. I did wonder if he had meant to interview her when he went to London, and if that was perhaps one of his reasons for going."

Crook groaned. " You're a honey," he said. " Didn't think of suggesting that to me before ? "

" It never occurred to me that a woman he might be going to employ who was in London could have any connection with his death at Hinton St. Luke, particularly as they'd never met."

" We don't know that for sure. Maybe she was the skeleton in his cupboard. Now, any reason to think Miss Beake was afraid of losing her job ? "

" She told me several times that she could get something much more attractive and better-paid, so why should she mind ? "

" Beefed about that a lot, did she ? Seems queer she didn't take one of the other jobs, in that case."

" I thought she hoped James would remember her in his will," said Rose, with the ruthless simplicity of a child.

" She knew at the last he wasn't goin' to do that, if she didn't before, according to herself, anyway. Her story is she was going to meet your husband at the lawyer's office and witness the new will or the alterations to the old one."

" Can you ? " Rose looked doubtful. " I never made one, of course. I haven't anything to leave. But I always thought lawyers drafted wills and codicils and sent them to you for your consideration before they were signed. Still, James didn't go up to London often, so I suppose he thought he could rush everything through."

" That's a point," Crook admitted. " You know, it strikes me as queer that Miss Beake hadn't made any dates for her day in London. You'd have thought she'd have got her programme fixed from minute to minute."

Rose looked up in amazement. " Are you suggesting that she knew she wouldn't be going ? Oh, but I'm sure she didn't think that. In fact, there's proof she didn't."

" What's that ? " Crook looked sceptical.

Rose told him. (What she told him will be obvious to all readers.)

Crook looked more sceptical than ever. " That's a woman's reason."

" Miss Beake is a woman."

" Only just," said Crook. " Well, time will show. Thanks for the memory—yours, I mean."

Rose was looking dazed, as well she might, by these lightning moves.

" Are you referring to Mrs. Carter ? "

" Sure. What else have you told me ? "

" But—what does it all mean ? "

" Ask me that next time I call, and you'll be surprised."

He bounced off, jaunty as ever, and shut himself up in a telephone booth, where he had a long satisfying conversation with London. Then he got back into the Scourge, and on his way back to Hinton St. John he worked out a possible alternative solution to James East's death.

" Item. Miss Beake comes down in the hope of making a bit for herself for life. She plays old East for a sucker, and finds it's no go. He's close-fisted and he may go on for years. She feeds his suspicion against his wife, but he, being nobody's fool, ain't going to make it worth another female's while to put out his light. So," continued Crook, taking a corner with what most people would have called reckless speed, " he makes it perfectly clear to her she don't stand to gain anything by his death. On the other hand, he don't want her to go. She suits him very well the way things are at present, and he gets her to promise to stay so long as he wants her. That means he's got something on her, and the something is pretty obviously that cheque. He says, ' I'll make a bargain. You play my way and we won't say anything about the cheque. But you try to double-cross me and you're for it.' So far, so good. Then Mr. East says he's going to London to see his lawyer. That puts the wind up her good and proper. People in his state of health don't go to London if they want to change a will. They ask to have it sent down or in his case brought down. Ergo, he's going to London to see somebody besides Merridew. And since it doesn't occur to her it could be to see a girl-friend, she jumps to the conclusion it's some-thing to do with her cheque. Anyway, he may be tempted to tell M. the truth and that would be just too bad. So—he mustn't go to town. How's he going to be stopped ? Suppose he has a heart attack and pips out ? But it ain't so easy to engineer a heart attack for an old codger who looks after himself as well as East does, and if she starts anything questions are going to be asked, and that's just what she wants to avoid. But—suppose something happens when she ain't on the spot ? Suppose he passes out before he has a chance to confide in his attorney ? No one's going to question the cheque then. But how come ? It's important she shall be well out of the way. Well, of course, the answer's as easy as falling off a log. She knows, every one knows, the old gentleman has three aspirins after every meal. If, instead of aspirins, he takes something he thinks are aspirin but are really a permanent quietus, her troubles are over. Only that's where the rub comes. She's got to be sure they will be over, that no one will suspect her . . . First of all, the agent. That's easy. Mrs. East has some sleeping tablets. You bet Nursie knew all about them, and knew how she could lay hands on them. Then—she don't mean to be the one to give them to him. That's why she makes a lunch-date, knowing that if there is any trouble, Rose East'll be for it, and not her."

CHAPTER EIGHT

IN THE MEANTIME Stuart had been renewing his acquaintance with Ventnor. The latter was clearly taking the affair hard, and though he seemed ready enough to answer questions, it did not take a man of Stuart's perceptions long to realise that his main preoccupation now was not to catch East's murderer, but to see East's wife acquitted. "Does he think she may have done it after all?" he asked himself. "It's a ticklish position for him too."

He set himself to break down the inevitable barrier that the years and their widely different post-graduate experiences had built up.

"It seems strange to find you in a place like this," he began, smiling. "I always fancied you behind a brass plate in Harley Street."

"It's where I used to see myself," Ventnor confessed. "This was only to be a stop-gap, a chance to pick up a bit of experience, I wasn't going to stay. But then Melhuish died, and I'd made some good contacts—oh, one more example of the bird in the hand, you know. The bush is always so infernally risky."

"In your case," said Stuart, "it might have turned out a gold-mine."

"I'm not Methuselah, yet," said Ventnor rather sharply. "Still, I know what you're thinking. A case like this doesn't do a doctor any good. And you're right, of course."

"I put my faith in Arthur Crook," said Stuart, and Ventnor replied more sharply than ever : "And I mine in that girl. If Rose East is a murderer I know nothing of human nature."

"She has been very sorely tried," said the specialist slowly. "I blame myself in a way. And yet we specialists are in a difficulty in affairs like these. I gave what seemed to me the best advice in the circumstances, the best Mrs. East could possibly take. Naturally the best of all would have been a complete break, and yet even that might not have been the right solution. She'd have worried even if they'd been apart— and then I knew you had the case in hand, and I had told you that if you thought there was anything more I could do to let me know at once."

"What could you do?" burst forth Ventnor. "What could

any one do? Goodness knows, trouble due to ill-assorted marriages is common enough. There are others even in this village. Mostly one has to advise the sufferers to grin and bear it. In ninety-nine cases out of a hundred they win through somehow without any outward scandal. This was the hundredth." He moved restlessly to the window. " Perhaps I took too much for granted. We have to grow a protective skin in our jobs if we're to keep sane, not to be weighed down, submerged by all the wretchedness, physical and mental, that comes our way. And perhaps I'm not a disinterested judge. You see, I'm in love with Rose East."

" And you've made the village a present of your feelings ? " Stuart's voice was dry but sympathetic.

" Oh, no. Miss Beake's done that, and she doesn't believe in half-measures. The only thing is she's not precisely popular so what she says may not carry much weight."

" On the other hand, she's the only person who had the advantage of being inside the house all along the line. You can't expect the whole place not to eat it, you know."

Ventnor turned back. " It's funny that I of all men should find myself in such a jam. I always meant to steer clear of emotional issues, and so I did until I met Rose. Not that it helped me much, come to that. I'm past thirty and I'm still just a lumbering G.P. in a village so small most maps don't bother to mark it. And yet—and yet—it's odd how hard ambition dies in a man. I still believe in my star, still swear that sometime, somehow, I'll make my mark. D'you remember the treatise I swore I'd write ? "

" There's still time, as you've just reminded me."

" That's what I tell myself, but it isn't true. When I'm less busy, I say, I'll really get down to it. When I can put some of this routine work on one side—but the days follow one another and sometimes I'm honest enough to confess that I'm never likely to have the necessary leisure. It's a matter of a couple of paragraphs typed at the day's end or the early hours of the morning . . ."

" So long as you don't give up hope," said Stuart gently.

Ventnor turned to him with a new eagerness. " I wonder if you'd look at what I've done sometime," he said. " It would be so encouraging . . ." Then his spirit seemed to droop again. " There I go, absorbed in my own affairs, while all this time Rose . . . Tell me, Stuart, how good is this chap Crook ? "

" I'd back him against the Lord Chief Justice."

" Does he realise that what we must have is a verdict of Not Guilty not just Not Proven ? We don't want any chance of Rose being pointed at in the years to come as the woman who poisoned her husband and got away with it. See who that is, dear ? That's Mrs. Ventnor, Mrs. East that was, you know, the one that did for her poor old husband and—wasn't it wicked ?—she inherited all his money and then she married the doctor. Of course, he was her accomplice, well, any one can tell that. You can see how impossible her life would be. Crook doesn't say much, though he seems confident enough. But how far has he really got ? "

" I can't tell you. I can only promise you this, that if he says he'll get her found innocent he'll do it. Try and believe that."

" These chaps who say the fault of the age is the lack of faith ain't so far out after all," exclaimed a new voice, and both men swung round to see Crook in the doorway. " But you can stop frettin'. I've told you I'll see Mrs. East through and so I will. Matter of fact, she's helped me quite a lot, and presently, doctor, I might ask you to lend a hand, too. I'll tell you this to go on with. Within twenty-four hours we ought to know just why Mr. East was so keen to go to town."

Cummings, the editor of the *Record*, liked to say that he gave his readers better value for their money than all the rest of the morning papers put together, and on the following day he seemed to have justified his claim. For the readers of the *Record*, though of no other morning paper, were informed that on the day after his death James East had intended to come to London to meet Mrs. Carter.

WHO IS MRS. CARTER ?

ran the main headline. And

MYSTERY WOMAN IN EAST MURDER
NEW DEVELOPMENT

The *Record* learns that the late James East was making a journey to town for the express purpose of meeting a Mrs. Carter of London. Now every one is asking

W—H—Y ?

When Stuart saw that he reflected, " Crook does it again."

When Miss Beake saw it she muttered, " The conceited brute. I don't believe he really knows anything, but if he does, why did he ask me what I knew ? A trap ? " And reflected with fierce satisfaction that she hadn't told him anything. She hung about the house all the morning waiting for Crook to appear. She even approached Merridew to get his reactions and to inquire why she had been told nothing.

Merridew said blankly, " I wasn't aware you represented the police. As for the information in this morning's paper, I can give you no assistance beyond the advice not to believe everything you see in print."

Miss Beake chose to regard this as a deliberate snub, with the result that when Crook did put in an appearance she fell on him like a starving dog on a bone, shaking the *Record* at him and crying, " Are you responsible for this ? "

" Sure I am," said Crook. " And if 'that don't score a bull's-eye I'm a Dutchman."

Like Merridew, he made it clear he had no time for her that morning, and went bounding up the stairs to his colleague's den. He found Merridew suffering the same reaction to the news as Miss Beake, though his disguise was different.

" This is what you meant when you told me to wait for the morning paper, or words to that effect ? "

Crook beamed. " Nice work, don't you think ? "

" But the fact that Mr. East did intend to meet Mrs. Carter has not yet been established," Merridew scolded. " It is sheer surmise, and as such is most dangerous."

Crook remained unmoved. " Dangerous to get born at all," he pointed out. " Got to take some chances, y'know! Why, the police are chancin' my client's neck. And if you don't know that James East meant to meet the mysterious Mrs. Carter on the fatal Wednesday, as the *Post* has christened it, you must be about the only chap in England who don't."

" No one knows of it even as a possiblity except readers of the *Record*," pointed out Mr. Merridew in his wintry way.

Crook grinned to show that a joke was intended. " The rest don't matter a tinker's cuss," he said. He settled down with the apparent intention of remaining on the spot.

" You are giving me the pleasure of your company this morning ? " inquired Mr. Merridew with icy politeness.

" Till Mrs. C. eventuates," Crook explained.

" Mrs. C. ? "

" Mrs. Carter. For, of course, she's the E.C. of the counter-toils. I wonder what E. stands for." He began to croon a litany of names all beginning with E. "Eliza, Evangeline, Eugenie, Eutychus—no, that was a fellow—Elsie, Eleanor, Emily, Engelina . . . What's your fancy ? " He looked as if he were prepared to make a book on the spot.

"You suppose she will try to get in touch with us ? But if your supposition is right and she was, in fact, blackmailing my client, it is unreasonable to anticipate any such development." He was back with what Crook called his B.B.C. manner and at his least helpful.

"Unreasonable ? It's pure bughouse. But then, we ain't dealing with a reasonable being. We're dealing with a female. And you know what moves them most—motivates, as the Americans say ? Curiosity. She won't be able to stand reading that piece about herself—and even if she don't take the *Record* one of its two million odd readers will point it out to her, to every Mrs. E. Carter in the country—and not know what we've got up our sleeves. Oh, she'll make contact sooner or later, and my bet would be sooner."

It was not long after this that the telephone rang. Crook itched to snatch off the receiver, but he assumed an air of patience and listened to Merridew's side of the conversation, oblivious of the latter's short pause to enable him to slide unobtrusively away and leave the library to its legitimate occupant.

"Well ? " he demanded blatantly the instant Merridew laid the receiver down. "Mrs. Carter, eh ? " Merridew had to give him best.

"She is coming round shortly. She is staying at the Park House Hotel. I understand she telephoned to my firm this morning and was informed that I should be found here. She proposes to stay for a day or two to see how matters eventuate."

"When she comes, any objection to me sitting on the side and pretendin' to be the office boy ? " asked Crook.

Anything less like an office boy than the burly London lawyer it would be difficult to imagine, but Merridew agreed. For one thing, he was convinced Crook intended to remain in any case, and it was better to have him in the open than to discover him lurking behind a curtain or crouching on the window-sill, and for another Mr. Merridew was by no means happy about the impending visitor and did not, in his heart of hearts, at all object to having another member of the profession on the spot. At all events he'd be a witness, and in Mr. Merridew's experience, though not always in Crook's, the profession hung together. A few minutes later the front door bell rang and Merridew said, " That may be our visitor."

" If so, she's like the young lady who travelled faster than light. Y'know, I've got a new idea. Suppose this lady was—is—James East's little mistake, and she thought she might as well get Pappy to support her ? "

" Since she is certain to be over the age of sixteen there would be no liability," pointed out Mr. Merridew with a return to his normal pomposity.

" How right you are. Well, perhaps she's the girl he loved and left and . . ."

Perhaps it was fortunate that at this juncture a resentful Miss Beake opened the door and said, " There's a woman downstairs. She says you're expecting her, and it's confidential. She won't state her business."

" What is her name ? " asked Mr. Merridew, and Crook cut in : " Unless her business is so confidential she can't even tell you that."

" She calls herself Mrs. Carter."

" Please show her up."

" And make it snappy, sugar," encouraged Mr. Crook, " before she changes her mind."

Miss Beake, whom not all Merridew's efforts had contrived to dislodge from East House as yet, since she claimed she had nowhere else to go, still looked mutinous and the lawyer added sharply, " The lady is here by appointment and I do not wish her to be kept waiting."

" Tell Mrs. Rumtumtiddley to bring her up if the stairs are too much for you," suggested Crook. This lady was a local widow who had agreed to ' oblige ' for a consideration, a handsome consideration in Miss Beake's opinion, who revelled in the position of being the sole link between the House of Mystery and the village. Miss Beake wouldn't have let Mrs. Ruff (which was her right name) poke her nose into anything she could prevent, and she disappeared with an indignant snort. At the door she turned to say, " So that's who it was on the telephone. Somehow it seems sacriligeous to me to ring up a dead man's house."

Since neither of her hearers could think of any adequate comment on such a bromide her remark went unanswered, and she disappeared, to return a moment later with a buxom female just on the wrong side of fifty, comfortably but by no means stylishly-dressed, wearing furs and high-heeled, open-toed pumps and nylons, and bringing with her a wave of what she and Miss Beake called perfume and the more old-fashioned Mr. Crook called scent. Mr. Merridew, rising to greet her, made no secret of the fact that this was not the type of client to whom he was accustomed, but the more simple-minded Mr. Crook reflected that she looked more like an armful of comfort than a blackmailer, though he reminded himself that you could never tell. In any case, it seemed highly improbable that the late Mr. East would have paid a pension on the scale of four hundred pounds in eight months to the most accommodating and unobtrusive mistress.

Mrs. Carter, entirely free from embarrassment, advanced towards the two men, putting out a plump hand bursting from a blue suede glove.

" Well, Jimmy certainly flew high in his old age," she observed, looking round her with amused eyes. " All these books. Wonder how many of them he read. Bought by the yard, I dare say, just to make an impression. He always thought that important. Half the secret of success is making a good impression, he'd tell me."

" What did he say the other half was ? " asked Crook, immensely intrigued by their visitor.

" Getting up while the other chap was still turning over and wondering what time it was."

" I've heard worse definitions," admitted Crook.

Merridew, outraged by this frivolous byplay, here invited the lady to take a chair. Mrs. Carter complied without ceasing her flow of chatter.

" Mind you, I guessed he was on the up-and-up or I wouldn't have troubled him in the first place. I reckon Jimmy and me didn't have much in common, but we neither of us liked writing letters if it could be helped. Besides, I never think there's any call to be nasty, and though, as it happens, it didn't do me any harm him going off the way he did, still you can't ever tell. I suppose he was as fat as a porpoise before the end."

" Madam," exclaimed the outraged Mr. Merridew, " my client is dead."

" I wouldn't be here if he wasn't." She seemed to be totting up the value of the room and its furnishings. " Very nice," she pronounced. " I suppose this is the sort of thing Jimmy dreamed of in the old days. He always said he meant to get on. It was just a question of time. Give me time, he used to say, and I'll die a millionaire. Well, according to all accounts that's what he has done, though what good all that money is to him lying in that bitter churchyard, goodness only knows. Still, it's his own doing and that's all there is to be said about it."

Merridew and Crook both stiffened. "His own doing!" repeated Merridew.

"I don't think Jimmy was dumb enough to let his wife poison him, so if he died of poison you may take it he knew more about it than anybody else. Always had an eye for Number One, had Jimmy. Had a nasty, jealous nature, too, as I should know. Revengeful. And touchy!" She threw up her plump hands. "Though, mind you, I never expected him to go to these lengths."

She stopped for an instant for a fresh supply of breath and Merridew took the opportunity to say severely, "You are making very serious charges about a dead man, Mrs. Carter. Presumably you can support them." Though you didn't need to be as perspicacious as Arthur Crook to see he didn't believe that.

Mrs. Carter tossed her head and her elaborate hat quivered to its last sequin butterfly.

"I know all that about not speaking ill of the dead, thank you, and a very silly idea I've always thought it. What you say about people who're dead can't hurt them, and anyway truth's truth, isn't it, and there's a saying that truth will out. No, you take it from someone who's known Jimmy East for thirty years, if he's anywhere where he can see what's going on he's having the time of his life. Not that taking an overdose, knowing that poor girl would be the one to find him and perhaps get the blame, is what I'd call the act of a gentleman. But then Jimmy never was a gentleman for all his airs." Here Merridew again tried to intervene, but he might as well have tried to stand up against a tidal wave. As for Crook, he was far too fascinated by the candour and rapid delivery of their visitor's revelations to want to open his mouth. "Nature's gentleman, that's the best you could say for him, and you've only got to look round you to see the number of mistakes Nature's made."

Here Mr. Merridew did contrive to get a word in. "Are you seriously suggesting, madam, that my client took his own life?"

Most women would have been shocked into silence by his tone, but not Mrs. Carter.

"Well, you know, Jimmy was always one for getting out of awkward situations if he could, and this was awkward all right. I mean, I didn't want to do him any harm, and so I told him when I wrote, but right's right, and I wanted a bit of justice. Well, after all these years . . ."

" Thirty years ? " put in Crook, thinking it was time they started getting some facts.

" That's right. It's a long time, isn't it ? Of course, I was just a girl then," she beamed at him over her hospitable bosom, " and Jimmy seemed wonderful to me. After a year the wonderful thing was that I'd ever seen anything in him. But there, you know what girls are."

Merridew gave her no encouragement along these lines. Leaning forward, he said clearly, " Madam, I shall be obliged if you will state your business, and if you have any information that can assist us at this stage . . ."

Mrs. Carter looked as if she were going to blow up. " Seeing I've come all the way from London," she began, " after seeing that piece in the paper . . ." And then Crook eased the situation by leaning forward and saying, with a grin that made him look like a friendly alligator, " I bet you were good and wild when you got to the rendezvous on the Wednesday and found he wasn't there."

Mrs. Carter relaxed. " Well," said she in her frank way, " I wasn't really so surprised as you might think. You see, I had known him pretty well years ago and it's my experience men don't change, and this wasn't the first time he'd run out on me."

" Am I to understand you are a relation ? " interposed Mr. Merridew, who clearly didn't approve of being overlooked in this outrageous fashion.

Mrs. Carter put back her head in its alarming hat and laughed heartily. " That's rich," she said. " That's very rich. Almost as rich as Jimmy was, according to the newspapers. Am I related to Jimmy ? " She snapped the catch of her agressively handsome bag—real crocodile, she told her friends, and wouldn't he (meaning the crocodile) be surprised to find himself walking down Bond Street on my arm ?—You tell me—and brought up a folded paper from its depths. " I know what lawyers are," she said severely, " so I brought my lines along with me. Mind you, they're pretty old, but that doesn't stop them being the real McCoy."

Crook watched her, entranced. This case was turning out even better than he had allowed himself to hope. Merridew seemed dazed. He took the lines without a word, stared at them, looked back to the lady who had passed them to him, looked once again at the paper in his hand, and then said faintly, " Do you say you are Mr. East's widow ? Is that what you claim ? "

" I'm not claiming anything I haven't a right to in law. Mind you, I'm sorry for that girl, the one they're holding, I mean. I don't suppose Jimmy ever told her there had been a legal Mrs. East ever, let alone one still living."

" I see from this document," proceeded Mr. Merridew, recovering a little of his customary weighty style, " that you were married in South Africa thirty years ago. I am bound to ask you if there were ever any subsequent proceedings."

" If you mean a family, why not say so ? Nothing indecent about a family, is there ? If you don't . . ." She completely ignored the scarlet-faced Mr. Merridew's attempts to stop her, " then all I can tell you is I'm as married to Mr. East now as I was on our wedding-night. I haven't set eyes on him for nearly thirty years but there was never any question of a divorce. I didn't know where he was, for one thing, and for another I didn't think it was necessary. I settled down quite nicely without him . . ."

" With Mr. Carter ? " Merridew apparently could not resist that prick.

" That's right. He was just my cup of tea, was Mr. Carter. It wasn't his fault I had a husband, more of a misfortune, if you get me. Anyway, we decided we were just made for each other. Which is more than Jimmy and me ever was. Mind you," her round merry face sobered suddenly, " we didn't fail for want of trying. We both did our best—leastways, I know I did, though I don't think Jimmy strained himself, because if he'd tried half as hard to make a go of it as he did making himself a millionaire it 'ud be me following the coffin to the cemetery in the morning. Anyway, it didn't work. Jimmy had such big ideas. He wasn't a gentleman then, not to my way of thinking, but he was going to be, he knew it, and he wanted to live like a gentleman before he was one. And being a gentleman he couldn't do a rough day's work, had to have nice clothes. See what I mean ? Mind you, I'm not blaming him. He knew what was in him, knew he was going to win out in the end. But I tell you straight,. I got sick of being expected to manage on nothing a week. I did what I could. My conscience is clear about that. Presently I let out a room. If you ask me, that was the only sensible thing to do. But the way he carried on ! He didn't want lodgers in his house. Well, I told him, half a house is better than the street. Things didn't get any better ; presently, I had two lodgers, very nice fellows they were, too."

" One of them called Carter by any chance ? " asked Crook, bright and inquisitive as a bird at daybreak.

Up came the lady's head. She must have been a good-looking piece when she was younger, he reflected ; she was what you'd call comely still. Nicely dressed, too, though a woman would have wondered how she managed to control that exuberant figure with utility corsets.

" Suppose he was ? " she demanded, with a sudden access of hauteur. " If a woman's husband walks out on her she's a right to make the best arrangement for herself she can."

" So that's what he did," said Crook sympathetically, and she nodded. She'd decided by this time that Merridew was no more good than a sick headache. No heart, no guts. Just the sort of machine that could add up a column of figures when his bill fell due.

" That's what my lord did," she confirmed. " I came back from a day's shopping to find a note on the table to say he'd got a chance at last, but only for a single man. I feel, my dear Elsie, you will be better off without a husband in the circum-stances, in view of the difference of our outlooks, and since this would appear to be a case of the grey mare being the better horse I feel I need have no concern for your future. And then a P.S. to say he'd taken the money out of the old tea-pot, knowing I wouldn't want him to start his new life without a bean in his pocket, and soon being in funds again through not having him to feed ! The cheek of it." Her double chin was convulsed with rage at the memory, her fine eyes flashed. Mr. Merridew looked shocked and disgusted, because his clients, though they broke laws all over the shop, did it in a gentlemanly way ; they didn't marry barmaids and then desert them, having robbed them first of their last shilling. To assert his authority he began to ask her how she had run her rogue of a husband to earth, but Crook jumped in with the suggestion that, after all, James East couldn't have been much of a loss. That, at all events, he intimated, was what his present wife had felt.

Mrs. Carter, however, wasn't having any. " It's always a loss to a lady when her husband goes off like that, even if he isn't much good at bringing home the bacon, as they say. You're a bachelor yourself, perhaps . . ."

" You know you don't really have to ask," retorted Crook jovially. " None of the ladies will look at me, anyhow not more than once." He grinned like the advertisement of somebody's toothpaste. "One thing," he went on. "I bet there was one person in the house who didn't shed any tears over Mr. James East's departure, and that was Mr. Carter."

"Mr. Carter was kindness itself," said the pseudo Mrs. Carter staunchly. "No husband could have been more considerate."

Mr. Merridew here did contrive to make himself heard. "Did you make any attempt to discover your husband's whereabouts?"

"How could I?" demanded the lady indignantly. "He just said in his letter he was going to England. I didn't even know the name of the boat or what his job was, or even if he really had one. I couldn't even be sure the whole story wasn't a yarn to stop me trying to follow him. Mind you, I was a bit put out at first, as anybody would be, seeing how hard I'd worked for him, but pretty soon Mr. Carter made me see it was a blessing in disguise, as you might say. He was in good work himself, and he was never a man for wasting his money, and pretty soon we found we could do without the other lodger. He was getting married, anyhow, and naturally I didn't want another woman in the house. It never works."

"So you and Mr. Carter set up house together?"

"Not there we didn't. But he was being transferred to another branch—he was in hardware—and doing well, too. He said we might as well go along as Mr. and Mrs. Carter, nobody was going to bother about us, so we did. And if you ask me, we were more married than a lot of people that have the words said over them in church. You may not believe this," she looked intently from one lawyer to the other, "but presently I felt a lot more married to him than ever I'd done to Jimmy."

"Did you ever hear from your husband, Mrs . . . ?" Mr. Merridew, that stickler for propriety, hesitated.

"Carter's the name," said the lady firmly. "It's been good enough for five-and-twenty years, and it'll do now." She settled her fur stole and continued, "As to hearing from Jimmy, no, not once. I dare say he hoped I'd think he was dead. Perhaps he thought I was. And being on the other side of the world, I never heard anything about him, never thought about him much, if you want the truth. When you haven't heard from a man for a quarter of a century he seems sort of no account."

Crook bounced in here and played his hand. "And when

did you find out he was really the bright boy of the family and had made a pile ? " he suggested.

Mrs. Carter was not at all disconcerted by this blunt approach.

" You might almost say it was providence. Mr. Carter was a year or two younger than me, and he looked less than his age. So when the war was declared he was hopping mad to get into it. They don't want old men like you, I told him, but he said he'd missed the first war through being the wrong age, and he didn't mean to be done out of this one. The long and the short of it is he managed to get over with one of the South African contingents, and he was killed in 1945. After that, well, I felt at a loose end. We'd never had any little ones, and when you've gone around with a man all your life you feel sort of lost going about alone. Besides, I couldn't take the same interest in things without Len, and that's a fact. Then I got a chance to come over as companion to a lady, and I jumped at it."

" Perhaps," suggested Merridew with deadly courtesy, " it occurred to you you had a husband in England."

Crook was amazed by his courage and expected to see him blinded on the spot, but Mrs. Carter didn't appear to be offended.

" I don't know if you'll believe this," she said, " but it was years since I'd thought about Jimmy. After all, thirty years is a long time, and I didn't know if he was alive or dead. After I got back, though, I didn't find things as good as I'd hoped. Everything was so different over here. I could get work of a sort, but I didn't see why, when I'd had my own home for years, I should have to go and look after other people's."

" Did Mr. Carter not make adequate provision for you ? " asked Merridew coldly.

" Mr. Carter gave up a good job to go into the army, and he was always sure he'd be coming back. He left me something to be going on with, but money doesn't last for ever, and the cost of living kept going up . . . Anyhow, I needed money and it was just then that by pure chance I came across Jimmy again."

" You mean, you met him ? "

" Not likely, and anyway I dare say I wouldn't have known him again after all that time. No, it was funny really. I was coming back from seeing about a job one day when I found myself thinking about him, wondering how he'd got on—you know. For all I knew, he'd been dead for years. Then I stopped to buy an evening paper and there was his name—Mr. James East, director of some company or other, and a note about where he lived and the wife he'd married in the war. Well, I told myself, he's not the only James East in the world, but I couldn't help wondering if it really was the same one. If so—well, he hadn't done anything for me for twenty years and more, and if he was doing well he mightn't object to giving me a hand. I was still his wife legally, and though I'd never have dreamed of trying to trace him if Len had been alive, everything was different now. Mind you, I didn't bear him any ill-will. I didn't want to upset his present wife, either, and as for going back to him—well, I didn't like that idea any better, I dare say, than he'd have done. I went to Somerset House and asked if they had a marriage certificate for a Mr. James East married in 1941. I couldn't tell them the name of the girl he married, but I knew his birthday and all that and where he was born—Tottenham, as a matter of fact—and when they found the certificate I was pretty sure my old Jimmy had committed bigamy."

Merridew was looking aloof, but Crook preserved his friendly air.

" Chance of a lifetime," he suggested. " Well, put us out of our agony. You contacted James East ? "

" I wrote him a letter. A real ladylike letter it was, saying I didn't want to make trouble for him, and hoping he was happy, and the young lady was well, but things weren't altogether easy for me now, not being so young as I was and stout, which makes it difficult to do the stairs, and if he felt like giving me a little bit, well, I wouldn't say no."

" Blackmail, in short ? " suggested Mr. Merridew.

She turned on him with a fine fire of indignation. " Nothing of the kind. A wife has a right to some support."

" I gather that for several years you had been supported by Mr. Carter," said Merridew, brutally.

" And suppose I was ? What was I supposed to do, left at twenty-three without a penny, and a husband who calmly marched off and said he wasn't coming back, and I could sink or swim for him."

" She's right," said Crook. " It wouldn't make a pretty story for the *Record*. Rich man deserts Penniless Bride. Magnate's bigamous marriage. Is that the way Mr. East saw it ? " he added to Mrs. Carter.

" I didn't put it that way, naturally. I'm sure I always try to be a lady. But, of course, Jimmy saw my point. He wrote that he thought there was a mistake, he had every reason to suppose his first wife had been dead for several years before his second marriage, but I sent him a copy of my certificate and said he could see the original any time he liked, but I wasn't letting it out of my hands. And I reminded him of a few things only a wife would be likely to know, and explained how I didn't want to make things difficult for him, and I wasn't suggesting a divorce or anything vulgar like that, and would he answer to Mrs. Carter, as I hadn't been using his name for a long while. Well, he was some time answering, but when he did he said he didn't acknowledge liability but he didn't like to think of me going short—and that was enough to make a cat laugh if there'd been one handy —and he sent a cheque for a hundred and fifty, and he hoped that 'ud tide me over till I found suitable employment. I had half a mind to write and say a married woman's suitable employment is looking after her husband's house, but then I thought well, sooner any job than that, and naturally I wasn't going out to work when I had a husband in the big money perfectly able to keep me, so presently I wrote and said the cheque was all gone and how about it? Mind you," she turned furiously on Merridew, who sat looking as though he'd got into an abattoir by mistake, " there was nothing wrong about what I did. He'd have liked it a lot less if I'd gone to court. Well, next time he sent me a cheque for two-fifty and said he'd write again later, and so he did. This time he thought we ought to come to some settlement and as he was coming to town to see his lawyer, would I meet him for lunch at the Liverpool Road Hotel and he'd get a table, and if I came at 12.45 there'd be time for a drink before lunch. And that was a come-out for him—suggesting the drink, I mean."

" And you agreed ? "

" I thought if we got everything cut and dried with a lawyer to witness the arrangement, I could be sure there'd be no hanky-panky."

" Very irregular," sniffed Merridew. " It would have been far better if he had been to see me first and got my advice."

" Better for who ? " asked Mrs. Carter, belligerently.

Crook said, " Didn't it occur to you that if he told a lawyer the truth he'd be making him an accessory in crime ? You can get five years for bigamy."

" Not if it's an accident," said Mrs. Carter, comfortably. " And anyhow we could have had a divorce, and he could have remarried the young lady, though, come to that, p'raps she wouldn't have been so keen."

"Still, it is a good argument," Crook agreed. "I dare say you meant to develop it at lunch."

"I've got to look after myself now I've lost Len. As I say, if he was ready to be reasonable I didn't want any fuss, and he needn't have been afraid I'd have wanted to share this house with him. I'd as soon live in a mausoleum. Well, there it was. I came as arranged and—no Jimmy. Mind you, I hadn't seen him for thirty years, but there wasn't any one there who could have been him. To begin with, they were all in couples or joined by someone within five minutes. I waited and waited and then I asked if a gentleman called East had booked a table. They said No, but even that wasn't proof. Because he might have called himself North, West or South. I ordered a drink and sat back to wait, and at half-past one I told the waiter the car must have broken down, and I had lunch. I had half a mind to come down to Hinton St. Luke myself, but then I thought I'd best give him the benefit of the doubt—after all, cars do break down—and if I walked into the house he might get into one of his paddies, so I decided to wait till the next morning. In case there was a letter, see ? And the next morning when I opened my paper there was just two lines about him ' Rich Man's Fatal Heart Attack '— something of that sort. You would think with all the news there is going on these days they wouldn't have even that much spare space, but there it was. Mr. James East, a company director, was found dead in his home at Hinton St. Luke on Tuesday night. Death is believed to be due to natural causes. And then just a word about the widow being forty years younger than himself. You know, when I read that, I was so wild that, if he hadn't been dead already, I could have killed him—cheerfully." She made the statement with perfect calmness and Merridew looked more shocked than ever. Crook, however, perfectly understood her attitude.

"Tough," he agreed. "Getting away twice before you had time to send in the bill."

"It was then I began to wonder what my position 'ud be. I mean, I was his wife in name, though not much else, but still in English law this girl—what's her name ? Rose, of course— is something it wouldn't be polite to mention. She didn't know, of course, but there it was. I wished I'd known the name of Jimmy's lawyer but there was nothing in the paper about him and Jimmy himself had been much too cagey to mention it in any of his letters. And then everything broke at once, about it not being a natural death but somebody having given him the stuff."

"It is somewhat surprising that you did not see fit to put in an appearance at that juncture," suggested Mr. Merridew.

"Be your age," retorted the sensible Mrs. Carter. "Where was the sense in me getting mixed up in an unpleasant case like this before I had to? Anyway, I thought I'd wait till after the funeral. Then, when I saw that bit in the *Record*, I reckoned that was my cue. By this time, of course, I knew who the lawyer was, so I rang up the office and they told me he was down here. And now," at last she turned squarely to Merridew, "you tell me how I stand. I'm the widow and that must mean something."

Mr. Merridew was frankly flummoxed. This sort of business was not in the least up his street, though on consideration it seemed to him obvious that if she could prove her story she could most likely claim the widow's portion of the estate. As for the unfortunate Rose, always supposing she would ultimately be in a position to claim anything, it seemed possible she might find herself turned out, a pauper in an unfriendly world. H · distinctly remembered the phrasing of the dead man's will. To my wife . . . no name . . . and in law the wife was this brazen harpy who didn't give a straw for the dead man and was only interested in his effects, an attitude of mind that Crook understood very well. At that moment Mr. Merridew knew that this case was going to hit the great British Public just where it lived. They were going to eat it, and the *Record* was going to be sold out half an hour after the morning edition reached the shops. Whatever Crook might think about that sort of notoriety, Merridew hated it like the plague. Crook at the moment appeared either to have over looked the publicity prospects or else to have taken them in his stride. Another point in this astonishing case had struck him.

"Holy Smoke!" he exclaimed. "That clears up something. This talk about divorce. He said he wanted to consult you about the rights of an unfaithful wife—and we jumped to the conclusion he meant Rose East. But as I see it now it wasn't her he had in mind."

The lady drew an audible breath. "What sauce!" she exclaimed. "Him speaking of me being unfaithful, if you please, when it was him deserted me, and took the bit I'd stowed away in the teapot, which was my earnings and nothing to do with him . . ."

Merridew said icily, " Thirty years ago, under British law, housekeeping savings were the property of the husband."

" And a very silly law, too. It's about time it was changed. And anyway it was me provided the housekeeping to start with. I mean, it was my money all along."

" But.not for very long at that," Crook reminded her.

" Anyway, what I want to know is, where do I stand ? As I've said before, I don't want to make trouble, and I'm sure I've only sympathy for that poor girl who thinks she's his wife, but I've more right to what my husband left than, say, that woman who opened the door to me, looking down her nose all the time, and she needs good eyesight to see the end of that."

" Make your mind easy," said Crook. " She don't get as much as the parson's proboscis. Eh, Merridew ? "

Mr. Merridew had turned quite pale. " If you mean Miss Beake is not a legatee of my late client, that is correct."

" Well, that's a comfort," acknowledged Mrs. Carter. " I couldn't have borne it if she had gotten a slice. Now, I know you two gentlemen are busy, and I dare say you'll want to talk over what I've been telling you, so I won't delay you any further. It'll be easier for you to speak your minds if I fade out. Now as for my address—I'm staying a day or two, just till after the funeral, at the Park House Hotel, but after that I'll be going back to town, and this is where you can get me." She flourished a copperplate visiting card at both men, and said, " I'm all right for the minute, for money, I mean, but it's nice to know there's more where that came from." Then, still mistress of the situation, she marched towards the door. Crook, not intending to give Miss Beake a clear field, jumped to open it for her.

" I can't drive you back ? " he suggested, as they came down the stairs together.

" Not if you mean in that red matchbox that's standing in front of the gate, you can't," she assured him. " The two of us 'ud make it collapse like a balloon."

Crook was inwardly hurt, though relieved that his offer had been refused. It was characteristic that he never cared what people thought about him but he was as touchy as dammit about the Scourge. Still, he reflected, he had better things to do at the moment than act as escort to the winsomest of widows, so he bade her a cheerful farewell and slammed the front door.

CHAPTER NINE

As HE CAME back through the hall he heard a rustling movement and called out, " It's O.K., sister. You can come out now," and out of the room on the ground floor that she called her office popped Miss Beake like a jack-in-the-box.

" Who was that woman ? " she demanded. " And don't just say Mrs. Carter."

Crook grinned. " Your late boss's past," he told her.

" And a long way past. She'll never see fifty again. What does she want ? "

" What all the ladies want. Their rights."

" What rights has she got ? "

" According to her own statement, backed up by the appropriate document, the rights of a deserted wife."

Crook had never actually seen any one knocked down by a feather, but Miss Beake gave a creditable imitation of the phenomenon.

" You mean, she . . ."

" She's got her lines. Thirty years old, but, as she says herself, the real McCoy."

" But surely after thirty years, even if she can prove her case, she can't have any rights worth mentioning."

" That's where you're wrong, sister. Murder and marriage have two things in common, they go on for ever. Get married and you've got liabilities twenty and thirty and forty years on. Same with murder, in case you didn't know. You can be brought up for a murder all your life. Makes you think, don't it ? "

" Neither contingency is likely to affect me," said Miss Beake frostily. " Of course, it's the money she's after."

" With interest," Crook agreed. " You know, your Mr. East wouldn't have liked it a little bit if she'd come out with her story. No man would."

" You mean, he was going to try and silence her ? "

Crook himself was silent for a moment, looking at her with what seemed like admiration. " You've got it. That's just what he did mean to do. And, as I say, you can't very well blame him."

" And then he was going on to see Mr. Merridew ? "

" That's the way I read it. You're sure he never said anything to you ? "

112

" I've told you once. This has come as a tremendous shock to me."

" I bet it was a tremendous shock to him."

" Of course, financially it doesn't affect me, but I suppose it makes a lot of difference to the official widow. Poor Rose ! "

" Very sympathetic all of a sudden."

" I mean—such a risk and all for nothing. Because I suppose if she isn't his legal wife she doesn't inherit. And if she doesn't inherit, where was the sense in killing him ? "

" No sense killing him anyway if she was going to get pulled in for it. But she didn't, you know—kill him, I mean."

" The police . . ."

" Lady ! " Crook's voice was stern but compassionate. " I hate to disillusion you, but even the police are sometimes wrong."

" And I suppose you know already who really did do it ? " She was openly contemptuous.

" I'll be able to tell you quite soon, I hope. But it would never do for me to make a bloomer, too, would it ? "

He shook her off and went bounding up the stairs to where a perplexed and disgruntled Mr. Merridew sat doing nothing but staring into space.

He looked up as Crook entered. " How justice ever gets itself accomplished in this country I simply do not understand," he observed bitterly. " I have naturally informed the police of the latest development and the inspector merely says that if the lady did not meet my client and no doubt it can easily be established that she did not, she can have had no hand in the crime."

" Pity about that," agreed Crook. " The Invisible Murderer. Make our fortunes, wouldn't it ? " Then he chuckled joyously. " This is a pretty kettle of fish, ain't it ? Just fancy. The great James East a bigamist. Mean to say the old boy never gave you a hint he'd been wed before."

" If he had done so . . ."

" I get you," said Crook, hurriedly. " Everything fair, square and above board, and as plain as a pound of sausages laid out on the table. But—there was correspondence obviously."

" Obviously."

" And not a trace of it among the old gentleman's papers ? "

" Not a trace. And it is hardly likely that so prudent a man as my late client would retain letters that might have a damaging effect if they got into the wrong hands."

" If you ask me, any hands 'ud be the wrong ones for a correspondence like that. Sure there wasn't a secret pocket in his wallet ? "

" You can see it for yourself, since you obviously share the Inspector's view of my mental development." Not a doubt about it, thought Crook, the old chap was knocked clean off his perch by this morning's interview. He rummaged in a drawer and produced the wallet, which he opened. " It contains a number of letters, one from myself confirming the appointment in London, one from an insurance broker, one from his stockbroker with a pencilled note of his instructions, a letter from his bank giving the figures of his balance in his current account which, as you will see, is considerable, his current cheque-book, three aspirins in a plain envelope marked aspirins, a book of stamps, four stamped postcards and his identity card. Like many wealthy men," added Mr. Merridew superfluously, " Mr. East was exceedingly careful about details, and would never write a letter if he thought a postcard would suffice. I have had a number of postcards from him during our relationship, which is unusual in my experience."

" Sign of an open conscience surely," suggested Mr. Crook. " Nothin' to hide. Most chaps writing to a lawyer put a blob of sealing-wax on the flap. At least, most of my clients do."

" Possibly," agreed Mr. Merridew coldly, in a voice that said that was precisely what he would have anticipated. " No, I am personally convinced that Mr. East believed his first wife to be dead at the time of his second marriage."

" Ask you to make any inquiries to that effect by any chance ? "

" Not me. But he may have employed some other agency."

" Anything in his bank record to back up such an idea ? "

" At this stage it would be impossible to select one particular name and identify it."

" Not for me," said Crook. " I know 'em all. Any notice of the wedding in *The Times* ? "

" I saw none."

" Well," said Crook, " that shows you, don't it ? "

" Shows what ? " Mr. Merridew was becoming testy.

" That he didn't want to advertise the fact. Once married, he kept the bride in this mausoleum where she hardly ever saw the light of day, and since he seems to have cut himself off from the world, there was no reason why any one should guess the truth. Say what you like, he'd abandoned the lady in South Africa, where he'd met her in the first place, and

there was no reason to suppose she'd come over here for the
the rest of her natural." He rubbed his big nose thoughtfully.
Merridew gave an excellent impression of a man who hopes
he's going to be left alone very shortly, and Crook took the
hint. In any case, there was nothing more he could do here
at the moment, and he had, as he would have phrased it,
other fish to fry.

It occurred to him that at this juncture Frank Ventnor
might be able to help.

Ventnor had just returned from his morning round when
Crook arrived, and he asked eagerly, " Anything new ? I saw
that bit in the *Record* . . ." He grinned. " Juicy, eh ? "

" And Merridew and me have seen an even juicer bit at
East House this morning. What d'you think of this ? Old
Man East was a husband of thirty years' standing when he
wed the lovely Rose, so the marriage don't hold good after
all."

Ventnor started and stared. " Talk about melodrama !
That's the one thing that never occurred to me. Does it help
us, though ? I mean, help Rose ? It doesn't bear thinking of,
remembering her in that black hole of Calcutta . . ."

" Black hole be damned ! " said Crook heartily. " It's a
nice modern prison and I've seen a lot of premises to let at
extortionate rents that were a lot less comfortable."

" All the same, it is a prison. That's what sticks in my
gullet. In her place I'd be crazy. And when you think of
what she's been through already—remember, I was on the
spot and saw it, month after month, and couldn't do a
thing "

" I wouldn't say that," Crook encouraged him. " You were
a lot of help really. I mean, you supplied the stuff that did
the old man in."

Ventnor looked at him as though he thought he'd taken
leave of his senses. " What exactly does that mean ? "

" Of course, I know that when a man or a woman is
determined to get rid of an enemy, he or she generally manages
it somehow. I only mean that in this case the stuff was
put ready to the willing hand. Now, there's something you
can tell me better than any one else. You knew the chap
better than most. Would you say he had a revengeful
nature ? "

" Personally I should say he'd stick at nothing. And, as
a matter of fact, if he could look up or down from wherever

he may be at this moment, he'd probably be rubbing his ghostly hands to see us all in this jam. If he thought he could ruin me as well as her, he'd be more pleased still."

" Right. Now, you don't have to answer this one, but—providing he could have died quietly like the gentleman he liked to think he was, you wouldn't have shed any tears for him ? "

" No one would."

" Except possibly Miss Beake ? "

" I doubt if he represented anything but a bread ticket to her. She sided with him because she thought it was in her interests to do so, and naturally she was jealous of Rose East, because she was young and lovely, and though Miss Beake may once have been young she can certainly never have been beautiful."

" Did she ever mention to you that she was anxious to leave ? "

" No. Was she ? "

" According to herself, she had the offer of a better job."

" Then why didn't she take it ? Or was she hoping to be remembered in the will ? "

" I fancy the old boy made it clear to her she could put that idea out of her head."

" Then—what reason was there ? "

" I give you three guesses."

" She couldn't have been in love with him ? No, that's out of the question. Then . . . ? " He paused, looking interrogatively at his companion.

" Right. He had a hold over her. Now what ? "

Ventnor shook his head. " I've no idea. Unless he knew something unprofessional about her past."

" Meaning she might have poisoned one of her other patients."

" No one can say you lack imagination," commented Ventnor, dryly. " You know, now you mention it, I do remember her asking me once how bad he really was and how long he was likely to hold out ? I asked her why she wanted to know and she said she didn't want to spend the rest of her life here. What are you really driving at ? "

" I'm trying to pin the blame for this murder on somebody who isn't Rose East," explained Crook patiently. " If I could show an alternative motive by someone else I can start buildin' operations. Now, Miss Beake had the opportunity, and precious little chance of being accused, because the average person would say she lost more than she gained by the old man's passing. Now—another leadin' question, just between you and me—when you saw the old boy, didn't it just cross your mind that somebody might have helped him out ? "

His voice was very persuasive, but Ventnor met his gaze steadily.

" No. I suppose that's enough to break me, but it didn't. I wasn't even particularly surprised, as I've already told the police. I wouldn't have been surprised if it had happened at any time. He was in a very dicky state, and he would get himself worked up about this London visit, and a heart in that condition can't stand a lot of strain."

" You didn't even think somebody might have worked him up deliberately ? "

" That's sheer speculation, a luxury doctors can't afford."

" Quite. Another thing. He had a special tonic for heart attacks, I understand."

" It was only a palliative. Nothing could have saved him for long."

" Still, if you'd been his nurse and you'd been going to leave him for several hours, wouldn't you have mixed a dose and left it by him ? "

Ventnor drummed his fingers thoughtfully on the table-top. " Difficult to say. I wouldn't like to be dogmatic. After all, his wife was in the house and he had a bell at the bedside."

" Very fair," approved Crook. " Now—do you dispense your own prescriptions ? "

" For my panel patients I do. They come and fetch 'em in the evening. I leave the bottles on the surgery mantelpiece and if all they want is their medicine they just come and in fetch 'em, instead of having to hang about till their turn in the queue is reached."

Crook looked dubious. " Isn't that a bit risky ? "

" It's mostly indigestion mixture or what they like to call nerve tonic. Wouldn't hurt a baby. The effect of a lot of medicine, you know, is pathological. You remember that cricketing chap who said that if the batsman thinks a ball is going to spin, then to all intents and purposes spin it does. If these chaps think the stuff I give them is going to improve their digestion or their nerves, then it will."

" Tactful lot, your patients," murmured Crook. " Don't they ever have anything seriously wrong with them ? "

" If they do, I mostly pack them into hospital, if I can

persuade them to go. If I can't, I go and see them. I certainly shouldn't put any medicine containing poison or a dangerous drug out where any one else could get hold of it."

" Still, you do have a supply of poison in your dispensary for the special cases ? "

" Yes." Ventnor looked puzzled. " What's all this leading to ? "

" I'll tell you. Did you ever leave East's medicine on the surgery mantelpiece? I mean, anything you may have made up specially for him?—even once? Take your time. This may be important."

Ventnor didn't hesitate. " I left his heart stuff there one evening, because I got a sudden call and couldn't get round with it. I rang up the house and Miss Beake said she'd come herself."

" And you left it on the mantelpiece ? "

" Yes. It was Tuesday evening when the surgery isn't normally open, but I told the old body who does for me that Miss Beake would be coming round. They all know her by sight, of course—well, we'll hope her sort don't come in couples—and I said she could leave the door open and lock up after Miss Beake had gone."

" I get you. Now—whereabouts is the surgery ? "

" It opens out of my consulting room, across the passage."

" And the dispensary ? "

" On the other side. Through that door."

" Also openin' out of the consulting room ? "

" A doctor has to consider his own convenience from time to time," Ventnor pointed out sarcastically. " Were you thinking of explaining all this rigmarole at any time ? "

" I was wondering whether you were certain the door to the dispensary was locked on that particular evening. I suppose it is locked, as a rule."

Ventnor coloured a little. " Officially it's always locked when I'm out, but actually, well, there's nobody on the premises but old Mrs. Pye and me, so I'm not too fussy."

" Then suppose, for the sake of argument, it wasn't locked on that particular Tuesday night, were there any of Mrs. East's sleeping tablets—I mean identical tablets, of course—in the dispensary ? "

Ventnor drew a deep breath. " So that's what you're driving at. Yes, it's possible. I mean, I do have a supply for emergencies, though how any one could positively identify them, unless they understood the Latin label . . ."

" And suppose, say, three or four had been extracted, would you be likely to notice ? "

" Probably not. All the same, how on earth do you hope to prove a case like that ? "

" The choice ain't wide, and as I've told you already I don't mind if I implicate the Lord Mayor of London if it gets Mrs. East off. Now, remember, Miss Beake went off deliberately knowing the old man had a big ordeal in front of him the next day and must be kept specially quiet. She didn't mix him a dose of his heart tonic for emergencies, she came back pretty late—by the way whose idea was it she should accompany the old boy to London ? "

" Hers. I'd never have suggested it. I didn't like the woman. I thought she was a mischief-maker, which I couldn't forgive, and a gold-digger, which I could understand more easily. Any one deserved anything they could get out of that old miser. All the same, it is a bit far-fetched. I mean, she'd have looked pretty silly if Mrs. Pye had found her in the dispensary."

" Had she ever come round to your place before ? "

" I don't believe she had."

" Then all she had to say was that she'd taken the wrong door. Or she could pop the bottle in her pocket and, if she was discovered rummaging among your things, say it wasn't on the surgery mantelpiece and you must have forgotten and left it in the dispensary, after all. Oh, a woman of her sort could lie her way out of that easily enough."

" But—wouldn't it have been simpler to abstract the tablets from Mrs. East's bottle and substitute aspirin ? "

" Much simpler, if Mrs. East had had the tact to leave the bottle lying about. But she kept it locked up. I dare say Miss Beake had thought of that for herself."

" It's very ingenious. Of course, you've got to get evidence that the old man had something on her."

" Don't worry about that." Crook sounded confident. " I dare say she had plenty of reason for wanting the old gentleman under the sod. And then, look at the way she's gone round trying to get the girl accused. What made her so suspicious it wasn't a natural death ? "

" I had wondered that myself. Of course, she was hideously jealous of Rose, and she loathed me like poison. She was always trying to set the old man against us both."

" Suggesting that, once he was out of the way, his widow wouldn't waste much time mourning for him. Now then, take it easy. Unless you go round with your ears pinned back, you must know what chaps are saying."

"Oh, I suppose it's true. You know, up till now I've never had much sympathy for chaps who go round falling in love with their patient's wives. There are plenty of unattached women who'd jump at them. But since I've met Rose, I've understood. At first, you know, I was just sorry for her, as I'd be sorry for any woman married to James East, but quite soon it was a lot more than that."

"And she knew it?"

"Not for a long time. I didn't mean to give myself away. After all, there was nothing I could do. James East was my patient. That was that. But one day I slipped my defences and . . . oh, Rose was loyalty itself. I don't think she'd even thought of such a thing. But Miss Beake had eyes all over the place. She realised the situation and decided it was just jam for her. That's a thing I'll never forgive her for. Don't you see how she's wrecked our future, whatever happens? Wherever we go people will point at Rose and say . . ."

"Don't you believe it," said Crook. "By the time this case is finished you'll be able to stop bothering about any considerations of that kind. You take an old pro's word for that. Y'see, I'm here to get the real criminal, and when I've shown my hand, the girl 'ull be dismissed from court without a stain on her character, and the great fool B.P. being what it is, any marriage she makes 'ull be a romance. No, let you stop worrying over that. Well, thanks a million. I've got to go along and talk to Stuart now. You know, I wouldn't be surprised if at the end it turned out the old man himself had a hand in things. Seeing the sort of cove he was, I mean."

And refusing to elucidate this mysterious statement he hurried away.

When he reached the Park House Hotel he was told that Stuart was out playing golf, so he had to curb his impatience until after tea. He looked round for Mrs. Carter, but there was no sign of her and he decided she had most likely gone to the cinema in the neighbouring market town. He left a message for Stuart and returned to the Barley-Mow, where later his friend found him, apparently doing accounts.

"Got something for me?" he asked expectantly.

"Who won?" countered Crook, without waiting for a reply. "By the way, did you chance to notice a new arrival at your pub, a dame with a bust like Venus and a hat full of butterflies ? "

" You'd have to be blind and deaf not to notice her," was Stuart's dry retort. " She just turned up with what I believe is called a pick-up, one of those fellows you find in every hotel, always on the look-out for whatever's going."

" He'll find he's got his match in Elsie," said Crook. " She's been there before."

" Friend of yours ? " asked Stuart.

" Did she look like a friend of mine ? No, but she may prove a friend to Rose East."

Stuart lighted a cigarette. " Do I take it she's the skeleton in James East's cupboard ? "

" Not fair," objected Crook. " You've been listening at key-holes."

" No need to. I'm a psychologist, remember, and when did you take an interest in women unless they were essential to a case ? "

" Toosh," said Crook, and Stuart stared.

" French," Crook explained. " B.B.C. pronunciation. All the same, you're going to get a shock when you hear who she is."

He told him, and Stuart registered appreciative astonishment. " All the same," he asked presently, " how much further does that get us ? "

Crook rubbed his nose. " A hell of a way, if you ask me. Y'know, Stuart, while I was waiting for you I've been putting two and two together, and twice two are ninety-six if you know the way to score. So, taking one consideration with another, I'd say Mrs. East was right when she said her husband helped himself to the sleeping tablets, but wrong when she said it was an accident. Now, hold everything, and remember that if you're a psychologist I'm a criminal lawyer with the emphasis on the criminal, and hold most of the aces. I think James East knew perfectly well which bottle was which and if he took three tablets out of Rose East's bottle he did it deliberately, knowing what the result of taking them would be."

" And the motive ? He must have known what it would mean to his wife if . . ."

" I fancy that was the idea. Y'see, by that time he hated her guts. And here he saw a chance of getting even. You may think it was a bit drastic, and so it was, but he was a natural usurer and he exacted a high rate of interest. Yes, he meant to do for her, whatever the consequences to himself—and you have to remember his expectation of life was pretty poor. Chaps in his state of health don't stand to lose much in any case. And how could he foresee that an eleventh-hour factor would upset his calculations and spoil his fun."

" Fun ! " commented Stuart, at his dryest. " I always thought you had a queer sense of humour, Crook. Anyway, how are you going to prove any of this ? "

" That's the rub. The trouble with dead men is they're so damned unco-operative. I know the one about dead men telling tales, but unless there's a witness it's not much help, and half the time their evidence is gibberish anyhow."

"It's an unsatisfactory case at best," agreed Stuart, in dejected tones.

Crook looked genuinely astounded. " What more d'you want for your money ? " he demanded. " Why, the case has got everything—beautiful young wife, rich miserly curmudgeon of a husband, dying just at the right moment for every one except himself, Galahad just round the corner, jealous nurse, even the mysterious voice from the past. Why, there's nothing missing except anonymous letters."

And, as it happened, they did not have to wait long for those.

CHAPTER TEN

THE FIRST of the anonymous letters came to someone who had no connection whatsoever with the East Murder. This was a Miss Stapleton, whose sister, Emma, a tiresome, tyrannical old woman, had died nearly a year before. The two ladies had lived together for many years and when the elder finally succumbed, after a long, painful illness, one of those fluctuating affairs that are erroneously said to cause as much pain to the relatives as to the sufferer, the whole village asked, " Poor Miss Stapleton. What on earth will she do now she is alone ? "

Miss Stapleton had, as they say, coped. Indeed, she had coped considerably better than any one had anticipated. She had waited a short, a very short time, and then had the drawing-room distempered—a barbarous practice, my dear Lucy, Emma used to say—and one or two of the more outrageous pieces of Victorian furniture disappeared. A few pictures were next bustled away to the attic, and Miss Stapleton satisfied a craving she had long cherished in secret and began to wear the heavy, handsome rings that had belonged to her mother every day, instead of only on state occasions, mainly when the Vicar and his wife, neither of whom noticed such adornments, came to call. But Mrs. Hilary, who was no fool, remarked to her husband when she heard the news, " Poor Lucy Stapleton. Really, I don't know that Emma's death isn't a blessing in disguise I know she subscribed heavily to the Organ Fund, but she led her sister no end of a dance."

Mr. Hilary, who was the Johnny-head-in-air type of clergyman, said simply that all death was a blessing in disguise —for the deceased, he hastened to add, for really, my dear, I don't know what I should do if you left me—and there the matter ended. Miss Stapleton did not suddenly break into orgies of entertainment, fine clothes (or as fine as the clothing ration would allow) drink, and give parties, but she did buy a geranium-coloured blouse and clip-on ear-rings and a gold wrist-watch, all small luxuries she had wanted for years. And every one noticed how quickly she lost the haggard look that had distinguished her during the dominant Emma's reign. Still, she missed her sister more than most people realised, and she visited the grave every Sunday, and herself clipped the grass with a pair of dress-making scissors, and sometimes, later in the evening, when she was playing a quiet game of patience and listening to the wireless (Emma had permitted the wireless on the understanding that it was only put on for the news) she would recall Emma's horror at the desecration of the Sabbath by card-playing—all card-games were alike to her—and she would sweep the pack together and shut it quickly into a drawer, feeling she was taking advantage of Emma, who couldn't now (unless she contrived to materialise) stop her sister doing what she pleased on Sunday evenings.

It was, then, to this inoffensive elderly woman that the first of the poison pen letters was delivered. It came through the letter flap with the fish bill and a Harrod's list and a letter from her only surviving school-friend, asking her to come and stay for a few days at her home at Malvern.

" We have no maid at present," wrote the friend, " and you would be such a help in the house. We remember the beautiful meals you used to cook for dear Emma."

Miss Stapleton, whose conscience sometimes nagged her because she couldn't be as sorry that Emma was dead as she felt she ought to be, glowed with pleasure as she read that. Yes, she really had been a good sister. Or, if not good, at all events adequate. Smiling, she picked up the last envelope. It was a cheap, white affair, square in shape, and the hand-writing was quite unknown to her. It was an uneducated hand, a local post-mark ; she supposed vaguely it was someone in the village who was in difficulty and wanted help or advice.

Inside the envelope was an equally cheap sheet of white paper, bearing neither address nor date.

So you're not the only murderess in Hinton St. Luke (the message read). *Only this one hasn't been so lucky.*

There was no signature.

Her impulse was to fling the letter into the basket, and this, in fact, she did, only to rise to retrieve it a moment later lest Flora, her elderly maid who had known Emma very well, should find it. Flora was a good sort ; in the ordinary way she wouldn't have dreamed of reading a letter she found in the basket, but this was different. And—alas !—she talked.

Miss Stapleton smoothed out the sheet she had crumpled in angry dread and examined the message again. Murderess. A horrible word for a horrible crime. It was fantastic, of course. She wouldn't pay any attention to it. Indeed, she hardly liked to touch the thing. Then it came to her for the first time that some human agency had penned that message, deliberately written out the cruel words, sealed them in an envelope, written the address, put on a stamp and thrust the whole into the mouth of a pillar-box, knowing that next morning it would lie on Lucy Stapleton's breakfast-tray and be opened by her. Not that any one could believe that she had had a hand in hastening Emma's death. Such a notion was unthinkable. (She took it for granted the writer was referring to Emma. There wasn't anybody else.) Then again second thoughts enlightened her. She could say it was ridiculous and nobody believed it, but X, the writer of the letter, obviously did. Somebody—incredible though it seemed—really believed that she, Lucy Stapleton, had encompassed her own sister's death.

A fact like that took some accepting and, when she had accepted it, she was first furiously angry and then suddenly desperately afraid. Because if one person could believe that, why not two or three, or thirty-three, or the whole village ? The letter, which had at first seemed no more important than a dirty sort of joke, now assumed immense proportions. Were people all over the village saying this sort of thing behind her back ? Oh, surely not. Emma had been dead nearly a year. She must have become aware of it if that was the legend that was circulating. Besides, someone would have felt it her duty to warn dear Miss Stapleton *what people were saying*. Every community has at least one such public-spirited member. And what conceivable ground could there be for such an accusation. Every one knew that she had nursed Emma devotedly, looked after her day and night (until the doctor insisted on a night nurse, saying he couldn't have two invalids on his hands), cooked her meals, measured out her medicine. And then when she had died, people had been so kind, brought her flowers and little dishes to tempt her appetite because, having cooked for Emma for so long, she couldn't feel it was worth while cooking only for herself. No, this letter was simply the fruit of a crazy brain and unworthy of consideration by any sensible person. But she couldn't make herself believe that. When the time came for her usual walk through the village she told Flora she thought she had a little cold coming on and would stay at home to-day. Instead of sitting near the window, where she could watch life pass, she sat in a corner of the room where no one could see her except by pressing against the window-pane. She had no appetite for lunch and by tea-time was so feverish that Flora of her own accord sent for Ventnor.

" It was quite unnecessary of Flora, doctor," said Miss Stapleton, folding and unfolding her hands on her lap. " I am just a little feverish, that is all."

" There's certainly not much use my coming in if you're going to try and throw dust in my eyes," Ventnor agreed. " What's happened, Miss Stapleton ? And don't say nothing. Say, if you like, it's something you'd prefer not to discuss, and I shall perfectly understand, though even then I should advise you to take someone into your confidence, but I should be a worse doctor than I am if I couldn't see you'd had a serious shock."

Miss Stapleton remembered with a great jolt of relief that doctors are like priests, you can tell them things you'd never tell an ordinary person, and they have to respect your confidence. And what a comfort it would be to show him the letter and hear him corroborate her own belief that it was all nonsense, the invention of a malicious or diseased brain, hear him tell her to put the memory of it out of her mind, reassure her that the whole village knew and appreciated her devotion to Emma.

"I really think I must tell you," she exclaimed breathlessly. "It is so astonishing, something quite outside my experience. I hardly know what to do."

And then she opened the drawer and took out the letter and showed it to him.

Ventnor registered as much indignation as she could have hoped.

"It's disgusting," he said. "You of all people. But you do understand how it's come about, don't you? It's this affair of Mr. East's death that is responsible. It has stirred up something in the mind of an unbalanced person. I can't go into a lot of explanations now, and you might be no wiser if I did, but my friend, Dr. Stuart, would tell you exactly how these things start. I do hope," he went on, "you won't give it another thought, unless you get a second letter. You see, every one knows what care you took of your sister, and if it were generally known that you had had this letter you would find every one else as indignant as myself."

"You think, then, there is nothing I can do? After all, you attended Emma, you provided the death certificate . . ." And there she stopped abruptly, colouring to the eyes, remembering another certificate he had given more recently that was still the subject of discussion all over the country.

"I know what you are thinking," said Ventnor steadily, "but you must remember it's possible for any man to make a mistake in such circumstances. One doesn't, after all, look for murder among one's patients. But in this case evidence of the cause of death was overwhelming. I warned you from the beginning that the illness was likely to end fatally and in the circumstances it was a blessing that it went on no longer. She was saved a great deal of pain . . My dear Miss Stapleton," for at this recollection of the past the poor lady had suddenly dissolved into tears, "you must either try and put the whole matter out of your mind or else you must take the letter to the police and ask them to try to trace the writer."

Lucy Stapleton mopped her face and tried to speak naturally. "Oh, I couldn't do that, Dr. Ventnor. I may be a coward, but the very thought of the police in this house—think how angry Emma would have been. And then, the publicity! If, as you say, this thought is in no one's mind but that of someone very nearly a lunatic, surely it would be madness to—to plant it there. Don't you see, that would be the sure way of starting people talking?"

"Only in indignation on your behalf," urged the doctor, but Miss Stapleton knew her village better.

"To begin with—yes. But then you would hear someone say there's no smoke without fire, and they would recollect that I didn't wear black for twelve months, and had the drawing-room chairs reupholstered, and was seen going to the cinema—such a vulgar entertainment, Emma always said —oh, no, Dr. Ventnor, pray, pray don't ask me to call in the police."

"You mustn't destroy the letter, though. There may be others—oh, not to you, but to other people. You see, people who write this sort of thing don't mind where they strike, and they generally have a working knowledge of—of the weak spots of their victims. In fact," a look of surprise flooded his own face, "it's only just occurred to me but I may be similarly honoured in the near future."

"But that's horrible. It means nobody is safe. Everybody has some secret grief."

"Well, nobody ever is—absolutely safe, I mean. You can't be sure someone won't break into your house in spite of all the police in the world. Or that a car won't skid on a greasy day and run you down, no matter how careful you are. There are chances we all have to take. Mind you, I think X will probably select people like yourself who are unlikely to call in the police. You see, once the authorities are on the track, the fun, if you'll forgive my using that word, is nearly over. Because such people generally give themselves away sooner or later, and when they are discovered they can expect no mercy at the hands of the community."

He picked up the letter and envelope. A cheap type that could be bought at any sixpenny store, disguised hand-writing —it could have been written by quite an educated person— postmark Hinton St. John, but that didn't debar any one except a cripple. There was a regular bus service and half the village had bicycles anyhow.

"You must try to remember that you are dealing with a very sick person," he went on. "There are sicknesses of the mind that are more dire than any sickness of the body."

Miss Stapleton shook her neat grey head. "Oh, I know you excuse everything nowadays, doctor, but when I was young when people did wrong we called it sin. I'm afraid I'm a very old-fashioned person."

Ventnor seemed to be thinking. " You say you haven't shown this to any one. Not Flora? Or the Vicar? No, doubtless you are wise. But, Miss Stapleton, you know I think, that I am very deeply concerned at poor Mrs. East's plight, and am quite convinced she had no hand in her husband's death. It's obvious to me that these letters—for I shall be most surprised if others are not received, if they have not been received already—are knit up with that death, and we have an unconventional but most efficient lawyer acting for Mrs. East. I should like your permission to show him this letter."

But Miss Stapleton instantly put out her hand. " Oh, no. I'm sure he is kind, but I really don't think—you see, it's not as if he were somone I know, and this is a very private matter. You do see? "

Ventnor retained his hold on the letter and put his free hand on Miss Stapleton's arm.

" Will you try and see this from another angle? A girl who, I am convinced, is as innocent as the angels, is going to be tried for murder. Try to realise what that means. To be shut up in prison, to know that presently you're going to stand in the dock and hear learned counsel argue that you deliberately poisoned your husband, to know you're innocent and yet to know you can't prove it, to know that everything, your whole life—think of it, Miss Stapleton, your life itself—depends on the case your counsel can put before the jury. In such circumstances, don't you agree that the smallest thing that may help the accused should be available to her lawyer? "

" Yes." Miss Stapleton looked distracted. " Yes, of course. But I cannot see what this letter has to do with Mrs. East. Naturally, I am very, very sorry—such a pretty girl, and though, of course, one mustn't speak ill of the dead, I never did like Mr. East—but I cannot like the idea of a stranger enquiring into my affairs."

" I promise you there will be no enquiry. But if there are other letters, Mr. Crook may be able to discover the author; it may even prove that he or she has some direct connection with Mr. East's death, though I admit that is a rather far-fetched suggestion. But I cannot believe we can afford to disregard anything that may be of assistance."

" I must be guided by you, of course," agreed the old lady painfully, after a pause. " But I do hope it will not involve my having to see this Mr. Crook. I have noticed him, I believe, in the village (Ventnor thought this extremely likely;

a roving tiger could hardly attract more attention) but I really do not feel I could discuss the sacred things of family life with a stranger." Her voice added, " And not even a gentleman," though naturally her lips, which were the lips of a lady, did not frame the words.

" That is very kind and very courageous of you, and I can promise you you needn't see Mr. Crook, unless you wish to, if you will undertake to let me know if you hear of any one else receiving similar letters, or if you should unhappily get another yourself. Though in cases like these, seeing that you can have no conceivable connection with the East affairs, the writers generally scatter their effusions over a wide field."

" You don't think this is an attempt to get money out of me ? " quavered poor Miss Stapleton.

" If there were any suggestion of blackmail I should tell you to take your letter straight to the police, but I don't think the writer has that in mind. At all events there's no suggestion of it here." He rose and held out his hand to say good-bye. Voice and expression were alike kind, and he held her hand warmly for a moment as though he could somehow reassure her. " Try not to worry too much," he told her, though Heaven knew he was worried enough himself.

" It's not just myself I'm thinking of, but other people who have been unfortunate enough to suffer bereavement or some kindred trouble and who may also be at the mercy of this— lunatic. And perhaps they won't all have someone as sympathetic and as strong as yourself to advise them."

" I will have a word with Hilary," said the doctor. " He may hear if any other letters have been received. I know he has the reputation of having his head in the clouds, but he receives a good many confidences notwithstanding."

" Mrs. Hilary," murmured Miss Stapleton in confused tones. " Such a nice woman. I am sure she would not allow her husband to be troubled."

Ventnor had a sudden vision of Mrs. Hilary going out with a carving-knife to decapitate any one who bothered dearest Lionel. He thought privately there were worse ways of dealing with people who threatened your peace of mind.

Driving away from Miss Stapleton, Ventnor wondered what sort of reception Crook would accord to the letter. He was an incalculable person ; he might say, " Only some jealous old judy having a bit of fun," or something equally heartless. Or, on the other hand, he might see in it a pointer to Rose East's freedom.

Crook, faced with the letter and Ventnor's explanations, said cheerfully, " How damned unoriginal these chaps are. Who is this old dame, and is there any chance that she did put her sister under the daisies ? "

" Not the slightest." Ventnor's tone was chilly. But Crook only said in absent tones, " You'd be surprised. Chap I know told me the other day there are about 10,000 unofficial murders a year. Well, I told him, they must be pretty unofficial if even I don't hear of them. Well, well, this is a beginning of a new campaign. Or could it have started somewhere else ? "

" That's what we've got to find out. This is the first that's come my way. I thought of having a word with the Vicar."

" Mrs. Vicar," amended Crook promptly. " If that dear old chap got one of these, he'd probably think an angel had written it and pushed it through the sky. Damn it, I don't believe he could think ill of any one."

" A very dangerous quality in a man in his position," was Ventnor's crisp retort.

" If you know any of the lawyers here you might try and pump 'em," continued Crook. " Old girls like this Miss Stapleton fly to the doctor or the Vicar, but some of the others might prefer a solicitor. Anyway, you keep your eyes and ears open and I'll do the same."

CHAPTER ELEVEN

Two DAYS passed without further incident. Crook went up to town to attend to business there and when he returned Ventnor had another letter to show him. This time the postmark was Shapley, the market town about a dozen miles the other side of Hinton St. Luke.

" Our chap gets about, don't he ? " said Crook. " But then you've a nice bus service here. I wonder what the idea is, though. How did you get this ? "

" I followed up your suggestion of visiting people who might be scarified. Come to think of it, it's horrifying to realise that five people out of ten have something in their history they'd rather keep dark."

" You're so moral in the country," sighed Crook. " In the towns it 'ud be ninety-five out of a hundred. Well, let's have it. What's the lady's name ? "

" Mrs. Abrahams. I'd been visiting her for a chronic internal complaint, and she surprised me by saying only this morning she thought she'd go away for a change of air. It would be beneficial. She's delicate and not very young, and though she has plenty of money, that doesn't cut much ice these days when most people seem to have more than they know how to spend. And this isn't precisely the time of year one would choose, particularly a woman in her state of health. I asked her if she'd any special reason, and she hedged a bit, as you'd expect, and eventually it all came out."

" She's had a letter too ? What's her particular skeleton ? "

" It's not known to many people. She had a son in the 1914-1918 war who was shot for cowardice. Some blundering fool of a major thought it the right thing to send the truth, and she had a collapse and apparently was half out of her mind for a time. Not so much for what her son had done—he was only eighteen and just lost his head—but that the authorities should have deemed it punishable by death. Melhuish, my predecessor, was her doctor and he got the truth out of her. But in consequence she has, as they say, kept herself to herself ever since, living like one of these marine creatures in her shell, peering out at the world and then hurriedly retreating. Of course, every one guessed there was some mystery, but I fancy most people don't know what it is. Now she sees the whole miserable story exposed, and though it was thirty years ago, that doesn't seem to make it any easier for her. In a sense, she's never moved on from that time. Even the last war didn't seem to make any great impression on her."

" She should have come to London," said Crook unsympathetically. " Don't she know you can't hide yourself from the world whatever you do ? Lock your door, seal your windows, but the wind comes down the chimney. It wouldn't surprise me to know half the village could tell you the truth."

But Ventnor said No, he doubted that, though, of course, there must have been local chaps serving with this boy who eventually came back, and most likely they knew the facts. But it wasn't the sort of thing a decent person would ever refer to.

" We ain't dealing with a decent person," pointed out Crook patiently. " We're dealin' with someone about as decent as an atom bomb. Well, step by step and silently— I wonder which of us the serpent will strike first."

" You think we're in for it ? "

" As I see it, there's no sense in all this correspondence

unless we are. Ah, well, I dare say we shan't have long to wait. In the meantime, mum's the word."

Crook was right in his supposition. As he was leaving his house next morning Ventnor was intercepted by Miss Beake, who was in a tearing passion.

" I was coming to see you," she announced, in a voice that must have been audible to the whole village, he felt. " Is this your idea of a joke ? " She waved a piece of paper at him.

" Hallo ! " Ventnor's voice was sharp. " Have you had one too ? "

" You mean, you know about them ? You've heard ? "

" Not yet. But I've no doubt I shall."

" Why should you ? "

" Why not—since you've got one ? When did yours come ? "

" This morning. I thought I'd come to you straight away. Since you say you don't know anything about them—how did you know what it was ? " she added, suddenly struck by this point.

" Because, though I haven't had one yet, other people have."

" Have they ? I suppose it never occurred to you to take me into your confidence ? As a matter of fact," she added, sullenly accepting Ventnor's offer of a lift, " I was going to consult Mr. Merridew. Perhaps he's heard. I wondered if it was your idea of a way to drive me out. But I promise you I'm going to stick here tighter than a limpet till the case is over."

" Wouldn't it be more comfortable for you in some other neighbourhood ? " suggested Ventnor sensibly.

" More comfortable for you, you mean. I'm sure it would suit your book excellently if I were to disappear altogether. If a thought of yours could strike me dead, you'd think it this moment."

" Why should I ? " the doctor inquired.

" If it hadn't been for me, Rose East would have got away with it."

" I wonder you don't accuse her of writing the letters."

" Even that wouldn't surprise me. I'm not much impressed by the way the police have handled the case."

" They've arrested the woman you hate. Isn't that what you wanted ? "

Miss Beake snorted. " What's the good of that when it's

132

simple to see that this Crook person intends to twist them round his little finger ? "

They reached East House and found Merridew hard at work, not, as it happened on East's affairs, but on papers he had had sent from London.

" Look at that," cried Miss Beake dramatically, casting her letter before him with the gesture of one offering pearls to swine. " What do you suppose that means ? "

Mr. Merridew read the message. " Be sure your sins will find you out," it said.

" Precisely what it implies," he suggested dryly.

" I thought Dr. Ventnor might have written it, but he says he didn't. Apparently other people have been getting them. Have you had one ? "

" Certainly not," returned Merridew. " Why should I ? "

" I dare say you will. You've probably got as many sins on your conscience as any one else. I wonder if this is some trick of Crook's."

" Do show some sense," urged Ventnor.

" I wouldn't put anything past him. What's justice to him ? Not so much as a word in a printed book. If Mrs. East hangs for a murder I haven't the faintest doubt she committed, I— I'll eat my hat."

" That 'ud be a pity, seeing you've only just bought it and, so far as my information goes, haven't even worn it yet," put in a new voice, and Crook swaggered cheerfully into the room. " 'Morning, Merridew. Just come to get the low-down on the day's work. Hallo ! " His sharp eyes had caught sight of the slip of paper lying on the table. " Who's been honoured this time ? "

" That," said Miss Beake in tones trembling with anger, " is mine. If you can throw any light on it . . ."

" Give me a little while. In the meantime, mind if I borrow this ? It may be important."

" How can a vulgar scribble like that be important ? "

" Murder's mostly a vulgar affair."

" Have YOU had one of these ? " demanded Miss Beake.

" Not yet. But then—I ain't the first in the queue. B still comes before C, in spite of all our modern educational improvements."

" Are you seriously suggesting that the crazy creature responsible for these letters is going to work through the alphabet ? "

" There's method in the craziest creature's madness. Still, that was just an idea of mine. We'll be able to test it. Merridew ought to come after me, with the doctor—V comin' at the tail of the alphabet—getting the last seat."

" Unfortunately," said Ventnor dryly, " this isn't the first."

" One up to you, doctor," agreed Crook, in no way discomposed.

" Since you know so much," snapped Miss Beake, " do you know who wrote them ? "

" My guess is as good as the next man's, I dare say. That's as far as I'd care to go at present. Well, thanks for this," he tapped the pocket into which he had thrust the letter, " and if you get any more, just pass me the word."

But the next person to be noticed by X was the doctor, which was, said Crook, only what you could expect. The fellow had a sense of method, he added. " Every other day, regular as clockwork. What does it say ? "

" Dad luck. You won't get the money, after all."

" That's illuminating," remarked Crook, with unwonted gravity. " I mean, it narrows the field, don't it ? "

Ventnor looked puzzled for a moment, then he said, " Yes, I get you. You know, I wish we could close this infernal case. It's beginning to get on my nerves."

" Don't tell me again about Rose in prison," Crook implored him. " She could be in worse places."

" But not many."

" There are coffins. Now it's obvious that X is either a maniac, and I don't think he is, or he's a pal of Rose East who, like me, don't care who's gated so long as she goes free, or X is hin s f the guilty party trying to lead suspicion away from himself."

Ventnor looked puzzled. " I don't quite get that. The police have already made an arrest. Until Rose East gets a verdict of Not Guilty I should have thought X was sitting pretty."

" Not with me on the track, he ain't. Now, you try and tap any legal pals you may have and see if you can pick up any more information about the letters—careful people do take 'em to their lawyers—it's odd if the only people to get 'em are our circle and your patients."

" You may have something there," Ventnor agreed. " Anyway, we could do with a bit of information."

" I like a man to speak his own mind," said Crook. " You don't think we're making much headway."

" Since you ask me, are you any nearer knowing who poisoned the old man ? "

" Cases like this break all of a sudden like a hurricane. One of these days I'll give you all a surprise."

He did not, however, appear to be in any hurry. Ventnor prosecuted his inquiries and thirty-six hours later said he had reason to believe that at least one person unknown to him had had an anonymous communication.

" I couldn't, of course, find out who it was," he told Crook, " but there's no doubt about it, there are more letters going round than we've actually seen. I let Beresford know that I'd been consulted, too, and he was prepared to take a serious view of it."

" Good of him, I'm sure," said Crook, a little huffily. " Nice to know that even lawyers find murder a serious affair. Of course," he went on in a more normal voice, " the trouble with anonymous letter-writers is that there's always a certain amount of truth in their accusations. That argues either that they're people who are well-established in the neighbourhood, or else they're the nosey kind who make everybody's business their business."

Matters looked up a bit when Miss Beake got a second letter, saying : ' The best-laid plans of mice and women gang aft agley.'

This time she came storming round to Crook, ready to accuse him of authorship if he gave her half a chance.

" What, another ? " exclaimed Crook, with ill-timed levity. " This chap does seem to have taken a fancy to you. And so far nothing for Arthur Crook. You'd think he didn't even take me seriously."

" Stop playing the fool ! " shouted Miss Beake, who, whatever else she lacked, didn't lack courage. " I believe you're behind all this. Oh, I know quite well you'd stop at nothing to get that woman off. It's nothing to you if she's killed half a dozen husbands."

" I'm only asked to show she didn't kill this one," Crook pointed out. " And surely you've been warned before to-day what happens to people who make these insinuations. Why not tackle Merridew ? P'raps he's behind all this."

" That little image ? "

" They say still waters run deep, and in my experience the most unlikely chap is often the one you want. Again like marriage. The fellow nobody thought had a chance tops the poll."

" He's certainly picking on the most unlikely people," was Miss Beake's bitter comment. " Months I've been here and nobody's taken any notice of me at all, except to look as if they thought I was trespassing just by being on the pavement, but now there's trouble brewing they suddenly remember me."

And with this she prepared to depart.

" Going to the police ? " asked Crook amiably.

" I've had quite enough trouble with the police as it is."

" Then, if you're agreeable, lend me that letter for a bit."

Miss Beake looked mutinous. " What have you done with the first one ? "

" Put it in my collection. I want to make certain they're all written by the same person."

" Why shouldn't they be ? "

" This sort of thing's catching. Like measles. One chap writes a letter and the story gets about and some other poor zany thinks, ' Why shouldn't I have a shot ? ' Fellows like Stuart would tell you it's an inferiority complex."

" What nonsense ! "

" If you've never had the limelight, never made a spectacular marriage, never been a film star or won a fortune at Monte, never even been asked to advertise somebody's face cream, you have to make your mark somehow, at least if you're what the expert johnnies call exhibitionists."

" You should know," retorted Miss Beake, with heavy sarcasm.

" So here's the idea. I've got several of these letters, and I'm going to take 'em up to town and get 'em vetted by a chap who knows what's what. If you set great store on yours, I promise you shall have 'em back when the case is over, and you can keep 'em as mementos of the first murder case in which you've been involved."

He did his alligator act. Miss Beake remained unimpressed. However, she seemed to prefer dealing with Crook to dealing with the police, so she gave up her second letter, and Crook went round to see Ventnor to collect his letter and ask if there would be any objection to his taking the letters for Miss Stapleton and Mrs. Abrahams with him. Ventnor said he supposed not.

" You see," explained Crook, " I haven't got one of my own. Not yet."

His last call was on Merridew, who merely looked disgusted when asked if he'd had a letter.

" Certainly not. Why should I ? "

" You have me there," Crook acknowledged frankly.
" After all, you're not trying to save Rose East's neck."

Merridew asked with a wintry smile if Crook was going to
London because the village had got too warm for him, but
Crook said no, he must have been a salamander in his last
incarnation, but he wanted to try out a theory, and then he
said he'd be obliged if he might take a last look at Old Man
East's wallet. Merridew looked as if he thought he'd taken
leave of his senses.

" You saw it only a few days ago," he objected. " I assure
you nothing has been added or subtracted since then."

" I'll bet," agreed Crook. " Still, it's just an idea I have."

Merridew, looking deeply mistrustful, produced the wallet
for the second time and put it on the table.

" If you are attempting to solve the mystery of the anonymous letters, you can hardly imagine that my client, my *late*
client   "

" Psychic news," grinned Crook. " Murdered Man Seeks
His Revenge. No no, it's not that sort of idea. Besides, these
letters weren't in spirit writing." He had opened the wallet
and was pouring the contents on to the table-top. Merridew
watched him like a cat at a mouse-hole. There was painful
fascination in his regard. So far as he could see, Crook wasn't
doing anything but examine the writing on the envelopes.

The telephone began to ring, and Crook jerked his head up
quickly " That could be for me," he exclaimed. (It couldn't,
of course, since he had told no one he was coming to East
House, but foxes had nothing on Arthur Crook.) The ruse
worked. Instantly Mr. Merridew snatched off the receiver and
half turned from his companion as though to exclude him
from even a one-sided conversation. Crook chuckled and went
back to his work. Whoever the call was for, Merridew seemed
to be having some difficulty in dealing with it. He kept saying,
" Who ? What number are you calling ? " and at last slammed
the receiver back on to its rest.

" A wrong number," he announced curtly.

" P'raps it's the murderer believing you have the essential
clue on the premises, and trying to find out if you're still on
dooty. By the way, shall I find you here when I get back ?
So far as you know, that is."

" My client's affairs require a considerable amount of
time and attention," said Merridew, a little evasively. As a
matter of fact, it suited him quite well to be at Hinton St.
Luke for a little ; an excellent local woman looked after the

house and cooked the meals ; so Mr. Merridew gave instructions to his partner to telephone him in any emergency, and he himself put through a number of calls to London. Since none of these, of course, was at his personal expense, their length and quantity did not trouble him.

" Good man," said Crook, who understood the situation to a hair. " Look out for yourself, though. And if you don't hear from me within three days, and I don't reappear in person, this is my partner's name and address. I'm goin' to leave a statement with him in case of emergencies."

Mr. Merridew looked really startled. " Do you seriously suppose you are in any danger ? "

" Well," said Crook, " what do you think ? " He shuffled the dead man's letters back into the wallet, and if all the envelopes didn't contain precisely what had been in them ten minutes earlier Merridew noticed no difference.

When Crook had departed, a kind of hush fell over the village. The tension lessened. People continued to fall sick, or have nervous breakdowns and summon the doctor, and Miss Beake, as always, contrived to keep herself busy and other people exasperated, but during the days of Crook's absence no more anonymous letters were received.

Two days later he came tearing back in the Scourge ; he had contrived to keep her on the roads throughout the war and, said he, he didn't intend to let a mere peace scupper either of them. He looked remarkably cheerful and told Stuart that everything was going according to plan.

" Whose plan ? " inquired Stuart, who was more perturbed about the whole affair than most people realised.

" Have patience with me and I will tell thee all," pleaded Crook. " Yes, as I say, it's workin' out accordin' to plan— X's plan, of course, but I'm adapting it to suit my book— but as the cops would tell you, theory's one thing and proof is another, and I don't think X has had quite enough rope yet."

" To hang himself ? "

" It could be me," Crook acknowledged. " But if so, Bill will see to it he's next on the list."

He dashed back to the Barley-Mow, to learn that no letters had arrived for him during his absence. But next morning on his breakfast table was a square white envelope of a familiar appearance. It was addressed in the usual clumsy capitals to Mr. A. Crook, and the message read :

Crook always gets his man, doesn't he? But make sure this time someone doesn't get him first.

" Nice of him to warn me, isn't it? " suggested Crook, reporting this to Stuart. " I'm going the rounds now."

" Whom are you going to visit? "

" Ventnor first. He may have got a letter too. Then Merridew and dear Miss Beake, on the bare chance that they can help. You never can tell."

When he reached the surgery, Ventnor's car was standing in front of the door, and when Crook, with his usual lack of ceremony, barged in, he found the doctor by his table, looking startled and shocked, holding one of those sheets of paper with which Crook was becoming familiar.

" What the devil . . . ? " he began as Crook burst in. " Oh, it's you. You're like a human cyclone, aren't you? "

" So you've got one, too. I sort of felt you might have."

" Have you heard? "

" At last. Well, this chap has overlooked me long enough."

" I believe you actually wanted to get one."

" I always like to be in the swim. What does yours say? You look a bit bowled over."

" It's more lunatic than usual. It says : ' Have you made your last will and testament? You are next on the list.' "

" You can't say he hasn't given you fair warning."

" What on earth does it mean? "

" To put it bluntly, that someone prefers your room to your company. Don't look so glum. It's a compliment if you look at it properly."

" The sort of compliment I could do without," returned Ventnor dryly " Do you suppose the writer is mad or simply malicious? "

" Probably enjoying himself like hell," said Crook. " Well, let's hope someone is."

" When you say he," began Ventnor, and Crook flung up his hands and said, " Oh, purely academic. X is always he. It don't mean a thing."

" Have you," asked Ventnor abruptly, " any notion who X is? "

Crook's red eyebrows climbed violently. " Sure," he exclaimed. " Haven't you? "

" Not yet. You don't feel like confiding in me, I suppose? " Again he looked with troubled eyes at the message he had just received. " Do you imagine he's in earnest about this ? " he asked.

" Could be," said Crook in unconcerned tones. " As for who X is, believe me, if I could tell you now I would. But I can't. Still, I fancy it won't be long now, and I promise you you shall hear as soon as any one, if I have any say in the matter."

CHAPTER TWELVE

WHEN CROOK suggested that the pair of them should now call on Merridew, Ventnor hesitated for an instant with a murmur about his patients, but Crook said heartily, " Didn't you tell me yourself one of these days that half the cures you effect are really the result of self-hypnosis ? Well, let your chaps get on with their hypnotic efforts without you for once," and because just then what happened about Rose East seemed more important to Ventnor than all his patients, he acquiesced, and they both drove away in his car.

" Yours broken down at last ? " asked the doctor kindly, but Crook said, No, he was giving her a day off and a merciful man was merciful to his beast. " Besides," he added, virtuously, " we're asked to save petrol, and one car's enough to take us round to East House. In fact, the Minister would probably suggest we might do it on our own feet."

When they reached East House they found Miss Beake with her nose pressed against the pane.

" Almost looks like she's expecting us," said Crook " Maybe she's heard, too."

As they entered the porch they saw the face disappear and an instant later Miss Beake flung the door wide.

" That woman ! " she panted in their faces. " It's a scandal."

" What's a scandal ? " asked Crook, pleasantly " Don't tell me you've another corpse for us. Who is it this time ? Surely not the first Mrs. E ? "

" I can't understand how you can be so flippant. No, I'm talking about Mrs. Ruff—you know, the woman who claims to oblige. I don't know how you could even think of another murder."

" Lady," said Crook, solemnly, " I'm like the White Queen, who could believe six impossible things before breakfast."

" What's Mrs. Ruff done ? " asked the more peaceable doctor.

" Wants a rise of wages already, and her only here a fortnight. Says there's more to do than she expected."

" Ah, well, the estate will pay those, not you or me," said Crook comfortably. " Every dog a bone. It don't come out of your larder or mine." He nodded as though to dismiss a triviality. " Now, have you had another of *the* letters ? "

" Why on earth should I ? "

" Don't overdo it," Crook begged. " Why shouldn't you ? The doctor and me have this very day. Anyway, time's drawing short."

" What does that mean ? " asked both his hearers simultaneously.

" I mean, zero hour's going to strike any minute now."

He went bounding up the stairs, followed by the doctor, with Miss Beake, determined to miss nothing, hurrying in their wake. Merridew seemed surprised to see them.

" Spare us five minutes," implored Crook. " As I've just been pointin' out to our mutual friends, we're nearing the place . "

Ventnor capped him neatly. " Where the element's rage, the fiend-voices that rave, shall dwindle, shall blend . . ."

" Thanks a lot," said Crook blandly.

Miss Beake stared. " More poitry," she said. " I can't think how you can read the stuff."

" I suppose it doesn't go very well with medicine," agreed the doctor

" Mrs. East was the same, Rose East, I mean. Always poring over poitry. That,' she added maliciously, " was something else you had in common."

Merridew here broke up the party by saying in testy tones, " What is all this about ? Have you come as a deputation . . ? "

" Not a bit," said Crook. " I've come for East's little wallet—you know, the one you lent me twice before."

Merridew looked downright angry. " Is this a joke ? "

" Not to me or the doctor or Mrs. East, it ain't.'

" What do you want with the wallet ? You saw it just before you went to town."

" I know I had an idea it might contain an essential cloo, as they say on the radio. And I was right. By heck, I was right. I took my suspected evidence up to town "

" Your suspected evidence ? "

" That I got out of the wallet."

" But there's nothing missing from it. I looked particularly after you had gone."

" Suspicious mind you have," Crook congratulated him. " All the same—got it handy ? Ah, many thanks." He took the wallet from the lawyer's reluctant hand and opened it. He shook all the envelopes it contained on to the table, then picked one out. " See this ? Blank envelope marked Aspirin. Break the flap, and what do we find ? " He shook three little white pellets out on to the palm of his hand and held it out for every one to see.

" Three aspirin," said Ventnor in troubled tones.

" You see ? Even you are deceived. One aspirin and two doses of death."

They were all hanging on his words now. Miss Beake barely repressed a cry. Only Merridew asked irritably. " What is this melodrama, Crook ? "

" While you were answering your wrong number the other morning I did a bit of quick change work. Y'see, I wanted to test an idea I had. And so when you weren't looking I opened the envelope and took out one of the tablets and replaced it with a genuine aspirin. And to prove there's no deception," he spread his big ruthless hands, then dived into the envelope again and snatched out a slip of paper. " All my own work, gentlemen, all my own work."

The three crowded round to see what his exhibit was. It proved to be a slip of paper in Crook's inimitable writing, containing a message which read. " One tablet removed 5. 9. 47. One aspirin inserted. A. CROOK."

" Now," he continued, obviously enjoying the sensation he had created, " that envelope was stuck down by me on the 5th, and it was in Merridew's possession since then, and you all saw it was stuck down when he handed it back to me. Is that good enough for the law that it hadn't been tampered with ? "

" I'm afraid I don't understand," said Merridew frostily.

" He's crazy. He ought to be in a circus," said Miss Beake.

" What are you driving at, Crook ? " asked Ventnor. " You've got something up your sleeve, of course."

" I'll tell you," said Crook. " You know, it puzzled me from the first why James East made the date with his wife, the legal Mrs. East commonly known as Carter, before he saw his lawyer. The reasonable thing for a chap in his delicate position was to tell you the facts," he butted his great head

in Merridew's direction, " and leave you to deal with the
lady. Of course, lots of people suffer from swelled head and
think they can do things better than the experts. But James
East, according to all accounts, wasn't like that. He reversed
the process for some reason of his own. First he said he'd meet
her and come to terms and then he'd get his lawyer to ratify
those terms."

" He was in an awkward position," Merridew intervened.
" He had already sent her two sums of money, thus acknow-
ledging liability."

" Have we any evidence that could be brought into court to
show that he did anything of the kind ? We know he got the
money in cash, in pound notes to be exact, from his bank.
All he had to do was to post them to her by registered post,
with a faked sender's name on the outside. And that was
queer, too. Why didn't he contact you right away when he
got her first letter ? If you were going to be dragged into it
anyhow, you'd think he'd get you to act from start to finish."

" If she had threatened a court action . ."

" Men as near death as he was don't generally bother their
heads much about court actions. And any judge would
treat a case like this sympathetically, at all events so far as
the second marriage was concerned. The lady had been
passing as Mrs. Carter for so long she hadn't much of a
case really."

" It is very unlike my client to do anything without due
consideration," intoned Merridew.

" I don't suggest he did. I think his first idea was to keep
the lady in the background, and perhaps he hoped the first
cheque would also be the last. But she demanded another
and got it, and after that he must have realised he'd got her
round his neck so long as they both should live. And having
thought everything over very carefully, he decided to go on as
he'd begun."

" Shutting her mouth ? " Ventnor sounded puzzled.

" Just that. Only the third time he wasn't going to do it
with a cheque, but with these," and he held up the envelope
with the single word aspirin scrawled across the surface.

" You mean—he meant——" but there Miss Beake stopped.

" I can't put it more plainly," said Crook. " I mean, he
meant to murder her. No, don't gasp like three fishes lying
out on the shining sands. It was the obvious solution if you
come to think of it. Murder often is. Trouble is, it's so
dangerous. But he turned the whole thing over and over in

his mind and he decided he could commit the perfect murder, the way amateurs always do."

" You are making grave assumptions," snapped Merridew.

" I'm like the perfect criminal, I've got my alibi. I took that i tle tablet out of the envelope to a pal of mine in London and got him to diagnose it, and—does this surprise you ?—it tallies identically with the tablets missing from Mrs. East's bottle."

There was no question now about his holding his audience's interest.

" I still don't get you," Ventnor confessed.

And Merridew chimed in with something about motive.

" He had all the motive there is," Crook defended himself vigorously. " He may not have been respected here in Hinton St. Luke, but at least he was respectable. He's rich and as powerful as any rich man can be these days, he lords it over his wife, who's almost reached the pitch of not being able to stand the sight of him, he's quite a big noise in the neighbourhood, and outside it for that matter. He's a company director, all the bundle, in short—and then he suddenly discovers he's a bigamist as well, and in pretty discreditable circumstances. He's got two alternatives—he can brazen it out, tell the woman to publish and be damned ; or he can buy her off. To begin with, he chooses the second, but pretty soon he realises he's like a chap sinking in a quicksand. Every step he takes he gets a bit deeper in. And though his money ain't much use to him, he'd a lot rather see it in his bank account than in any one else's. And the way the lady's shapin'—that's how I read it, and I've met the dame, mind you—quite a heap of it's going into her account. And what's more, when he's dead there's nothing to stop her coming forward and proving who she is and throwin' mud on his name. You might think a dead man wouldn't bother about that, but you'd be wrong. This dame has got James East worked up to anything.

" Now he's a sick man and he don't have much to do all day but lie back and think about himself. I dare say his thoughts haven't been worth much for a long time, but now he's really got something tough to bite on. Because, y'see, it's occurred to him there is a third way, and it's the third way he finally chooses to follow."

He stopped, waiting for comments, but, like the oysters, answer came there none, so he resumed.

" Y'see, nobody but him knows about the first Mrs. East's

existence. The money he sent her went in cash, and the envelopes were addressed to Mrs. Carter. I miss my guess if he said anything in his letters to give the show away, and, of course, he'd destroyed hers. In fact, if it wasn't for her story and the initials in the cheque book, we wouldn't have anything to go on. But we do know he had a date with her and she kept it. He told her to bring her marriage certificate and any other documents she had to prove her case. He invited her to meet him at a station hotel, where the waiters would never recognise her again, he didn't book a table, he didn't leave any traces of his presence there."

" And what do you imagine he intended to do ? " Merridew inquired.

" I think he meant somehow to put her out of the way and Mrs. East, Rose East, that is, inadvertently helped him. Mind you, I don't for a minute believe he didn't know about the sleeping tablets. He was the sort of chap who made it his job to ferret out everything that went on under his roof. Anyhow, he got hold of his wife's tablets, as you know, and like everybody else, he realised they were exactly like aspirins. So my view is that it was he who took the three tablets out of the bottle and replaced them with the three aspirins he generally carried in his wallet. Now you see how easy it was going to be. He would arrive first, order drinks—incidentally he's not a drinking man, I understand, but this was the only way he could put his plan into practice—and when Mrs. East arrived she'd be welcomed with a drink, and she wouldn't guess there was more to the glass than a cocktail. This stuff works slowly ; it would give them plenty of time to have lunch, and probably she wouldn't feel the effect till after she got home. East would persuade her to give up the marriage certificate, say he must have it to show the lawyer or some poppycock of that kind. Then he can just walk out, ask to be excused for a minute—or maybe suggest she'd like to powder her nose while he pays the bill—and then he vanishes. The car would be waiting for him wherever he'd told it to pick him up— not, you may be sure, outside the hotel—and by the time Mrs. Carter realises what's happened—that he's made off with her evidence and she doesn't know the lawyer's name— he's miles away."

" She could come down to Hinton St. Luke and make a stink there," suggested Ventnor.

" Walking in her shroud, I suppose. You've forgotten the drink she's already taken, haven't you ? No, no, she'd go home presently and start making plans. But not for long. She'll feel sleepy, she'll decide to have a nice bit of shut-eye, and—she won't wake up again. Maybe there'll be a couple of lines in an evening paper to say a woman died of heart failure from an overdose. There won't be any other tablets found in the place, but cause of death will be certain. Even if awkward questions are asked she'll be listed at the mortuary as Mrs. Carter, and who's going to link up Mrs. Carter with James East, that respectable citizen of Hinton St. Luke ? "

He stopped, looking eagerly from one member of his audience to the other.

" How's that ? " he inquired.

" Far fetched," returned Mr. Merridew " Very far fetched."

" All right," said Crook, with unimpaired good-humour. " You give me a better explanation of the tablets bein' found in East's wallet. I'm always ready to learn."

Mr. Merridew, not unnaturally, found himself at a loss.

" If he meant them for himself, what's the sense of putting them in his wallet ? " Crook continued. " He could take 'em on the spot. And he wasn't in a position to tamper with the drink of any one else in the house. Miss Beake waited on him hand and foot, and I dare say he kept a pretty sharp eye on her to see she wasn't playing any monkey-tricks."

Miss Beake, pale with rage, said, " You're always very ready to warn other people about slander, but you ”

" When you're dealing with a nasty-minded, suspicious old cuss like James East you must be prepared for everything," explained Crook. " Then, don't forget he makes a date with an unknown without takin' even his man of affairs into his confidence. If these tablets weren't meant for the pseudo Mrs. Carter, you tell me who they were meant for."

" He's got us there, Merridew," acknowledged the doctor, after a pause. " Miss Beake, I don't know whether you . . . ."

" Why do you ask me ? " shrilled Miss Beake. " I don't know anything. I tell you, I never saw the wallet open till to-day. Unless, of course," she looked suddenly sly, " Mr. East didn't put them there himself."

" Meaning that Mrs. East . ? "

" It's possible," she flared

" But not likely. I mean, there'd be no sense in it. And then she didn't have the stuff, not for both fatal doses, I mean. There are only three fatal tablets missing altogether, so if her three were in the wallet, what about the three James East is

known to have taken ? No, I bet you I'm right. James East
wasn't a murderer only because somebody else got in first.

Merridew looked more shocked then ever. " You canno
advance such an argument in a court of law " he protested.
" My client is dead."

" Don't they say the evil that men do lives after them A
for not advancin' this or that in a court of law I thought I'
made it perfectly clear that I was going to advance an
argument that could help my client. You know, it's goin
be very difficult for a jury to make up their minds why Jame
East should have these tablets in his wallet unless he mean
use 'em. and nobody in his senses is going to suggest he mean
them for himself. So unless he meant them for you." h
nodded cheerfully to Merridew, " and I don't think he did
because if so it would have been much simpler to get you down
to Hinton St. Luke, what other explanation is there ?

" It's certainly a poser," agreed Ventnor frankly. A
the same, Merridew's right when he says you can't use
speculation like that in a court of law."

" I've told you already, this won't get as far as a court
law."

" And why not ? " asked Merridew frostily

" Because we shall have nailed X before then."

" And your evidence ? " inquired Merridew, more coldly
than ever. " Or do you propose to manufacture that ? "

" I shan't need to," said Crook. " that job will be done for
me."

" By ? " insinuated three voices simultaneously.

" The murderer, when he strikes again."

And with this hackneyed but undeniably effective curtain.
Crook made a magnificent exit.

CHAPTER THIRTEEN

THE THREE he left behind him looked anything but happy. Merridew was the first to speak.

"The fellow's such a charlatan," he complained. "You never know where you've got him."

"He's like quicksilver," corrected Ventnor. "He's never on the same spot for two consecutive seconds."

"If you ask me," contributed Miss Beake venomously, "it's all bluff. That's what the man is. Like a tremendous gas-balloon. It looks wonderful till someone pricks it, and then it's just a shrivelled wreck."

"Were you thinking of pricking it?" Merridew inquired, who seemed to have endless capacity for disliking his fellows, male and female. But for once Miss Beake was too intent on her own thoughts to take offence or even to answer him.

"It's perfectly obvious that all that interests him is getting his client off. Truth—Justice—they're just words to him."

"That was an interesting theory of his about Mrs. Carter," observed Ventnor. "It could even be true. If so, it's a case of the biter bit, only, as Crook points out, he was bitten first."

Merridew surveyed them both thoughtfully. "It's neck and neck," he observed in rather a disagreeable voice. And then the telephone rang before he could be asked to explain what he meant. But it was quite obvious to both his hearers, who presently went off looking not a little agnized

That every one's nerves were badly frayed seemed obvious from a series of events that took place next day For a start, Miss Beake had a flaming scene with Mrs. Ruff, who said she couldn't be expected to get three midday meals, and since Merridew insisted on having his alone in the library, she suggested that Miss Beake should have hers in the kitchen. It would have the advantage, she added, of saving coal by not lighting a fire downstairs till later in the day Miss Beake protested furiously, and fired a bolt in the shape of window-sills. She had noticed, she said, that when Mrs. Ruff did a room she seemed to forget the window-sills existed They were thick with dust.

"Window-sills?" sneered Mrs. Ruff "Well, if you aren't

old-fashioned. If anybody wants window-sills dusted these days they can do them themselves."

Miss Beake, whose nerves were certainly in a poor way, seized this opportunity to point out to the technical " obliger " that people who took wages for scamped work were no better than thieves. That, as they say, tore it. Mrs. Ruff dragged off her apron, kicked off her " working " shoes, snatched up her hat and jammed it on her head, pulled on her coat and stuck out her hand.

" What's that for ? " demanded Miss Beake.

" I'll trouble you for my wages."

" Your what ? "

" Wages. I suppose you never heard of them. Salary to you I suppose."

" If you leave without notice you're not entitled to wages. They're forfeited."

But when it became obvious that Mrs. Ruff was in earnest and intended to repeat her version of the interview to the neighbourhood, the spinster observed furiously that it would be worth double wages to be rid of Mrs. Ruff's presence, though in the circumstances it was charity rather than wages, which nearly precipitated a battle royal, with blows flying as well as words. Mrs. Ruff took the money and marched off, pausing at the door to say that wages of sin would very likely be more in Miss Beake's line, and men being the fools they were you could believe anything. But of the two it is probable Mrs. Ruff regretted the breach most. For some time now she had enjoyed a unique privilege ; she was the only outsider free to come and go to the House of Mystery, and now, through her own silly temper, she had lost her position.

" What on earth made you do it, Ma ? " inquired her outspoken daughter, Flo. " Your tongue'll be the death of you one of these days. I'm sure enough people have told you that."

" I suppose you think your mother should let herself be called a thief without a word," stormed Mrs. Ruff.

" It all depends," said Flo. " Sometimes it's worth it."

" Not to me," retorted her mother, and then Mr. Ruff came in and asked disagreeably why it was that two women could never carry on a sensible conversation and he dared say there was something to be said for Miss Beake, though she did remind him of a bottle of vinegar.

Miss Beake, having watched Mrs. Ruff's dignified exit, stormed up the stairs to acquaint Mr. Merridew with this development. The lawyer looked at her disapprovingly as had the departed Abigail.

" In the circumstances," said he, " it would, I consider, be in order to sanction the employment of a substitute until my client's affairs are straightened out."

" I always thought Mr. East was about as straight as a corkscrew," agreed Miss Beake, who appeared to be giving herself full license for the day, " and anyway you don't get women like that. You join the queue and put your name down. And in the meantime I'm told The Pheasant's quite good for lunch. There won't be any in this house to-day."

Mr. Merridew found himself wishing quite fiercely that James East had left this human scourge a legacy so that he might have the pleasure of somehow screwing her out of it. As it was, he waited till Miss Beake was out of earshot and then rang up his partner in London, instructing him to send an urgent telegram forthwith, recalling the speaker to town without delay. When, a couple of hours later this telegram arrived, Mr. Merridew spoke weightily to Miss Beake of integrity and responsibility and the dignity of the law, which implied, so far as she could make out, that such dignity did did not permit Mr. Merridew to seek his lunch in the saloon bar of The Pheasant or make his own bed. Not that Miss Beake was at all sorry to see him depart. The man was nothing but a nuisance anyhow, to her way of thinking, and her indigestion had unquestionably been worse since his arrival.

After he had gone she settled down to make her plans for the next day. But something she had not foreseen happened to upset them.

In the late afternoon she went down to the village and ran into the ubiquitous Mr. Crook. He said he thought of coming to see Merridew to pool a few more ideas he'd got, and Miss Beake said he'd have a job to catch the last train to town, unless, of course, he meant to go in the car and it was wonderful how some people found their way into the Black Market. Crook said, " Merridew bolted ? Why ? Nobody's got anything on him, have they ? "

Miss Beake explained.

" Pity," said Crook. " Not thinking of following his example, are you ? "

Miss Beake looked startled. " Why should you suppose . . . ? "

" It's only that I'd like to have one or two of the old hands in the auditorium when I bring the rabbit out of the hat."

She twisted her hands together. " You mean, you've learned something new ? "

" I mean, I'm waiting to learn something new. I want the murderer to make just one more mistake."

" And if he doesn't ? " said Miss Beake.

" Trip the blighter up. No other way. But it's my experience they mostly do—make mistakes, I mean. And the funny thing is it generally comes of being too careful. Remember what they say about kids ? An ounce of neglect is worth a ton of care. There's a lot to it, you mark my words."

He marched off, leaving Miss Beake very perturbed indeed.

Her subsequent movements were a subject of close inquiry by the authorities. It was established that she left East House in time to catch the 9.40 bus into Hinton St. John. Here she went first to the local registry office. Miss Hunt, the lady in charge, remembered her quite clearly, and in any case had a record of her name and address. The situation, said Miss Hunt, was an unusual one. Miss Beake could not be regarded as the lady of the house, and Miss Hunt did not care to do business with employees.

" Well," said Miss Beake with deplorable taste, " the lady of the house is in prison, and is likely to remain there. The gentleman is dead, but the lawyer has agreed to pay the necessary wages out of the estate until the house is shut up or offered for sale."

" Then it would only be a temporary post ? " objected Miss Hunt. " My women all want a steady situation."

" If that's true, you ought to exhibit them and charge a shilling entrance fee," retorted Miss Beake. (It was no wonder that Miss Hunt remembered her.) " Most of them are as changeable as the weather."

Miss Hunt next asked if Mr. Merridew was in residence and was assured that he would return as soon as there was someone to look after him. The duties were perfectly ordinary, simply keeping the place clean and cooking the meals. Then there would be the job of shutting the place up, as she had explained before. Miss Hunt looked more dubious than ever. She didn't like the sound of the job, and she doubted whether any of her women would.

" I don't suppose they will for a moment," agreed Miss Beake, tartly. " No one likes the sound of work nowadays.

Not that it matters to me if the place does go to rack and ruin. I'm not there for long."

She marched out, leaving a telephone number, and was next recalled by Mr. Pope, a stationer, who sold her some cheap white paper and envelopes to match, and a fancy penholder, a bottle of ink and a sheet of blotting-paper, all in an artistic shade of green. These purchases she took away with her.

A neighbour who had come in on the same bus saw her at The Copper Kettle having elevenses, and, though she wasn't intimate with Miss Beake, she had paused to say a friendly word. Miss Beake had seemed very much engrossed in her own thoughts, but had said that the East affair was making her a martyr to indigestion, and if there was any justice in the world she would be permitted to see a specialist and have a course of treatment out of the East estate. The lady, feeling snubbed, withdrew.

" And none too soon, either." she added. " The way that woman looked at me ! Now if Mrs. East had put *her* out of the way, every one would have understood."

After that she was seen by Frank Ventnor to enter a chemist shop where he was purchasing a commodity temporarily in short supply at Hinton St. Luke. There were a good many people in the shop, and she didn't notice him at first. While she waited for her turn she began to talk to the woman next to her about her health. Like a lot of people, men and women, of her age, whose interests are narrow and personalities boring, she assumed that every one would be interested in her symptoms. She said she suffered from chronic indigestion and had tried every remedy on the market. She had at last found a special mixture, not, of course, stocked by that stupid Mr. Headley at Hinton St. Luke, and she had come absolutely to rely on it. She was, she confided, down to her last dose, and it was so fortunate she had been able to come in this morning. Even when her reluctant hearer was called away to the counter to state her needs, Miss Beake went bumbling on. Ventnor, who had overheard all this, and who had no desire to be recognised and publicly claimed, laid down his money on the counter and slipped out. He knew that the mixture she had chosen was just the same as all the others, but more enterprisingly coloured.

Miss Beake lunched at Ye Olde Cherry Tree—No meal more than 2s. 3d.—and caught the 1.20 back. At half-past two Ventnor telephoned to know whether Merridew would be back on the following day. Miss Beake replied sharply that it depended how soon she could get some slut to wait on his lordship, and rang off. That was the last piece of definite evidence the police were able to get, though later on a tramping woodman testified that he had called at the house in the afternoon—he thought about four o'clock—in the hope of making a sale, and had heard the noise of the typewriter.

"So she was alive at four o'clock," said Mrs. Ruff to Flo. (The pair had quite buried the hatchet in the excitement of this latest turn in affairs.) " Must have been busy, too, though what she was writing no one seems to know. But she never so much as stopped for a cup of tea, so she must have been in a rare taking."

It was, as might have been expected, Mr. Crook who precipitated matters. Marching down to The Four Horsemen —because only a fool takes all his drinks in the same bar when he wants information almost as badly as he wants beer —he noticed that there were no lights burning in East House.

" Gone on a bender," he thought charitably, pushing open the swing-door of the public-house. Here he found himself in close juxtaposition to the lady who had seen Miss Beake at The Copper Kettle earlier in the day. The talk naturally turned on the local mystery. Crook had already established friendly relations with the locals, saying that a chap with his living to get couldn't afford to turn up his nose at any one. You never knew when you mightn't run up against the identical piece of information that would complete your puzzle.

" She come back on the 1.20," the lady volunteered.

" Must have had a date," said Crook. " She ain't in now."

" Funny if she's found a boy-friend. Shows there's hope for us all. Not that it isn't a bit cold for hanging about behind hedges this time of the year."

Crook made some suitable retort, said Same again and What's yours ? and a little later left the bar. From the Barley-Mow he rang up East House, but as might have been expected he got no reply. He began to wonder where Miss Beake could be. When you came to think, the choice of places where she might be found was pretty restricted. There was no local cinema, she wasn't the sort that attends religious meetings, even if there had been any on that evening, she had no friends. The idea that she might be wandering about under a cold, inhospitable sky at the dinner-hour was fantastic.

Presently he rang up Ventnor. " Miss Beake ? " exclaimed

the doctor. " Of course she's not here. Why should she be ? "

" Seen anything of her to-day ? "

" She was at Hinton St. John this morning, giving the chemist hell. P'raps she's still there."

" She came back on the midday bus. I've seen an old girl who remembers her. I've telephoned East House, but I can't get any reply."

" Come to think of it, *I* tried to get her about four o'clock. I wanted to know when Merridew's coming back. There wasn't any reply, but I assumed, if I thought about it at all, she hadn't come back yet. It was not as urgent as all that. Have you tried the Hilarys ? "

" She's not—what's that toney phrase ?—*persona grata* there. On the whole she'd be more likely to come to you."

" I'd be sorry for any one who came to me this afternoon. I'm deep in accounts. This income tax is the devil. Well, look here, about Miss Beake. She must have gone to see a neighbour."

" Pigs might fly," agreed Crook politely. " You didn't speak to her this morning ? "

" No. But she looked the same as usual."

" I'll have a little something in the bar and then I'll take a little ride, just as far as East House, I think."

" And if you can't get in," Ventnor began, but Crook laughed.

" I'll make it somehow, if I have to bust a window."

" There's no need to do that. There's a side-door—I expect you've noticed it. At one time I used to come in that way, when the old man didn't want to advertise the fact that he was using a doctor. And afterwards I used to come in that way so as to get into the house before he realised I'd arrived, or he was quite capable of locking himself in and refusing to see me. Not that I really cared if he died at dawn every day of the week. Apart from the fact that he was the one rich patient I had, of course."

" I could try that," agreed Crook. " Unless the lady's locked it. She's no Juliet."

" You might ring me and let me know how's tricks," Ventnor suggested. " By the way," here he allowed his curiosity to put out its head into the light of common day, " why are you so deadly eager to contact the old girl ? "

" Because I'm practically at the end of the road, and I have an idea she may be able to supply the final note. Just a notion of mine. Don't say it'll come to anything."

" You're so modest," sighed Ventnor, and asked if Crook would like him to come, too, but Crook said No, thanks. When he couldn't tackle one jane single-handed you could put him down for the O.A.P.

" Besides," he added, " she hates us both like poison. One dose of poison she might stomach. Two would probably polish her off."

But, as it proved, one had been sufficient.

When Crook reached East House there was still no sign of a light in any of the windows. Nor were the curtains drawn, and this in itself was an ominious sign, since Miss Beake was of those who, to quote Crook, loved darkness rather than light, by which he meant that she always drew the curtains, " though what she has to hide is more than I can tell you," he would add in his ribald way. He marched up to the front door and pulled the bell. Then he waited. Looking through the letter box he could see there was no light in the hall, and this convinced him that something was wrong. Either Miss Beake had bolted or she had come to some grief. He wondered for a moment if he'd find her lying dead drunk under the kitchen table, but consoled himself, so far as this supicion was concerned, by the recollection that James East might have been a teetotaller for all the liquor he kept on the premises.

" Still, she ain't one of those beloved by the Fuel Minister for her economy programme," Crook reminded himself. Miss Beake's renegade theory was that if all householders cut down consumption to a minimum there would be even less incentive to the miners to produce coal. Anyway, she didn't pay the electricity bills for East House, so what the hell? Crook went round to the side door. If anything was wrong he'd be the most popular man in Hinton St. Luke in the morning. That uncultured community found a murder in their midst (or even a sudden death if there was just an element of mystery about it) far more enthralling than any of the pep talks Cabinet Ministers crowded to the microphone to deliver to jaded listeners. He reminded himself that nobody had seen her leave East House since her return at midday and she hadn't visited any of the village's four shops.

" If she's diddled me at the eleventh hour I'll never forgive her," Crook assured himself, as he came thrusting through the side door, which wasn't locked, as he had thought possible.

It was just as well, he decided, that Ventnor had told him of its existence ; it was so well concealed by shrubs that he might easily have missed it altogether. The house inside was as dark as a tomb. Crook fumbled his way into the hall and switched on a light. Wherever he looked emptiness met his eye. He was quite sure by now that she had gone. Otherwise she would have come bouncing out, wanting to know his business. As a mere matter of form he called her name once or twice in tones which would, he told himself, wake the dead.

But this, it appeared, they were unable to do.

When he received no reply he began a formal examination of the house. Drawing-room—empty and sheeted, dining-room—empty and dark, curtains undrawn. Stairs untenanted. Cupboard under the stairs ditto. Oh, well, he told himself, I didn't expect anything else. It's only in films that brooms suddenly prove to be corpses in disguise. His heart heavier than usual, Crook opened the last door at the end of the passage. This was the room Miss Beake liked to call her office. Although Mrs. Ruff had been gone less than two days the place already had an uncared for look. There was dust on the cupboard and the desk, the china ornaments stood askew, no one had emptied the waste-paper basket or swept the floor. Cake crumbs, testifying to Miss Beake's secret orgies, cigarette ash and odds and ends of those cottons that seem to materialise from the air itself, strewed the dingy carpet.

" Not particularly spinsterish about her surroundings," decided Crook. " Still, no one else ever came in here, so I suppose . . " He left the sentence unfinished. A bit of dust and a lot of untidiness didn't worry him either. It wasn't at first sight a very revealing room. It held no books—Miss Beake was practically illiterate, he remembered. On the table was something that caught his attention. Lying on the sheet of new blotting paper that had clearly been used this afternoon for the first time, beside the jaunty green pen and the bottle of green ink was the last of the anonymous letters, the usual cheap white writing-paper, though search where he might he didn't in this instance find any trace of an envelope. The anonymous writer had flown higher this time. The message read :

> *The shroud is done, Death muttered, toe to chin.*
> *He snapped the ends and tucked the needles in.*

The writing, like the paper, was identical with the other messages.

Crook laid the paper down again and looked round. Then he picked up the sheet of blotting-paper. Miss Beake must have had a busy afternoon. There were no fewer than five signatures imprinted on it. Writing cheques ? he asked himself. Or letters ? But she had no friends. On the table was the uncovered machine that had belonged to James East. But there was no sign of any letter or manuscript and he had to go upstairs to find Miss Beake.

She lay on her bed, as if she had dropped down there to take a nap after her exhausting morning. But when he came closer he saw that she was as dead as the proverbial door-nail, poor wretch, and realised that the case against Rose East was virtually at an end.

He knew that his duty was to go downstairs and straightway report his discovery to the police, but unaccountably he lingered. There was, he recognised, nothing he could do, since it was waste of energy blaming himself for not having somehow stopped the hapless woman from taking the stuff that put an end to her days. For, without being a doctor, Crook was pretty sure that she had got out by the same door as James East. Alone in this gaunt house, virtually alone in a friendless world, she had calmly poured out the fatal draught and taken it. After that, she hadn't spoken to another human being this side of eternity. He saw her handbag lying on the table and opened it. It contained just what you might expect, purse, ration book, comb, powder-case, a very small inexpensive lipstick, handkerchief, wallet for identity card. Nothing else. He thought, with a moment of insight, how impersonal they all were. You couldn't build up her character from these trifles. Everything about her was drab, even the way of ending her life. Sad, unwanted women should die peaceably in their beds. Even mystery, even crime can hardly invest their passing with glamour.

At last he went downstairs and lifted the receiver from its hook. " Police," he said absently, and grinned in a sudden unhappy way, wondering if perhaps a zealous local authority would try and run him in for house-breaking.

157

CHAPTER FOURTEEN

RUMOUR FLIES apace in villages. Before the lights were out in the Barley-Mow the whole neighbourhood seemed to have heard about Miss Beake. The landlord besieged Crook with pleas for an inside story.

" What was it, sir ? " he begged. " Don't tell me she just died in her sleep, too."

" As a matter of fact, that's precisely what she did do."

The landlord looked horribly disappointed. " Like Mr. East ? "

" Exactly like Mr. East. These criminals never have any originality, that's why they get caught." He instanced a number of the more famous cases—George Joseph Smith, who drowned one wife after another in a bath in a hired lodging ; Landru, who took his girl-friends by the dozen to the infamous cottage at Gambais and, it is supposed, interred them in the woods where doubtless many of the bodies are rotting to this day ; the Bulgarian rascal so oddly named Kiss, who put his girl victims in orderly rows in the garden until the day came when there was no more room, and he had to start an annexe in jars in the cellar.

The landlord's eyes were like those of the dog in the fairy tale, as big as saucers.

" You mean, she . . . ? "

" Now, do a bit of simple arithmetic," suggested Crook. " Old Man East dies suddenly in his sleep and it turns out he's been poisoned ; I come down to make some investigations, not agreein' with the police's findings, and a lady closely connected with the deceased is also found dead, though this time on, not in, her bed."

" You mean, it was the same stuff ? "

" You'll have to ask the doctors that, but—I wouldn't be surprised " He then said he was going out for a bit, and might be late Before he left he rang up Ventnor, only to hear he was out on a case.

" Another chap who won't be popular with his Union," he remarked " If he calls me back," he added to the landlord, " you can tell him I'm at the Park House Hotel."

He hung about for a little after that in case the doctor should telephone, but nothing happened, so he clapped on his brown bowler and set off, thanking whatever gods there be that the real Mrs. East wasn't in residence at the moment. She had gone back to London some days ago to consult a lawyer on her own account. In any case, she'd nothing to grumble at, since she could claim a fat slice of the estate; if not all of it. And if he knew Rose East, she wouldn't contest the claim, and you could hardly blame her. She'd had publicity enough as it was.

Crook found Stuart up and waiting for him, flanked by jugs of beer.

" I guessed you'd be over. What's the betting at St. Luke? "

" What could it be ? " asked Crook. " You know, I didn't like the woman but I can't help being a bit sorry for her now. It's one thing to go out in a motor smash or die triumphantly with weeping relatives round the bed, but hers is a nasty, furtive end. A mean, sordid life and a death to match."

" You'd better have some beer," said Stuart sensibly, and then a car came racing up to the hotel and stopped abruptly outside.

" Police ? " wondered Stuart, but it turned out to be Ventnor, whose case had been a local one, and who had looked in at the Barley-Mow on his way back. The doctor came in, looking tired and apprehensive. He said briefly he'd lost the baby and the mother was half out of her mind. Then he stopped talking shop and asked :

" What's this yarn that's going round about Miss Beale ? The village is simply humming."

" You'd better have some beer," suggested Stuart, upon whom the visitor's wan appearance was by no means lost. " Or would you prefer a whisky ? "

Ventnor said in absent tones that beer would suit him very well, and Crook continued in an unwontedly sober voice, " I suppose you've heard that Miss Beake is dead. Yes, it's quite true. I found her myself."

" I never knew such a fellow," complained Stuart, who also looked worried—perhaps on account of the appalling exhibition he had made of himself on the links that afternoon. " Wherever you go, something happens."

" Ah," said Crook quickly, " but you must remember that I shouldn't be on the spot at all if something hadn't happened first."

Ventnor put down his glass of beer untasted. " Is this what you expected ? " he demanded bluntly. " If so, you do consume your own smoke, don't you ? "

Crook refused to become excited. " Answer to Part One—

no, or at all events, not yet. I was sure there'd be a shot at me first. Two. If you mean I kept you in the dark, well, I dropped a pretty hint and—the murderer picked it up."

The doctor leaned back in his chair. "Think of it. Miss Beake, after all. So much violence and hate. By the way," he looked suddenly more alert, "did she leave anything in the nature of a letter or a confession? It seems pretty pointless to get out like this unless she was going to exculpate Rose East."

"What makes you think she cared two straws about Rose East?" said Crook in astonishment. "I thought she'd made it clear to the world she even hated her shadow."

"All the same—it's virtually murder."

"When you've got one murder on your conscience," said Crook, but Ventnor, as though he hadn't heard him, went on, "And she left nothing but that anonymous letter?"

"I was just coming to that." Crook nodded in a friendly manner towards Stuart. "Yes. Rummy thing. No envelope."

"Thrown it away, perhaps?" hazarded the doctor.

"Nowhere in the house. I looked."

"But it couldn't have come . . ." Ventnor stopped. "Oh, of course. There was no envelope to be seen because it didn't come in an envelope."

"That's the way it seems to me, too," Crook agreed.

There was an instant's silence. Then Stuart said slowly, "So she wrote them all to cover up what she'd done?" and Crook said, "I don't say that. I only say that that last letter which was found on her table never came through the post."

"So the implications are obvious," added Ventnor heavily. "It's been a nasty case all through."

"Well, look at some of the people connected with it," said the sensible Mr. Crook.

Ventnor thought of another point. "Whom do you suppose that letter was meant for?"

"I don't suppose at all," said Crook. "I'm pretty sure that was meant for me."

Both his hearers pondered that for a moment. Then Ventnor said in disappointed tones, "You mean that was her oblique way of leaving a confession?"

"Oh, I don't think she'd have been satisfied with anything so subtle. And it is subtle, you know."

"What did it say?" enquired Stuart, and Crook looked across to Ventnor and asked if he'd seen it. Ventnor said No, he hadn't, but if it wasn't more subtle than the others there couldn't be much to it. Crook fished out a bit of paper on which he'd copied the two lines, and read them out.

" Who wrote them ? " asked Stuart.

" Search me," said Crook. " Ask the doc. here. He's our literary gent."

" John Masefield," said Ventnor absently. " I wonder where she ran across them. She was always down on poetry. But it's a neat way of saying she found herself in a blind alley."

Crook rubbed his big nose. " I never understand that about blind alleys," he confessed. " Being foxed by them, I mean. If there ain't a secret way out, me, I'd make one."

Stuart reminded him of the biblical injunction to those who kick against the pricks, but Crook replied that he was no St. Paul, and at the moment he wasn't looking for a heavenly vision. He just wanted a bit of proof to tail off his story.

" The inference being that Miss Beake committed suicide ? And the anonymous letter on the table is the pointer ? "

" I take it that's what we're being told. Still, there's more than that to go on, or will be shortly."

Both his audience looked startled. Stuart asked him how he made that out. Crook said, " What about the five signatures on the blotting-paper ? " and Ventnor said, " What are they ? You haven't mentioned them before, have you ? "

" There was a brand-new sheet of blotting-paper on the table with no impressions on it but five signatures, all made more or less at the same time. That looks as though she wrote five letters or five documents or drew five cheques, only I don't think it was the last, because if she was blotting a signature the odds are she'd be blotting the amount of the cheque and the payee's name."

Ventnor said simply, " I didn't know she knew five people. But, look here, Crook, don't you see where that may get us ? Suppose she had written some sort of confession—she may have drafted more than one and then been dissatisfied . . ."

Crook looked a bit dubious. " Five's overdoing it, ain't it ? Besides, where are the ones she didn't send. There was nothing at all in the waste-paper basket."

" And where's the confession in any case ? " Stuart enquired. " Shouldn't it have been on the table ? "

" I suppose she might have posted it," suggested Ventnor in doubtful tones.

" I'm darn sure she posted it," agreed Crook. " And I'm darn sure I know why."

Both his hearers said, " Well ? " in impatient tones, and

Crook said, " For the reason most letters are posted—to make sure it gets into the right hands. I think whatever is in that confession, and I agree with you there probably is one, is meant primarily for Arthur Crook, with the police a bad second. I may be wrong, of course—just a hunch of mine—but that's what I think. Besides, ever hear of a murderer not making a statement, a self-killer, I mean ? " he went on, looking in friendly fashion at Stuart. " I probably have met more murderers even than you, and they're all the same. Vain as peacocks."

" They need to be," Stuart agreed, " to think that their personal affairs are more important than a man's life. But I see your point, particularly in a case like this. The unfortunate woman never had the luck to attract anybody. In fact, until now probably no one so much as realised her existence. This is her one chance of the limelight."

Ventnor intervened grimly that if she'd waited a bit she could have had even more limelight. Though the country didn't blench much at capital punishment for men, a hanging involving a woman was still first-class news.

" On my sam," exclaimed Crook, " I thought I was pretty tough, but I'm a kid seethed in its mother's milk compared with you. And there are some forms of limelight practically no one can afford."

His voice was reproachful, but the doctor replied in hard tones that he needn't look to him, Ventnor, for any sympathy for the woman who had tried to get Rose East hanged.

" And I take it you expect an interesting post in the morning ? Why you ? "

" Murderers are showy birds," said Crook. " They want to be sure you realise how clever they are. And take my word for it, it's damn difficult to impress the police."

" So this is to tell you how she did it, put James East out of the way, I mean ? Do I follow you ? "

" Like a camel through the eye of a needle. Like a small bet on it ? " But Ventnor said dryly he was sure Crook only betted on certainties and declined.

Stuart moved restlessly and Crook took the hint. " See you in the morning," he said, rising with alacrity. " If by any chance either of you two gents should hear from the deceased, just give me a ring. But I don't suppose you will."

Ventnor found his assurance depressing. No man, he thought, engaged in such a case had the right to wear such an air of being on top of the world. Stuart looked preoccupied, not to say wretched.

" No one will be more thankful than I to see Mrs. East at liberty again," he said. " All the same, I can't help thinking of that miserable woman, playing her hopeless game and realising, alone and in desperation, that she'd lost. And then in desperation sitting down and putting an end to herself. I suppose it was an overdose ? " he added abruptly.

" There was a glass by the bed and an empty bottle of her patent mixture next to it. Looks to me as if she'd just drained the last dose."

" That would be it," said Ventnor. " She was in Fox's this morning, buying another bottle." He looked accusingly at Crook. " That doesn't look as if she meant to take her own life. What happened between midday and evening ? "

" When I get her letter, assuming I do get one, I'll tell you," said Crook. " But don't press me now. I hate stories told on the instalment plan."

Stuart was still weighed down by his imagination. " If her life had been a little different she need never have come to this. Some people murder for gain, the thugs and gangs, but she wasn't like that. There's some tragedy in her past, probably the commonest of all tragedies among women, which is that nothing ever happened to her and nobody ever wanted her. There's no better breeding-ground for every kind of anti-social germ than loneliness, and I suppose you could call murder the greatest of all anti-social acts."

" You could," agreed Crook. " You would even be right."

" Murderers are exhibitionists, I know, but they're also the loneliest people in the world. They daren't have friends. Friendship implies confidence, and in a rash confiding moment they might give themselves away. I wonder how she's been feeling since the old man's death."

" I still don't see why she wanted to put him out of the way," said Ventnor. " If she couldn't stand the sight of him she could have walked out. She knew he wasn't going to leave her anything. And if she'd contrived to separate him from his wife there might have been something in it for her. It was a pretty bad mistake, wasn't it ? "

" Murder's always a mistake," said Stuart sharply, but Crook said, " So you've got there at last."

Ventnor's astonished gaze met his. " You mean, she never meant to murder the old man ? It was an accident ? "

" I don't say it was an accident, and of course I stand open to correction, but—no, I don't believe she did mean to kill him."

" Then why . . ? "

" You remember her anonymous letter—the one that came to her, I mean. The best-laid schemes of mice and women . . . So long as Rose East was in prison I don't think Miss Beake was in any danger. Rose would be convicted and be hanged or get life imprisonment and Miss Beake would be as free as air. But once I came on the scenes and started operations to get Mrs. East out of quod, then she—the Beake, I mean—couldn't be too careful."

" And she still wasn't careful enough ? "

Crook said with sudden passion, " In a murder case nobody's ever careful enough. I thought I was watching every mouse-hole, but you see I was wrong. I thought I should be next on the list—seems tame not to try to do for the man who's out to hang you—I didn't think of being by-passed. I meant to pounce when that attempt was made, instead of which I've been caught napping. I can't do anything about it now, except just tie up the threads if and when that letter arrives."

As Crook and Ventnor drove back to Hinton St. Luke, Ventnor said, " Assuming that she did for herself in the same manner as she did for the old man, where did the tablets come from ? She couldn't have borrowed Rose's bottle this time, and she couldn't have got at the old man's wallet either."

" Perhaps she had a whole store," murmured Crook.

" You mean, helped herself to more than she needed in case of just such an emergency ? But where could she keep them all this time ? "

" There's a thing that occurred to me," said Crook. " We assumed that there were three dangerous tablets inserted into a bottle of innocent aspirin. But suppose the whole bottle had been substituted ? Ever thought of that ? "

" I hadn't, but you're wrong. You see, I was on the scene on the day of the old man's death before Miss Beake returned, and I collared the bottle of aspirin on the bedside table, and I can assure you every tablet in it conformed to the label. No, that's not the answer."

" To-morrow is also a day," said Crook, placidly. He stopped at the Barley Mow, and his last words to Ventnor were : " If there is anything I'll let you know right away, and we can chew it over before the police come on the scenes. If there's anything I hate, it's the print of a bobby's boot all over the nice pattern I've made."

CHAPTER FIFTEEN

As FREQUENTLY HAPPENED, too frequently to please his de-tractors, Crook's expectations were justified. Stuart was going through the obituaries in *The Times* about ten-thirty the next morning when he was summoned to the telephone. Crook's voice said : " It's come. And, seeing you were in at the birth, you should be in at the death, too. I'm going to contact Ventnor and ask if he'd like to make a third, seeing he is in a way implicated, because of Rose East, see, and we might mill the thing over together before calling up the police."

" Perhaps the police have had a replica of your letter." Stuart suggested, but Crook said No, he didn't think so, because he'd met the Inspector when he, Crook, was on his rounds, clearing up one or two minor points so as to put a high polish on the whole, and he'd asked him point-blank if there were any developments, and the Inspector had said No.

" You won't be popular with the police when the story breaks," Stuart warned him, but Crook said as a matter of fact he had invited Finch to come along and make a foursome and he hoped Stuart didn't mind. Stuart said bring the whole town if he wanted to. Personally he'd be thankful when the affair was over, and he didn't envy Crook his job if it was worth twenty thousand a year. Crook said that was all right, he wasn't complaining, and rang off.

Stuart called for one of the more sensational papers and looked at the headlines. The *Record* was running the story for all it was worth.

EAST MYSTERY   NURSE FOUND
POISONED.

They were a cautious lot in Fleet Street. No hint of suicide. They'd wait for the official verdict for that.

Soon afterwards Crook arrived with his two companions. Ventnor looked pale and Finch grim. Stuart supposed he didn't much like being dragged at Crook's tail. It was a good thing the curtain was just coming down. Even Crook didn't seem quite as buoyant as usual. He'd be happier when he got back to town to the odd world in which he lived, whose language he understood so well. It couldn't satisfy him really to have hounded that wretched woman to her death, and he found himself thinking that James East really wasn't worth all this pother.

" No," said Crook unexpectedly, making Stuart jump. " He wasn't. But it's law and order you have to think of. If we all went round bumping off the chaps we didn't like who were spivs on the community, there'd be a boom in undertakers' shares and nobody 'ud get firewood because it 'ud all be wanted to make coffins."

They sat down and Ventnor offered cigarettes, and Crook said he would waste no time, but satisfy the curiosity of them all, by reading the document that had arrived on the morning post, and if any points seemed to warrant discussion they could be discussed at the end of the reading.

Finch looked rather as though he would like to tear the typewritten statement out of Crook's hand, but he restrained himself. Ventnor said nothing, and Crook, having made it clear that he wanted no interruptions, no matter how startling the admissions in the ' confession,' immediately got down to work.

Just as he was going to begin, however, he looked up to say, " I've been making the rounds and can't discover any one else who heard from the lady. I suppose neither of you . . ." They both said No, they hadn't heard, so Crook said, " Here goes. One thing, it comes to the point right away. No time wasted in civilities," and began to read :

" Don't let any one suppose I am writing this because I am sorry in any way for what I did. I am only sorry that you, you human ferret, have learned the truth, and I prefer taking this way out to waiting for what is absurdly called official justice. Official murder would be nearer the truth. There is no justice in life, anyway. My experience has proved that. It's a tooth and claw existence and you get as much as you can grab from your neighbour, no more and no less. My trouble has been I could never grab enough to make life comfortable, and I thought at last I saw my chance. I suppose the truth is, though, I'm only an amateur which is why I bungled the last and the most important risk I ever took, and since my end is inevitable I may as well clear my mind of her murder as well as his. Mind you, if I could have kept the secret I'd have gone to her hanging without a qualm, but somehow I made a mistake, and you have learned the truth. It's a pity you can't establish connections with the dead. If you could, you would be able to tell me where I tripped up.

And now, here are the facts. I killed James East deliberately and without pity, and if I thought I could do it safely I would do the same again. If it hadn't been for you I should have got away with it. The police never suspected me, nor did Merridew nor Ventnor, that lovesick booby. Nor his clever friend at the Park House Hotel. But after all, why should they? What motive had I? Wasn't James East what Americans call my bread-ticket? But that's just the point. He wasn't, not any more. He was a threat to my future. You see, he was planning to dismiss me in circumstances which would have made it practically impossible for me to find another job. You and he are alike in that way—the life of the individual doesn't matter to you a tinker's curse. You'd string up the whole village if it would save Rose East, I've heard you say so, and he'd make use of me so long as it suited his book. But if I died of starvation it would never lie on his conscience.

Mind you, I missed my opportunities. If I'd opened even one of those letters from his real wife, as I could easily have done if I'd dreamed what was in the wind, I'd have had him on a string, and I'd have kept him dangling there until he died. But I didn't know. I thought it was a very different person he was going to meet. He let me think that, and I knew, of course, he was going to see his lawyer afterwards. James East had the power of life and death over me because of something I did long ago, and he found out. It's cruel that old sins should have such long shadows. If he didn't choose to ruin me it was because it suited him better to have me at his perpetual beck and call, to spy for him and cheat and wait and slave for him. I came to hate him and that doll-wife of his as I'd never hated two human beings before. I used to lie awake wondering how to get even with them. And it wasn't till he began to talk of this trip to London that I saw my opportunity.

After that, it was absurdly easy, so easy I ought to have been warned. He knew that if he wasn't careful he'd never make the journey and he'd set his heart on doing that. I did not know then why he thought it mattered so much. I know now. It was absolutely vital for him to get to London, if he didn't want the whole disgraceful story to break. He meant to get rid of that wife of his, as mercilessly as I later got rid of him, destroy the evidence and be free again. But he failed then just as I did later. He failed because of me and I've failed because of you, Mr. Arthur Crook.

On that Tuesday, before I went out I insisted on his taking a dose of his heart-medicine. I told him it was touch and go whether he got to London the next day anyhow, and this would buck him up. He was so madly anxious to be all right for the journey that he took it practically without demur. I hadn't expected it to be so easy. I had some of the sleeping tablets that I got out of Dr. Ventnor's dispensary one day when I went round for Mr. East's medicine. He's like most doctors, leaves everything unlocked and enough poison on the premises to bury the entire parish. All I had to do was mix the medicine, drop in the tablets that I'd crushed to powder, and watch him drink it. Yes, I stood by the bed and watched him. Then I took the glass away and rinsed it and filled it with cold water. He always took cold water to wash down the aspirins. As I brought him back the glass I remember thinking that by the time I got back from Hinton St. John he'd be dead. I didn't tell the doctor on purpose that I was going to be out that afternoon. I was afraid he might tell me it was risky, I ought to stay, and I didn't mean to be on the premises when James East died.

I wasn't quite sure how long the tablets took to have an effect. I didn't want him so sleepy that he forgot about taking his aspirins after lunch, so as I went down I called out to Mrs. East that he was quite ready. Then I went out, knowing I'd seen him alive for the last time.

Thus far everything had gone according to plan. I knew, of course, that when Rose East found him dead, her first act would be to ring up Dr. Ventnor. And this she did. What I never thought of was the pair of them plotting together to make it look like death from natural causes. And if it had not been for me they would have got away with it. You might say that if I had had any sense I should have let sleeping dogs lie, but I wanted to hurt her as well as him. After all, what had I gained by James East's death? My liberty—for what? To work for my living in some other house, to be some other employer's servant. And she had everything—money, youth, beauty and her future assured. Quite soon, I knew, she would marry Dr. Ventnor or some other man—and it was I, I who had made all that possible for her. When I laid my plan I meant that she should pay. She deserved to. Why couldn't she have treated me like another woman in the house instead of hating and resenting me from the first ? You might have thought my presence about the place was an insult. I would never have played the spy if she had wanted to be friends As a matter of fact, I would even have let her off if she hadn't been so greedy. That led to her undoing. She had so much, couldn't she have left Ventnor alone ? I hadn't had many chances, but she was like David and the ewe lamb. She had to have everything. That's why I put the idea of divorce into James East's mind. If she was going to have the doctor, then she should pay dearly for him. I couldn't prevent them getting married, but I could wreck that marriage. I couldn't supply enough evidence for a divorce, but at least I could stir up sufficient talk for the neighbours to say as people stupidly do, There's no smoke without fire. I didn't believe she really cared for him, and she certainly wouldn't want to marry a ruined man, but if the story broke her hand would be forced. I thought that would be a charming revenge.

And revenge was what I wanted. Think of it, Mr. Crook ! Years and years of hard labour at poor pay, always passed over, the plain woman, the undesirable woman. he woman with no power, and then suddenly— power put into my hand Here was my chance to be revenged on all three of them, James East, his wife and the doctor, and, through them, on the whole world of sneering stupid superior men and women who'd made my life so worthless it hardly mattered if I went on living or not. I tell you, I was intoxicated at the thought of that power. Long before my plan had taken shape, I was playing with the idea. I kept my eyes open and presently my chance came. I should have been more than human to let it go. Everything, it seemed, had come my way at last.

And yet—and yet—there's always something it is impossible to count on, what you, Mr. Clever Crook, have called the unseen witness, the person or factor you do not allow for, not because you are stupid, but because you haven't got second sight. How could I guess you would pick on me as the guilty person ? What evidence had you ? What mistakes did I make ? Looking back, I can't see where I went wrong. What a pity I cannot return for half an hour from the other side of death, and then you could tell me where I had blundered."

Crook had been reading this in a level voice to an audience who sat spell-bound. Even Finch had ceased fidgeting. Stuart looked absorbed. Only Ventnor stared at the floor so that no one could see his face, but then the reading must have held some embarrassment for him, with its candid suppositions and admissions. Finch said after an instant, " Is that the end ? " and Crook said, " That's the story, but there's another paragraph. I'll read it," and he went on in his deep impersonal voice :

" I suppose the truth is I gave myself away somehow over the anonymous letters, and that led you to me, and adding two and two and making it five you ran me to earth. I do not intend to furnish a spectacle to men and angels by standing my trial and fighting a losing battle. It's lucky for me I kept enough tablets for just such an emergency as this. In a moment I shall seal this letter and take it to the post, and then I shall go upstairs and take my last dose of indigestion mixture, and it will look as innocent as James East's dose of heart tonic did, and be just as deadly.

" That's the real end," said Crook, " and that's where the signature comes, but there's a sort of P.S. as if at the last minute she wanted to register her hate of me for what was happening to her.

" Yes, you're very clever, I know, but do you know how I see you, Mr. Clever Crook ? As the loathly bird ' stationed always in the skies, waiting for the flesh that dies.' "

Crook's hand clenched rather hard on the manuscript after he finished the final line, but all he said was, " And now, I take it, I hand this over the the police. Exhibit A. Does police procedure allow me to have it back later, seeing it's addressed to me ? "

Finch took the manuscript and looked at the hasty typing with some of the words run together, the big blue signature sprawling across the page. " We shall have to get proof that it was actually typed on Miss Beake's machine," he said," to which Crook replied, " Not much doubt about that. You remember the woodman who called hoping to make a sale and testified to hearing the machine being driven along ? "

This was new to the doctors, and Finch explained that when the news about Miss Beake's death became known, a foreigner, as they still called people of another locality, had come forward with a story of calling during the previous afternoon with a cartload of wood and trying to get an answer to his bell, but without success.

"The fellow seems to take particular umbrage because he could hear the typewriter, so he knew, of course, the house wasn't occupied."

"I still don't understand one thing," began Stuart, and Crook exclaimed, not rudely but in genuine surprise, "Only one? There are half a dozen that stagger me. But let's take yours first."

"How did the woman give herself away? I admit I haven't been on the case from the inside as you have, but I can't see where she slipped up."

"She didn't," said Crook. "That's one of the things that puzzles me."

"She didn't? Then how did you know she'd done for the old man?"

"I didn't," said Crook.

"Then it was bluff that made her write that letter?"

"Oh, but surely you don't believe Miss Beake wrote that," exclaimed Crook.

His three hearers goggled at him. "Not Miss Beake?" repeated Ventnor in incredulous tones. "But   " He stopped.

"But what?" asked Crook.

"I was going to say she'd told us everything, and if she didn't do it how did she know?"

"You're going round like a dormouse on its wheel," said Crook. "Try and bear in mind that Miss Beake didn't write this."

"Then who did?"

"The murderer, of course. When I first read it I thought what a curious document it was. I mean, if Miss Beake was leaving it as her last will and testament you'd think she would be careful to clear up all the outstanding points, instead of which she tintillates one's curiosity."

"Not nearly so much as you're tintillating mine," protested Stuart.

"It's like a serial story. You read Part Two to clear up points raised in Part One, and then you find you've got to read Part Three to clear up the points raised by Part Two. Now, the murder was Part One, and this letter is Part Two. But that ain't the end. We've still got Part Three ahead."

as they still called people of another locality, had come forward with a story of calling during the previous afternoon with a cartload of wood and trying to get an answer to his bell, but without success.

"The fellow seems to take particular umbrage because he could hear the typewriter, so he knew, of course, the house wasn't occupied."

"I still don't understand one thing," began Stuart, and Crook exclaimed, not rudely but in genuine surprise, "Only one? There are half a dozen that stagger me. But let's take yours first."

"How did the woman give herself away? I admit I haven't been on the case from the inside as you have, but I can't see where she slipped up."

"She didn't," said Crook. "That's one of the things that puzzles me."

"She didn't? Then how did you know she'd done for the old man?"

"I didn't," said Crook.

"Then it was bluff that made her write that letter?"

"Oh, but surely you don't believe Miss Beake wrote that," exclaimed Crook.

His three hearers goggled at him. "Not Miss Beake?" repeated Ventnor in incredulous tones. "But " He stopped.

"But what?" asked Crook.

"I was going to say she'd told us everything, and if she didn't do it how did she know?"

"You're going round like a dormouse on its wheel," said Crook. "Try and bear in mind that Miss Beake didn't write this."

"Then who did?"

"The murderer, of course. When I first read it I thought what a curious document it was. I mean, if Miss Beake was leaving it as her last will and testament you'd think she would be careful to clear up all the outstanding points, instead of which she tintillates one's curiosity."

"Not nearly so much as you're tintillating mine," protested Stuart.

"It's like a serial story. You read Part Two to clear up points raised in Part One, and then you find you've got to read Part Three to clear up the points raised by Part Two. Now, the murder was Part One, and this letter is Part Two. But that ain't the end. We've still got Part Three ahead."

" And what do you expect to find in Part Three ? "

" The answers to my questions, which are :

(a) Why are there five signatures on the blotting-paper and only one signature on the manuscript ?

Any answers ? "

" Presumably she wrote to five people," said Ventnor.

" That's the point. She didn't. The Inspector and his chaps have gone all round the place seeing if any one else heard from the lady this morning and no one did."

" It wouldn't have to be a local person, would it ? "

" According to Barrows, the postman, she never had a letter and she said herself she had no friends, so why should she suddenly develop five correspondents ? And how is it that only her signature appears on the blotting-paper and no name or address of any one to whom she might have written ? "

" She typewrote," said Ventnor, simply. " Doesn't that supply your answer ? "

" It could be," agreed Crook, reluctantly, " it could be. But the inspector here will tell you that the packet of envelopes and the writing-pad she bought yesterday are still intact. If she meant to take her own life she wouldn't go round buyin' writin'-paper."

" It could be a sudden impulse," suggested Stuart.

" It wasn't one of these spur-of-the-moment affairs," Crook assured him. " She'd taken the trouble to put the stuff in the bottle of indigestion mixture. There are traces in the empty bottle."

" That is unusual," Stuart had to admit. " Well, suppose she didn't write five letters. Perhaps she re-typed the last page more than once."

" Five times ? " asked Crook, sceptically. " Even suppose she did, where are the spoiled sheets ? Not in the waste-paper basket and not in the grate, for there was no fire there. And if you're thinkin' of suggestin' that the letters or whathaveyou were written the day before, don't forget the blotting-paper was only bought yesterday. The Inspector here has been in touch with the shop and they say it's the first consignment of green blotting-paper they've had for three months. Any more suggestions ? "

" Get on to the next point," said Ventnor, and Crook continued :

" (b) The anonymous message."

" What about it ? "

" Quite a lot. To begin with, it had been blotted and one or two of the words were smudged. But—where was it blotted ? There's no impression on the green blotting-paper and the only other piece on the premises, in that room, I mean, is a crumpled bit that certainly hadn't been used for that purpose. The Inspector here has got it under a microscope and he knows."

" You and the Inspector seem to be working hand in glove. That's a new development, isn't it ? " inquired the doctor.

" Remember the yarn about the cockroach that was afraid of being eaten by the tortoise, so he hid under the tortoise's armpit ? If you think you're in any danger of a chap, the safest place to be is right beside him. See ? Now—about that message ? How do you explain that ? And who was it meant for ? "

" You said yesterday it was intended for you."

" Then why not send it to me with that ? " He nodded towards the document in Finch's hand. " Or if the lady was going to the post, why not send it on to whoever was meant to get it ? And that starts another hare—what that play-writing chap would call the time factor. According to the postmark on the envelope this confession was posted to catch the six o'clock collection. Since there was another collection at four, it means the letter wasn't finished or taken to the post till after that time. Right ? "

No one had any fault to find with that argument.

" That means Miss Beake was able to walk down to the post, a matter of five or six minutes, after four p.m. But the medical evidence puts the kybosh on that. We know she got back to the house about 2 o'clock and then we're supposed to think she sat down and wrote out this letter—wrote it straight on to the machine, mark you, with no alterations, no second thoughts—we've searched the house from roof to floor without finding any trace of the draft—and when it's finished she addresses an envelope to me, and walks down to the post and pushes it through the box. The earliest she could be back would be, say, four-thirty, and it's worth noticin' that though various people were coming and going nobody happened to see her. Then she came back and took the sleeping draught, which takes around four hours to work. So that at nine o'clock, which is roughly the hour I stormed the fortress, she'd still be warm, only just passed out, in fact. Whereas the fact remains

—she was lyin' in a room without a fire—she was stone-cold, had clearly been dead some hours."

Stuart began to work that out, speaking aloud. " Then we have to assume that she took the indigestion mixture at the usual time, after lunch, as soon as she got back."

" That won't work," said Crook. " If she'd done that, she certainly wouldn't have been in any state to walk down to the post at four-thirty or possibly later. That was a big job, that confession, to say nothing of the five vanished letters."

" Look here, Crook," said Stuart, " you're making pretty serious allegations. What it boils down to is that Miss Beake didn't write this document at all."

" Explains the five signatures, don't it ? " said Crook unperturbed. " Someone wanted to be sure no questions would be asked, so he sat there testing signatures till he thought he could pass muster."

" And who," asked Ventnor, " do you suggest that person is ? "

" The visitor of yesterday afternoon."

" Visitor ? But—how do you know ? "

" There was cigarette ash on the floor. I've seen Mrs. Ruff, she did out the room as she calls it, on the day before, the last thing I'll ever do for that Miss Beake, she said—and how ! Miss Beake was a non-smoker, Merridew was in town, nobody else had access to that room. Yet somebody sitting at that typewriter smoked incessantly—the butts of several Players were found outside the window—somebody remembered to chuck the butts away but didn't notice the ash on the floor. That was one mistake, but it was only the last of a series. I mean, those anonymous letters were a complete giveaway from the start. If you think it over, you'll see why. I mean, Miss Beake couldn't have been responsible for them."

" Why not ? "

" Because she didn't know enough. Not from beginning to end. Take the last one first. Don't it surprise any of you to find a dame that can't stick poetry quoting from the Poet Laureate ? And how about that bit at the end of the confession ? I don't know who wrote that . . ."

" It's pretty well known," explained Ventnor. " That is, it's in all the anthologies. A fellow called Ralph Hodgson wrote it."

" I'll bet all my national savings Miss Beake didn't know that. And there's the last, in a way, the most important point of all, I happened to go through Miss Beake's bag, and the one thing I didn't find was a fountain pen. It wasn't in the morning-room either, and that's not so surprising really, since the girl at the stationers at Hinton St. John remembers the old dame leaving her pen to be repaired when she bought the blotting-paper, etc. So, you see, she couldn't have signed that document."

He looked round, without triumph but with the air of a man who has presented an unassailable case.

Ventnor leaned forward, trembling with tension. " Interesting, Crook. So even you can slip up sometimes. Miss Beake's fountain pen may have been at the stationers, but there was one of these ridiculous quill pens and a bottle of ink on the table."

" I know," Crook agreed. " I saw them. But they were both green, and the signature to the document was blue. Besides, the pen had never been used. And come to think of it," he added, coming slowly to his feet, " that's curious, too. I knew about the pen and ink because I was in the room that afternoon, but—they were only bought that morning, so *how the hell did you know ?* "

CHAPTER SIXTEEN

" IT's LIKE I told you," said Crook later to Stuart. " Those letters gave him away, if nothing else did. Well, just think for yourself. The first two came to old residents, whom Miss Beake didn't even know. She always complained that every one was unfriendly and no doors opened to her. Only two kinds of people could have written those letters—those who had lived in the place for years and knew local history, or else someone who had come in later but managed to win the confidence of the old-timers. I ask you, does our Miss Beake fit into either of those categories ? So how the heck did she know about Miss Stapleton's sister or Mrs. Abraham's son ? And don't it strike you as a bit peculiar that the first anonymous letters to arrive come to two people who ain't connected with the case, both of whom consult dear Dr. Ventnor and can be pretty well depended on to confide in him ? He admittedly knows their family histories, he's one of the few who remember about young Abrahams, a thing Miss Beake couldn't conceivably have heard. No, it's like what you said, murderers are a conceited lot. They will show off. Take

Ventnor. If he hadn't been so keen to prove what an educated chap he was we might never have nabbed him, or, anyway, not for the same reasons. He was a literary bloke, you see, read poetry, wrote a nice classy style himself, and couldn't forget it even when he was supposed to be writing for someone else. You never really believed Miss Beake wrote that letter, did you?"

"There was one thing that did strike me," said Finch, who had no intention of giving himself away to an outsider, as he inevitably regarded Crook. "She was pretty cagey about the nature of the hold East had over her. Now if she was really planning to commit suicide she wouldn't have wanted to hold out on you."

"There's more to it than that," said Crook gently. "She knew I knew about the cheque, and she knew I had a pretty good idea what it was all about. Whoever else she tried to faze she wouldn't have tried to faze me. The answer, of course, is that the chap who wrote the letter didn't know what that hold was but he knew there was something."

"How did he know?" inquired Finch.

"I dropped a hint," returned Crook airily. "A sensible chap wouldn't have been so detailed, just let it be understood there was something. But these educated chaps can't let well alone. And he quite forgot that Miss Beake wasn't an educated dame. Not that I think the worse of her for that. A lot of this education is hooey, and it's my belief it's all wrong stuffing it down people's throats. If chaps want to be educated they'll manage it somehow, and if they don't, then it's a waste of time and money." He didn't actually say, Look at me, I was never educated, a fact indeed which sprang to the least perceptive eye, but his manner said it for him. "Well, only an educated person would have written that letter, everything in its right place, arguments all dovetailin' and followin' in the right order. I don't know if you've ever tried writin' a document where all the ends have to tie up—probably not—but if you have you'll know that the first time you get just a jumble of facts. Mind, they're all there, but it's like a jigsaw puzzle, they ain't all in the right place, and the thing to do is to jam everything down and then go through it and put things in the right order, so as to make it simple for the chap who's going to read it. But that letter of hers was child's play. I mean, any one could understand it, police, public, press, any one. And she didn't make a draft—that's what looks so damned odd to me—because if she had she

177

must have destroyed it and put the pieces somewhere. I've had a tidy look round and Finch and his merry men have been through the house with a tooth-comb but there's no sign of that draft, and no coal fire had been lighted, so she couldn't have burnt the pages."

" Do you suggest that though Miss Beake couldn't have written such a letter without a draft, Dr. Ventnor could ? "

" Of course not. Why, I wouldn't like to have to do it myself. *But* the draft would only have to be made at East House, if it was Miss Beake making it. Any one else— Ventnor, say—could make and destroy half a dozen drafts on his own premises. And did you think to ask how the doctor spent the afternoon ? No ? Well, I'll tell you. He was doing accounts. Doing accounts, mark you. People dyin' all over the place and he spends the afternoon obliging the Income Tax collector. Does it sound likely to you ? And he had a hell of a lot of trouble with them to judge from the amount of burnt paper there was in the hearth."

Stuart looked perplexed. " I suppose you must be right. But tell me this. Were you sure it was Ventnor from the outset ? Did you never suspect Miss Beake ? "

" I considered her, of course. Don't do to underrate even the ship's cat. But Mrs. East—Rose—persuaded me it wasn't her."

" How on earth did she do that ? "

" She said no woman would buy a hat she knew she wasn't goin' to wear. Well, she's a woman, she should know. So that proves Miss B. did expect to go to town on Wednesday —ergo, she didn't polish off the old man."

" As simple as that ! All the same, let's get this straight. You're indicting Ventnor for James East's murder as well as Miss Beake's ? "

" I'm not a ruddy dick," retorted Crook, in some indignation, " but since you ask me, there was no sense murdering the old girl if he hadn't done for the old gentleman first. But if you mean, did he murder James East and intend Rose East to hang for it—No, definitely not. Nobody could have had a worse shock than he did when he saw how things were breaking. His plan wasn't bad as plans go, but it didn't go far enough. Or rather, he wasn't careful enough to see there were no loopholes. He took a lot of trouble and a lot more risk than he need have done, but that's the amateur all over, but at the end you could have driven a coach and four through his crime. And all because he forgot—or never knew—the murderer's first rule. If ever I have to give classes to would-be criminals I'll tell 'em all to write this out in letters of fire and hang it where they can see it wherever they turn their eyes. If possible, hang it opposite a mirror, so if they have eyes in the backs of their heads they can see it twice over. 'It's the little things that matter.' Because it's the little things they don't think about that hang men ; the little things he overlooked are going to hang our Dr. Ventnor in due course."

He nodded with the air of a man satisfied with what he has achieved.

" Poor devil ! " muttered Stuart.

Finch said nothing at all.

" I bet you anything you like he was cut to the heart when he realised where he was standing," Crook went on. " Well, what had he taken these frightful chances for except for his own advantage ? And here at the end we have Rose East in quod and he doesn't know how to get her out. She's no good to him there, not according to his plan. Of course, I grant you, he couldn't guess that, as things turned out, she wasn't even going to be a rich widow, and a poor one is simply a liability. Still, he made other mistakes, too, all little ones, and all mistakes he could have avoided with a bit more care. He's a thus-far-and-no-farther chap, and that sort always loses the count. Y'see, he remembered to take away the bit of paper on which he'd practised the signatures, but he forgot about the blotting-paper. He remembered to chuck the cigarette stubs out of the window but he forgot about the fallen ash. He left the last of the anonymous letters on the table, minus an envelope—a good touch that, and one he knew the police couldn't miss—but he forgot he'd blotted the lines and there wouldn't be any impression of 'em on any of the blotting-paper at East House. That's the fault of the age. You ask any of the employers or the Labour bosses. Chaps ain't thorough. They scamp. And though, if you scamp a house the odds are it comes down on someone else's head, if you scamp a murder it comes home to roost with you in the death cell. And, of course—I've pointed this out already—Miss Beake couldn't have quoted any of those flim-flams because she wouldn't know them. The trouble is murder has to be committed by amateurs in 999 cases out of 1000. The law don't give them a second chance, so they can't profit by experience. I bet you if our Dr. Ventnor could get away with this he'd bring off a second murder that 'ud be a credit to him."

" A second ? " asked Stuart.

" They mostly do. Ask the Inspector here. Still, he won get the chance now."

" There's one thing I'd still like to know," suggested Stuart. " What did he really expect to get by poisoning the old man that made it worth his taking the risk ? "

" James East's money-bags," said Crook simply. " On, know there was nothing definite between him and Rose East but he didn't make any secret of the fact that he wanted her to like him, and you have to bear in mind that she was young and attractive and quite alone. No relations, no friends When the old man died who would she turn to ? Not Miss Beake. Not any one in the neighbourhood. There was only the kind, sympathetic doctor who'd already let her see h was infatuated with her What more likely than that he'd persuade her after a decent interval to become Mrs. Frank Ventnor ? And it needn't be so very decent either, since they wouldn't stay in the district."

" You seem to know a lot about his plans," observed Finch dryly.

" I have such big ears," said Crook in an explanatory voice " Anyway, he told any one who'd listen to him. He wa bitten by the bug that destroyed Wolsey. Ambition. By tha sin fell the angels, and by that sin falls Dr. Ventnor of Hinton St. Luke, right down into the bottomless pit. When he started out on his career he meant to be one of the big names That so, isn't it ? "

He nodded towards Stuart, who replied, " I always though he would be. I couldn't understand how he ever settled in little place like this."

" You should know that all the brains in the world withou the cash to back them don't carry a chap into Harley Street And the further away from Harley Street he seemed the more he wanted to get there. Not that he played his cards too well His one rich client was James East and he managed to antagonise him. Still, he always thought of his job as just a stepping-stone to higher things ; what he needed was money and plenty of it, but he didn't see where it was to come from Until he got to know Rose East, and then he began to ge ideas. Mind you, I don't say he wasn't taken with her , she's the taking kind—but if she'd been in Miss Beake's shoes he wouldn't have thought of her twice, not as Mrs. Frank Ventnor. Don't you see how the idea would grow in his mind ? If James East were to die—perhaps one day if James

East dies—until after a bit it was When James East dies. When a chap starts thinking like that he's got to back-pedal like hell if he don't want to end up in the little covered shed. But usually by the time they've reached that stage they don't want to back-pedal. All they think of is how to do their murder and get away with it. And to do him justice Ventnor did think of practically everything to ensure that James East's murder should never be brought home to him."

" Are you suggesting he didn't mind Mrs. East being suspected ? But if that happened what became of his plan ? "

" His original idea, I'm sure, was to get a verdict of death from natural causes, and if it hadn't been for Miss Beake he'd have succeeded. But, because he was far-sighted enough to realise that somebody might ask inconvenient questions, he used a poison that was known to be on the premises."

" In Mrs. East's possession," insisted Stuart.

" He didn't think she'd be dragged into it. That was the first, indeed almost the only mistake he made over his first murder. He didn't make sure enough that everything was watertight. When you're planning a crime of that scale you can't afford to take anything for granted. Because the nurse usually went out on Wednesday it didn't occur to him to make sure that this particular week wouldn't be an exception to the rule. It was part of his plan that Miss Beake should be on the premises and in charge of the invalid. Then, if questions were asked, she'd be held responsible as having given the aspirins, which, of course, you realise weren't aspirins at all."

" Ventnor having substituted sleeping tablets ? "

" That's right. And not just three, according to my guess, but a whole bottle. It would be very simple. East always bought 25 aspirin tablets at a time, because the bottles were small enough to go comfortably in his pocket ; the bottles of sleeping mixture were about the same size, though naturally I don't imagine Ventnor was careless enough to substitute a bottle rather like the one containing the aspirins. Obviously he'd get an actual aspirin bottle, fill it with the right number of tablets and when the moment came ' effect a substitution. That 'ud be simple enough. He'd only got to barge against the bedside table, knock the bottle over and replace it with the deadly one he'd meantime taken out of his pocket. Then, when Rose East discovers her husband's breathed his last, what will she do ? I give you three guesses."

" Ring up Ventnor."

" Right first time. He'll come beetling over, get her out of
the room and change the bottles over again. What could be
simpler ? Of course he had to hang about round his surgery
all through the last part of the afternoon to make sure some
other doctor didn't get in in front of him. Then he pulls his
chin and nods his head and pats the widow on the shoulder
and says it's all for the best really, he's saved much suffering
and, of course, though he doesn't mention this, the old gentleman has petered out before he had time to change his will.
It's all been too easy. And in the days to come who is the
sad widow to turn to but Dr. Galahad Ventnor ? Oh, he had
it all worked out. His murder was a honey, and then that
helion ruined everything by calling in the police. That must
have brought him out of his fool's paradise with a rush. For
a few hours he'd seen himself in Harley Street with a lovely
wife and an even lovelier bank balance—My chance at Last,
that kind of thing—and then he's brought down to earth with
a rush. Though even then it must have been a shock to him
when he heard they were goin' to take Mrs. East for the crime."

" A diabolical piece of irony on the part of Providence,"
agreed Stuart, and Crook said, " You're such a toney chap.
What you mean is he was ham-strung all right. In fact, he
was worse off than he'd been before. Because the chaps in
the village were all lookin' sideways at him and suggesting
that if he didn't know the difference between a heart attack
and death by poison adminstered of malice aforethought he
wasn't really good enough for Hinton St. Luke, let alone
Harley Street. And he either had to confess himself an
accessory after the fact or a plain damn fool. It's like the
picture of that chap with a crocodile on either side of him,
both sayin', Of two evils choose the least. Trouble is, how's
the chap to know which is the least ? "

" And if his plans had gone right and Miss Beake had been
arrested your theory is he'd have let her hang ? "

That was Stuart. Crook looked at him in amazement.

" I thought you were one of these psyches," he observed
inelegantly. " Able to read other fellow' minds and all that.
Of course, Ventnor hadn't gone to the trouble of workin'
out a long, elaborate scheme of murder to muff the dividends
when they fell due. He wouldn't have cared if Monica Beake
had been hanged every day for a week. When she suddenly
popped up and started makin' trouble, then he was in a spot.
For one thing, he didn't understand her motive, specially
when he knew she hadn't stood to gain anything from the

amended will. But Miss Beake genuinely believed that Mrs. East had murdered her husband, and she didn't see why she should get away with it."

Finch said something about justice, but Crook swept that off the board at once.

"I wouldn't say she worried any about justice. Dames don't as a rule bother much about the law. You know that as well as me. But she didn't see why Rose East should have everything—liberty, money and ultimately another younger and a lot better-looking husband while she, poor old horse, had nothing to look forward to but another trip to the Labour Exchange. So she chucked her spanner into the works, and like most amateurs, Ventnor hadn't the sense to lie low and say nuffin. No, he had to make things safe for himself, and the only way to do that was to fake up a case against someone else. He knew I was there to get Rose out of durance vile, and there wasn't much choice. That's the trouble about real life crimes. On the films and in tales there's always a house-party full of chaps and dames to choose from, but in real life it generally boils down to two people at most. The two in this case—since the first Mrs. East may have had the will but certainly hadn't the opportunity—were Miss Beake and himself. So what he had to do was build up a case against Miss Beake."

"What opportunity did she have?"

"All the opportunity in the world. She was with the old gentleman right up till the time she left the house. What could be easier than to have given him the heart medicine, just the way he tells it in his 'confession'? And nobody could prove it wasn't true. Oh, he had some ideas, but the trouble was he didn't have quite enough. He tried to think of some other way of involving her and all he could think of was the anonymous letters, and there again he tried to be too clever. She couldn't have sent those messages to Miss Stapleton and Mrs. Thingmajigg, but I thought I'd put it to the test. So I sent him a letter."

"You did?" exclaimed the two men simultaneously.

"You remember I took all the letters to town to show them to an expert. The expert was Bill. Always clever with his hands, Bill Parsons was, as the police could testify. He drew up a couple in the same sort of writing—the paper was no trouble at all, you can get it at any sixpenny store—and—I suppose you didn't notice I got my first letter the day after I got back from town? I dropped in to see Ventnor next morning, and I found him with the letter in his hand, looking as if a dead man had walked through the window. Y'see, he didn't know whether someone had rumbled him or if some other chap was poaching on his preserves. Then I went round and had a word with Miss Beake. She didn't care if I'd had forty letters, it didn't mean a thing to her, but when I showed mine to Ventnor he was plain panicked. I suppose Ventnor thought if he sent himself a letter no one would suspect him. Bless you, that's what they all think. Mostly they start with themselves. And then, of course, he made his final, crashing mistake, and there I do blame him, because that alone was enough to hang him. He took it for granted that Miss Beake carried a pen in her bag. I admit most people do, but when you're risking your neck you can't be too careful. Mind you, he's got his wits about him. As soon as he heard me say the pen had been left for repair he remembered the pansy quill on the table. But on the spur of the minute it's only the genius in crime who can remember everything. He didn't remember it had only been bought that day—perhaps he didn't even know that—and he forgot or never found out that the ink in the bottle was green, whereas the document was signed in common or garden blue."

" You have him hip and thigh," agreed Stuart, but his tone was sober. " He knew how to typewrite. In fact, he sent me part of a treatise that he'd typed in his spare time, and a pretty sound piece of work it was." It hardly bore thinking about that the man who had produced that work was heading straight for the gallows and nothing, nothing could save him. With an effort he wrenched his thoughts away and went on, " I suppose he poisoned Miss Beake's medicine with the same tablets he had used for the old man. When ? "

" While she was still at Hinton St. John—obviously. Don't forget he was in the chemist's and heard her ask for a new bottle of indigestion mixture. That would give him the idea. Think how easy it was. He knows she can't get back till about two o'clock, while he, in his car, can go beetling home in twenty minutes. There's the side-door—he knows all about that—all he had to do was get the stuff from his surgery, leave his car there, and go quietly round to East House. There won't be a soul on the premises—he knows that. No Mrs. Ruff, no Merridew. He marches in, finds the bottle with the one dose in it, adds the powdered tablets—that's why the stuff was found in the bottle, which was odd enough, you'll admit—and there's the stage all set."

" And the letter ? "

" He couldn't type it then, of course, in case someone heard the machine going at a time when Miss Beake was in Hinton St. John, someone like the woodman, for instance. Besides, he'd have to get it ship-shape. When you're fighting for your life, as he was, you can't afford many chances. He took more than he could afford as it was. No, when he tells his story, if he's ever persuaded to tell it, you'll find that's how it happened. Didn't he say he spent the afternoon doing accounts ? Accounts my Aunt Fanny. He was drafting that confession. He had the sense to realise it must be finished off on her machine, and naturally he had to be sure she would be out of the way when he arrived. Didn't you wonder why he rang her up at two-thirty ? What did it matter to him when Merridew got back ? But he had to be sure she really had returned."

" And she answered that call ? "

" It's a pity she can't confirm it, but I'd say Yes. Then he rings again at four o'clock and gets no reply like he says. That means the plan's working all right. The old girl's passed out, and it's safe for him to pop round."

" She might have gone out," objected Stuart.

" Oh, she might. But I think he'd ring the front-door bell, and then, if he got no reply, he could get in by his private entrance and march upstairs and make sure she'd taken the stuff. Even if she hadn't then she'd be bound to sometime, and as it happened, of course he found she had."

" Suppose she hadn't ? "

" He'd have waited another day, that's all. Still, seein' how things were, all he had to do was get out his copy of the confession, sit down at her machine and type like billy-o. In a way it was luck the woodman coming, because he could swear the house wasn't empty, and most people would think she was workin' so hard she didn't hear the bell. Or else didn't mean to be interrupted. Well, there it was. He found the empty bottle and the used glass, and this was his opportunity. Y'know, he's a cool chap. She was lying on the bed upstairs all the time he was typing. No wonder he made a few blunders in the script. Still, most of the time he kept his head. He was careful not to leave a cigarette-end, a scarf, a pencil, anything that could be traced to him—and yet he might as well have left a note—All My Own Work—and signed it, for all the good it did him."

" There's one more point," said Stuart. " Why post the letter ? Why not leave it on the table ? It was bound to be discovered sooner or later, and then your argument, one of them, I mean, would have fallen to the ground."

" Well, not really," deprecated Crook, " because I'd never have thrown it into the air. But he wanted to establish for sure that the letter came to me. If it had been found on the table by the bobbies they'd have had first pull at it. .Besides, Miss Beake bein' nobody's darling, she could have disappeared for days, I dare say, without anybody worryin' much. If any one did telephone and get no reply, they'd jump to the usual conclusion that she was out. And he wanted to fix the date."

" He could have done that, surely, by putting a date on the manuscript."

Crook looked at him with pitying eyes. " Aren't you innocent ? What proof's that ? You or me or the Inspector here could write a letter and put last week's date on it, and if it didn't carry a postmark, how would that prove anything ? "

" I see." There was a long pause. Then Stuart said, " What happens to Rose East now ? She'll be discharged, of course, when various formalities have been complied with, and I dare say the Inspector will see they don't take too long. But what will she do ? She's not the legal widow, so presumably she gets nothing from the estate. Circumstances have debarred her from making friends, she's no relations . . . It's an appalling position for her. Of course, she'll be beset by the usual maniacs and publicity hounds offering her marriage —that always happens, I understand, in cases like this where the girl is as young and lovely as she is—but what security has she got for the future ? Doesn't the law make any provision for her ? "

Crook scored neatly. " It won't have to, the medical profession's going to see to that. No need to look so coy, Stuart. You ain't the only psychologist in the world, even if we don't all have brass plates nailed on the front door. And when a golf-fiend like you stays away from his usual haunts and fluffs his shots and forgets his dates and slices like —like a bread machine, there's only one reason." He clapped the astounded Stuart on the shoulder, nearly bowling him over. " Don't tell me you've suddenly turn:d the Good Samaritan or Mrs. Doasyouwouldbedoneby. Why, even the Inspector can't have missed that one."

But the Inspector was looking primly at the carpet. Crook picked up his loud brown bowler and clapped it on.

"Good luck," he said in a voice as loud as the hat. "You'll have to go a bit slow, of course, but take the word of the man who's never wrong—twelve months from now you'll be a Benedict and wondering how the hell you ever thought you knew a thing about the psychology of a jane."

THE END

9 781471 909863